KU-576-025

THE QUIET SHORE

by

ERNEST RAYMOND

CASSELL · LONDON

271075WRL

CASSELL & COMPANY LTD
35 Red Lion Square, London WC1R 4SG
Sydney, Auckland
Toronto, Johannesburg

© Ernest Raymond 1958

All rights reserved. No part of this publication may be reproduced, stored in a retrieval system, or transmitted, in any form or by any means, electronic, mechanical, photocopying, recording or otherwise, without the prior permission of Cassell & Company Ltd.

First edition 1958
Second edition, second impression 1973

I.S.B.N. 0 304 29162 5

Printed in Great Britain by A. Wheaton & Co., Exeter

872

For

PATRICK, PETER

and

CHRISTOPHER RAYMOND

PART ONE

THE BEACH

So said the Dream, and left him where he lay,
Pondering hopes the Gods would overrule,
Thinking that Priam's city in a day
Would fall to him—oh, he was Fancy's fool
And little knew the pains, the wails, the woe
That tarried there for Greece and for the foe.

The *Iliad*, II. 35–40.

CHAPTER ONE

It was an odd little craft in which we beat down the long channel. Its bow was high-peaked; oriental rugs were slung over one side for our comfort, and in the stern it had an old motor engine whose endless detonations shocked the wide silence of water and cliffs like a machine-gun. My wife and I sat against the gay-coloured rugs; the young brown man with the Tartar eyes, our guardian or watcher or escort (his function was obscure to me) sat opposite us and did not speak since he had no English, but watched us curiously and grinned whenever he caught our eyes. Whatever his function was he seemed to think it amusing. The motorman at the tiller was hardly more than a sea-tanned boy, and he showed no interest in us at all but dreamed behind his dark brown eyes and over his trembling tiller.

There were strange things about the channel too. At the point where we embarked in this odd boat it was barely a mile wide; now it had broadened into five miles at least; far ahead we could descry that it narrowed again where it flung its waters into the sea. That sea beyond its mouth was calm today and presented to the clean sky a blue more royal than a peacock's breast. In mid-channel a current hastened towards it, running at some four or five knots with this north-east wind behind it—that old north-easter which once we knew so well. Perhaps it was this current that caused the dreaming tiller-boy to hug the western shore; but this suited me well because I could not take my eyes from those continuing cliffs and the sand and scrub that dressed them. Sand and scrub; persistent sand and scrub. The other shore was different. There the hills lay further back and rolled away to become the foothills of grey mountains; near the water we could distinguish gardens and vineyards and a long coast road. Our strait might have been a hurrying, wind-blown river unless you knew—and, God, how well I knew!—that while this eastern shore was the edge of a vast continent, the western was but a long appendage to another continent, a narrow tongue of land with the open sea beyond its hills. I could almost *feel* that blue sea on the other side of these continuing hills; and I thought, 'If it's a long serpent-tongue of land, what a sting it once had.'

'Now don't talk,' I said to my wife.

'But I haven't said a word for twenty minutes,' she complained. 'You've done nothing but stare at those cliffs.'

'Naturally. Don't talk. I've waited forty years and more for this. That's nearly half a century. We're almost there. It's incredible. Incredible. But I see it must be more wonderful for me than you.'

'It's rather wonderful for me to,' she pleaded, chidingly.

'I know. Of course it is.' I said this gently when I remembered why it could mean much to her, even after forty years. 'But to me it's all so vivid it could have been yesterday. Nothing else has ever been so vivid. Yesterday. Lord, it's hard to believe that I'm now old and battered and slightly senile.'

'You *will* talk such nonsense,' she protested. 'You're not all that old.'

'My dear, four years to go, and I am seventy.'

'Nine for me, and I too.'

'Yes, but women are immortal. They go on for ever. We softer creatures die easy.'

'Don't talk such nonsense. Why all men want to be clowns, I've never known.'

'Nonsense? It's not nonsense. Look at me—but look at those birds first.' Overhead a flock of wild duck whirred towards the south faster than the wind or the funnelled water. It was autumn now. 'Heavens, they went just like that forty years ago. They went before we did, and we wondered if they were an omen. We shot some down for our supper, and perhaps that was a sinister thing to do. But now consider me: I am clearly a ruin, and I only just got here in time. If I'm to speak truth, my hearing isn't what it was; without my glasses I see most people with a ghostly aura around them; I have to go easy with my false teeth; my memory is going, and I tell everyone everything several times. I'm much too heavy; and thanks to something diabolical in my left heel I limp on one foot. I'm clearly beginning to die.'

'Which is rubbish, my pet.'

'But all too many who were with me here are now dead. All too many. And some of them years ago. So let me see this place and die. But first, perhaps you'll tell me why, in company with all other old fools, I try to conceal from everyone that I'm getting slightly deaf but brag to all the world about my shortsightedness.'

'Because the one is interesting, while the other——'

'No, no; don't talk. You're only saying what I said—just saying it over again; don't talk for quite a while. I must look . . . I must look.'

Throughout these exchanges, our guardian or watcher (or whatever his function was) grinned to hear us baiting each other—this surely was extremely funny—and either picked his teeth or bit his dirty nails, spitting the outcome into the current. The tiller-boy dreamed behind his palpitating engine, his dark eyes far away, probably with some brown girl he loved.

The boat sped and bumped on, down this water-lane between the continents.

'Twenty-four I was then, and, as it seems to me now, strangely naïve and immature,' I continued while gazing at the cliffs. 'Colin, with Balliol behind him, was very different. A year younger than me, but much more adult in some ways. He was something of a scholar, of course; which I never was. Not really.'

'From all you've told me, I think you must have been rather sweet.'

'Sugary, my dear. A sugared lad from a very genteel Victorian suburb. Largely the product of pious women and parsons. But he's such a stranger to me now——'

'Who is?'

'That romantic youth who once bore my name. I can feel little shame for the things he did, though many were absurd and some were hateful. A point, my dear: how many decades must pass before one forgives oneself? I still feel some shame, I suppose, because I've never dared tell them to any but you. But stop! *Now*—now we're there!'

Our strait had narrowed again and we were thrashing through its doors to the open sea. And at once, as we swung west, the beach came into view. Oh, my God—this clutch at the heart! There it was: of scimitar shape with its mouldered fortress on this nearer headland and the tall cape beyond—the cape which gave its grand and terrible name to all. There was the low bank of sand with the drowsy ripples slinking up towards it in their sleep. That tiny cliff of sand! But how quiet—how utterly quiet it all was. Surely if one listened one must hear ghostly reverberations. Surely a swarm of grey phantoms should sweep over sand and hills. But no: it lay there facing the calm blue sea like some Cornish beach after the summer visitors have gone.

Our tiller-boy swept the boat round a spit of rocks beneath the tumbled fort, where there were the ruins of a stone causeway.

That spit of rocks! That ruined causeway!

I stepped out of the boat on to the rocks and helped my wife to do the same; but I could not speak nor look her way. I could only look at sand and slope and rolling plateau above. I was looking at a doubly haunted scene: haunted by the sweetness of an early love and by the greatest terrors of my life. And here too, most strangely, once, terror and peace sat side by side in my heart.

Suddenly I heard the lap and drag of the water on the sand, and with that sound more memories came back to me than I could have believed. They went with me as, taking my wife's hand, I limped ashore, our watcher following.

CHAPTER TWO

OUR sleek grey ship lay at anchor, along with a hundred others, in the great loch; and Colin and I leaned upon its rails. The loch was almost enclosed by a sweeping cyclorama of barren hills; it was not a lake but an arm of the sea stretched into the heart of an island. Colin said that it reminded him faintly of a Scottish loch, and I kept quiet because I had no knowledge of Scotland.

The wind was still, and therefore the undulating hills were green and yellow and the water blue. Lucky indeed that on this signal afternoon all should be still; because the moody wind could often come down through the hills at breakneck speed and shock like an earthquake all the tents and hutments ashore, and drive veils of dust from the dry summits over the water, which it whipped up into such an inland sea that ships careened and dragged their anchors.

But on this April day the light was as limpid and many-hued as it could so often be among these islands; and Colin and I, crammed like all the other soldiers against the rails of the mine-sweeper, could see on the hills a stony village, some wheel-winged mills, and a few hairy sheep trying to find sweet food among thistles and stones. Colin, who was a hearty liar at times, said he could see the bees at the same occupation among the wild spring flowers.

Nevertheless the contrast today between the sterile hills and the peopled water was something, I am sure, that this island, in all its immemorial history, had never foreseen. Here were ships without number. Why, neither Clyde nor Mersey, neither Southampton Water nor Plymouth Sound, had ever known an array like this. Colin spoke of Homer and his naming of the beaked ships assembled against Troy (what else could he do with Balliol only two years behind him? I hastily nodded and showed that I knew what he was talking about, though I had no such scholarship as his. Once he spoke some of the Greek lines, showing off, and I said 'Yes . . .' pretending that I understood, and showing off too.) Oh, that I had Homer's space, page upon page, in which he numbered the ships and named the great captains. I must content myself with dividing the enormous assembly into the black ships and the grey.

The black ships were the liners, huge and medium and small. They belonged to all the shipping lines but were troopships now, packed with khaki soldiers and painted a dead black for their present enterprise. Around them fussed trawlers, colliers, tramps, picket boats, and the coloured sailing ships of the natives bearing wares of fish, fruit, goat meat, and goat's milk cheese.

The grey ships, the ones that drew our eyes and exalted our hearts, were the ships of the Navy. Majestic, many of them; sleek and beautiful some of them; terrible all of them. Dreadnoughts, battleships, cruisers, destroyers, submarines, and the White Ensign drooping from all. And we ourselves—were we not standing on one of them, His Majesty's grey minesweeper, *Guelder Rose*?

'Gerry.' Colin turned to me. 'Do you think it's quite fair, assembling such a power as this? Isn't it rather like bullying?'

'Yes, but——'

'No one's ever stood up to the British Navy yet. Not in the end.'

'No, but——'

'No, but what, damn you? Damn you, Gerry.'

'They're beautiful ships, but unfortunately they can't come ashore. They can only knock at the door for us and then stay outside. They can't come upstairs.'

'True, but they can blow the door to hell.'

'Yes, but who's on the stairs?'

'They can blow them to hell too.'

'Christ, let's hope so.' I had only just begun to take some pride, after my suburban and pious upbringing, in a few soldierly oaths.

'Gerry, would you be anywhere else in the world at this moment?'

'Hell, no.'

'Nor I. I simply can't believe in my luck. France? Pooh! It's nothing to this. Can you really believe you're here?'

'No.'

'I'm glad of that. I can't either. We *are* here, I suppose? It would be too awful to wake up in England and find that the whole thing was an extremely quaint dream. After an adequate luncheon at the Club. Maybe I'm asleep in the Library at the Reform.' Colin was very proud, I could see, of his recent election to the Reform Club.

I had no ready answer. It was sometimes a strain, trying to match Colin's dry Balliol fooleries, though I thought that, every now and again, I did quite well.

Our minesweeper was near the mouth of the harbour and the boom. Outside the boom were some grey French warships—waiting; and this reminded me that somewhere among the transports a division of the French Army waited with us, the Corps Expéditionnaire de l'Orient.

'When do we move?' I asked.

'About five or six, I think.'

A launch came fussing towards us from the steep grey hull of H.M.S. *Marathon*. In its bows was a small figure in a grey sweater, wide breeches and high Russian boots, with an Indian civilian topee crowning all. The topee made an exotic figure of him, because few of the troops were in pith helmets yet.

'Look who's coming,' I said.

Colin looked. 'Oh, my God! The Colonel. Now for his bandobast. Last Orders, I suppose. He's not dressed for dinner, is he?'

'No.'

'No. He's dressed for action.' Colin said it with a rich appreciation. 'He means to come ashore too, laddie; mark my words.'

'He's never going to shin up that rope-ladder?' The launch was now against our hull.

'Oh yes, he is. He's quite hot stuff at it. Been practising it with the boys for days.'

'What? In those boots?'

'Yes; and with a Tommy's pack and all. He believes in setting an example to the boys. Besides, you forget: he's probably used to shinning up a Himalaya every now and then.'

Colonel Harby was an officer of the Indian Army attached to us after our colonel from England fell ill. He was a little man of fifty, and because his grey moustaches were smartly dressed to left and right; because his grey sweater was woolly and came up to his ears; because his Russian boots were knee-high with crumplings about the ankles that caught the sun; and because the pith helmet made him look even smaller than he was; the men called him 'Puss-in-Boots'. An obvious nickname; so was his other, 'Punjabi Harby', because his regiment had been the 27th Punjabis and he was often followed by a turbaned Indian bearer twice his size. A third nickname, 'Kiss-me Harby', needs more elucidation. He was a kind-hearted, simple little man, with most of a soldier's virtues, but with some vanity too; and he had told us more than once in the mess— perhaps twelve times—of some flattering thing said to him by a high-placed general who lay dying. Most of us had forgotten what the flattering thing was; so Colin had suggested that it was probably 'Kiss me, Harby'; whereupon the officers' mess, if not the men, adopted this as a new nickname.

'Mr. Dester, sir.' A voice speaking to Colin. And to me. 'Mr. Browning, sir.' Our Company S.M. To both of us briskly.

'Yes, Sergeant-Major?'

'All officers to the Colonel, sir. He's over there on the port side.'

'Right-ho, Sergeant-Major. Come, Gerry. Come along. Hear the worst.' He followed the S.M., swinging his arms smartly and turning to me to say, 'I always like to give an impression of zeal.'

We found the Colonel leaning back against a rail and facing

the rest of C and D's officers, all of whom, though young enough to be his sons, were taller than he.

'Where's his savage?' I whispered, referring to his handsome Indian bearer, and hoping this was witty in Colin's manner.

'Making him a chupatti, I should think,' whispered Colin.

The Colonel saw us and, satisfied that all were now present and correct, began: 'Well, gentlemen, since we're on the ships of the Navy we shan't move out till tomorrow. Only those on the transports are going today—see what I mean? You'll join 'em all at their station tomorrow night. The show'll be in the morning. Yes, Sunday; dawn; see?' His utterance was crisp as a machine-gun's. 'You'll get into the ship's boats, as rehearsed, and the bluejackets'll tow you to the shore. And if any of you ever pray, dammit, pray like hell that it's calm. See that all the fellahs have their two hundred rounds, their entrenching tools, their three days' rations, and their water-bottles full. God knows when we'll see water again. Any questions, gentlemen?'

Our O.C. Company, Bill Drewer, spoke first. Bill Drewer was a big, broad, oiled dandy with a curled golden moustache. 'Yes, sir,' he said. 'What exactly is this beach like?'

'Like? It's rather like a nice little Cornish beach, Drewer.'

'Yes, but . . . I mean——'

'It's kind of semicircular, with a grassy slope to the cliff tops. There are some rocks about. Not many.'

'Yes, but what I mean is: they've fortified it terrifically, I suppose?'

'Oh, yes. Yes. Certainly. Aerial reconnaissance reports a damn lot of wire and that they've been digging like beavers. Their trenches seem well sited. Their German allies'd look after that.'

'I see, sir. And they're well supplied with machine-guns?'

'Oh, I think so. Naturally. And the ruins of the old fort are a damn fine spot for machine-guns.'

'I see.'

'That all, Drewer?'

'That's all, sir.'

So Bill said, but I thought he still felt dubious and sought comfort from feeling and fingering the golden moustache. He nodded quietly and mysteriously to himself.

'Any other questions? Anyone?'

I was too little at ease with colonels (and with all my superiors social or military) to ask a question, even if I could have thought of an impressive one. But Colin, always more socially at ease, spoke up, and Bill Drewer turned towards his subaltern's voice, while he fiddled with his golden moustache, curling up its ends. When Bill Drewer did this, I always suspected he thought he looked like a Viking. Usually he did look like a Viking, but not so today because he'd had all his blond hair shaved down to a yellow stubble: he stood ready for a battlefield with its lice and its dirt. Neither Colin nor I, nor indeed any of the new, inexperienced officers, had offered up this great sacrifice, and strange our Bill Drewer looked among us with a moustache too long and elegant for the Army and a head severely bald.

'Is the ground mined, sir?' Colin asked.

'Oh, no doubt. Remember the damn Germans there.'

'I understand, sir, that the old Germans are saying it'll be impossible to land.'

'They are, are they? Well, we'll prove 'em wrong; that's all, what?'

'Yes, sir.' Colin smiled. 'Certainly, sir.'

Pirrie, in temporary command of D Company, took over from Colin; perhaps he thought he must not be surpassed as an intelligent questioner by Drewer of C. 'Say we carry the beach, sir, what's behind it?'

'Oh, acres of wire and machine-guns and howitzers and all that sort'a thing.'

'I see. Thank you, sir.'

'Is that all, Pirrie?'

'Well, yes, sir.'

'Satisfied, Pirrie?'

'Perfectly, sir.'

Manifestly Pirrie was *not* satisfied but didn't like to bombard a colonel who thought he ought to be. So, having no handsome moustache like Bill Brewer's to seek comfort from, he just stepped back and stood there with an awkward smile, like a batsman ashamed of having been defeated by a rather quick ball.

'Yes, well . . .' Obviously the Colonel now felt that it was time he said something encouraging. 'We hope that the Navy'll blow their wire to blazes and most of their trenches too. They'll be uncomfortable in their trenches. Don't forget, dammit, that the flagship's fifteen-inch guns fire shrapnel with ten thousand bullets. That should make 'em think. But we shall have casualties too, of course,' he added, after thought.

'Half of us, I put it,' murmured Colin. 'Oh, well . . .'

As he said this, I admitted the thought, which so far I had not dared admit, that he might be killed—he, not I, because this latter was a thought still to be unleashed—and my heart sickened into a death. Alone in this company I knew how absurdly, and with what a shamed secrecy, I loved him. It was my shameful secret that I had loved him at first sight because his profile seemed to me beautiful. Ever a soft thinker, I drove from me the thought that in less than thirty-sixhours he might be killed.

Since all were silent now, and the Colonel couldn't think of any more to say, he began, 'Well . . . good luck, all. Don't know what else I can say. Dammit, you'll all do your damnedest, I know. And you can be pretty sure of one thing, gentlemen: this job they've given us to do on Sunday morning, if we do it properly, will go a hell of a way towards bringing the war to an end. Yes, by God! The whole conception of this new front, in my humble opinion, is the one bright idea that has come to the big-wigs at home so far—as a strategic idea, I mean. Tactically I might have ordered it rather differently.' Here spoke the small vanity. 'However, that's only my opinion. And I'm no one. I just do what I'm told as loyally as I can, as I know you all will. Well, thank you, Drewer. Thank you, Pirrie. And all of you. Good-bye—at least, not good-bye. The General wants me to go ahead with him this evening, but we shall meet ashore, I sincerely—— Hell and be damned—by God!—what's that?'

A great noise of shouting, cheering, and singing seemed to be filling the air on the other side of our sweeper. We all, the

Colonel no less quickly, hurried round to its starboard rail. All the soldiers and many of the ship's company were pressed against the rail.

The transports, thronged with their khaki freight, were moving out of the bay. Great and small, and all in their guise of black, they were heading towards the place of battle, in line ahead, and slowly. And all in the standing ships were cheering them. Their line had reached our grey naval ships, and all the sailors, officers and ratings, on high decks and low, were hurraying and bellowing, and waving caps. I saw an old captain on his bridge holding his cap high as the Army went by. Nor did he once lower his silent salute but, as his arm tired, changed the cap from one hand to the other.

The passing soldiers cheered back. This was the great hour, after weeks of drills and preparations and practices. Ahead was adventure . . . a fight . . . war real and tremendous . . . the greatest of all games. Probably not one of them, in this high-kindled excitement, entertained the thought that he might be moving towards death or agony. Each in this afternoon hour, when the sun's bright western glow matched the glow in their hearts, was less an individual than a cell in any army eager for battle. They were young, and youth is ever proud to visit the margins of death, whether on the North Face of the Eiger or among the sound barriers of the air. They hurrayed and sang, and the whole bay between its enfolding hills seemed a basin of young men's voices, tumultuously cheering, laughing, chorusing, exulting.

A sound like a gulp behind me. I turned. The Colonel was standing there with lips tight closed over so unsoldierly a sound. The lips, however, being autonomous, were trembling. Since his men were happy and cheering on the rails he had not liked to push through them but was rising up on the toes of his top boots to see the ships, these carriers of loud acclamation and song, go slowly by. Seeing me, he hastened to speak that I might not suppose his voice was temporarily disabled.

'Good fellahs, all of 'em,' he said. 'Very fine show, that, don't you think, Browning?'

'Yes, sir,' I stuttered, a little shaken at being directly addressed by the Colonel.

'Yes, good lads. Damn good lads. What I mean: it's moving, rather.' And he gulped.

'Yes, sir; yes, it is.'

'God . . . God be good to them.'

I managed to stammer another, and inappropriate 'Yes, sir,' and he, after watching longer, said, 'Yes. Makes one rather proud, you know . . . it does, really. In a way.'

One behind another the black troopships stole out through the boom, and the French warships waiting there roared their hail and farewell. Soon all these old travelled liners were clear of the still gulf water and out on the restless and vanishing highroads of the sea. They stood out for Tenedos.

CHAPTER THREE

NEXT day at two in the afternoon the grey ships went: that is to say the Navy followed the Army to shepherd, protect, and watch over it; to be, as the C.-in-C. had said, its father and mother. Very slowly, in line ahead, the procession passed our minesweeper: battleships, cruisers, destroyers, frigates, and submarines, with a humbler line of followers-on: trawlers, drifters, tugs, and water-boats, far less beautiful, some even rather rusty and scrofulous, but all bent upon the King's business, just the same. The big flagship, leading the armada with all guns cleared for action, bore a message from the King.

Colin and I tried to name the lean destroyers as they went rolling and vaulting by: *Whirlwind, Unity, Tempestuous, Windflower, Javelin*—for we'd been studying the ships for days past, leaning on our rail and identifying them, as schoolboys identify locomotives, leaning on a railway gate. 'Comforting, I must say,' said Colin, 'but, Gerry, what a moment in history! Is this, or is it not, the most romantic show in the world?'

'I don't know about that,' I answered, 'but you should have seen the old Colonel yesterday: he was almost weeping.'

'Well, I don't wonder. I'm a strong man too, but I was very nearly unstrung. Here come the sweepers, Gerry . . . *Jasmine* . . . *Gladiolus* . . . *Torbay* . . . *no, Wolfhound* . . . *Stormbird* . . . *Dogfish,* I think——'

But now our own sweeper, *Guelder Rose,* was curving into its place. It joined the line and went out through the fairway.

Lemnos Island with its great Mudros Harbour was now behind us—perhaps for ever.

Outside the harbour there was a wind and a menacing heave on the sea. This troubled and silenced us, and I went alone to the ship's stern to look down its wake. Sometimes I looked northward and saw far away the isle of Imbros standing like the tops of a purple-shaded mountain submerged by the sea. Yet further, and veiled in mist, Samothrace rose sheer into the sky like some platform built for the gods behind the vague horizons of our world.

But mostly I looked down the wake, and inevitably it made me think of all the past from which we were steaming away. I thought of my small grey genteel home in the Baron's Court Road, and of my school on the City's embankment to which I would go daily in an underground train. My father had been a master at the school and so I got my education there for nothing. But he had died when I was sixteen, and from that day I was left in the hands of a devout and simple mother, her only child. I had to leave school when I was just seventeen, and my education incomplete. However, with much lamplight swatting after a day's labour in a certain great store, I passed a Civil Service exam with some credit and went to a humble job in Whitehall—little dreaming then that forty-odd years later I should retire with the rank of Principal Assistant Secretary. From my place in the Civil Service, and with my show of education, it was not difficult, during the famine of young officers in 1914, to leap straight into the gentleman's rank of a second-lieutenant.

As I remembered this, the wake before my eyes turned into another wake—the wake of H.M.T. *Carpathia*, a black troopship steaming through the Channel and bearing thousands of us, officers and men, in singles, drafts, and whole units, to Alexandria and the Mediterranean Expeditionary Force.

This old trooping liner was but three hours out of Devonport when I first saw Colin. He was leaning on a rail of the promenade deck and staring out to sea (just as I was now on *Guelder Rose*). I saw his straight-featured profile under the waved brown hair which the head-wind was lifting, and in my shame-filled habit of those days, I wondered if he was the one I could love.

Let me say at once that the young man who thus looked at

Colin's face, being the child of a narrow middle-class home and a church-loving mother, was still virgin at twenty-four, and of somewhat inhibited sex, so that his hunger to love someone carried no physical desire; it was simply a hunger for the exquisite emotions of a purely cerebral love. Before seeing Colin I had twice found someone to fill my need, the first a new boy at school with a pretty face, and three years younger than I; the second a junior clerk at my store. Each was lost to me now, and day by day during my six months in the Army I had secretly looked for their successor. No doubt I was approaching full heterosexuality because I had searched also among the faces of girls—but the love I wanted would not rise at my call. And now I looked at Colin on the rail and instantly selected him as a candidate for the long vacancy.

At twenty-three he was as slim as at eighteen, and his fine-boned face was narrow; I on the other hand was somewhat thickly built, and since my face, in addition, was full-cheeked and rather rosy, some of my friends had dubbed me 'Beefy Browning'. I did not mind this nickname—at least not much—so long as they knew that the heaviness was formed of muscle and sinew only. Sooner or later, if they didn't realize this, I told them so. Actually I was a powerful slogger at cricket and might have got close to county standard if I hadn't left school so early. I contrived sometimes to let them know this.

Delighted to see the badge of my regiment, the King's Own Sussex Light Infantry, on Colin's tunic, I rested my elbow on the rail beside him.

'I see you're going out to the Koslis too,' I said.

'Yes, thank God.' He had turned towards my voice, and his full face with its merry eyes was no declension from the appealing profile. 'It's the devil's own luck because I'm not a regular. Are you?'

'Good gracious, no. Just a New Army amateur. One of Kitchener's bright hopes.'

'Same here; but have you done any fighting? Ypres or France?'

'Heavens, no. I'm not even properly trained yet.'

'Nor am I. I only joined up last August. I am still guiltless of blood. Cigarette?'

'Thanks. August? Then you're a month senior to me.' Proud of my early commission, I was always disappointed when I encountered someone younger and yet senior to me.

He evaded this. 'But do tell me: how did you get to a regular battalion? One of the finest in the Army.'

'I just don't know. Probably it was a mistake. There are heaps of Brownings, and the War office probably meant a Lord Browning or someone.'

'Your name's Browning?'

'Yes. Gerry Browning.'

'Mine's Dester. Colin Dester. It was merely improper influence that got *me* into the Koslis. Father's an old pal of the Brigadier, Lord Wesborough. They hunt together with the Coldstock.'

I didn't dare ask whether my guess was right and the Coldstock was a pack of hounds. So I said, 'Oh, I see.'

'I met the old bird myself once when Father and I were out with the Duke of Melfort's. I was only a kid at the time but I was feeling pretty good, and rather cocky, because I was on my first real hunter.'

My heart fell into a deepening sadness as he said this. I was thinking of the Baron's Court Road with the District Railway grinding along behind it and the waste ground across the street in front, where we would play cross-touch or stump cricket. I was contrasting our London street-play with the Duke of Melfort's hounds. Plainly this Colin belonged to a different world from me. His words seemed to be carrying him out of my reach; and as he receded he became the more desirable.

'Do *you* hunt?' he asked.

'Good lord, no!' In my despair I flung my poverty before him. 'I could never afford anything like that. My father was only a junior master at my school, and even so he died young and left us poor'; but hardly had I said this before I tried to heighten my social standing by adding, 'He was a Classical Master. If he hadn't died I might have gone to Oxford or somewhere.' Doubtfully true, this last statement; and, ashamed of having spoken it, I set about being humble again. 'My father being a master there, I got my schooling for nothing.'

'Which school was that?'

'City of London.'

'Damned fine school.' But I knew from his tone that he was being polite and generous, while thinking in his heart that it was one of the lesser schools.

'Which was yours?'

'Eton. There's quite a sea running. A south-west wind too. It'll be stormy in the Bay of Biscay. Are you easily sick?'

'I don't know. I simply don't know. I've never been on a big ship before.' Eton. So I might have guessed. 'And you went on to the Varsity?' Should one say 'Varsity' or 'University'?

'Yes. To Oxford.'

'Which College?'

'Balliol.'

Just so. Balliol. Eton, Balliol, and—'And you got a good degree, I expect?'

'No, only a Second in Greats. I think the old man was disappointed. I had managed to get a Classical Exhibition at Balliol, and it was his idea that I should only take Pass Mods in my second term and take the Greats School at the end of my third year, and get a First of course.'

I didn't know then what he was talking about, and I'm not sure that I'm clear now; but I didn't let him see this. I hid my fog behind a further question, 'And after Oxford, what did you do?'

'Oh, I had a year at the F.O.'

So glad was I that I could translate something at last that I had to display my knowledge before him. 'The Foreign Office. And where was your field of activities?' I asked pompously.

'The Embassy at Rome.'

Oh, dear.

'Luckily the Ambassador was a Balliol man too and he knew my father well, so there was no difficulty in getting on to his staff.'

Oh, dear, oh, dear. Nevertheless, though awed, and increasingly sad at heart, I didn't want to give in. Especially since the love I longed for was rising in my heart. I fought for it. 'Have you chosen your table in the dining-saloon yet? Or could we perhaps sit together'—but, instantly afraid that this was impertinent and silly, I tried to justify it. 'After all, we belong to the same battalion and it'd be rather fun.'

Strange, but he was obviously delighted by my invitation. He turned to me, the pleasure in his eyes. 'Yes, *rather*! That'd be absolutely top-hole,' he said in the language of those days.

Perhaps he's lonely too, I thought, and thinking of his home. Perhaps he was, but now I know also that he was just approachable and affectionate and that whatever other sins found a footing in his life, snobbery never got near to it.

Pleased with this first victory I did not say much more. I was nervous of being a nuisance and, to speak the truth, felt that I should be rather more comfortable away for a while from all these allusions to Mods and Greats and Lords and hounds. I smiled awkwardly and strolled off along the deck.

Dester? The name was uncommon, but surely I had seen it in the papers? Lord This, Duke of That—was it the family name of some noble house? In the lounge of this old liner there was a 'library': a glass-fronted cabinet of old and recent novels, with a shelf of reference books among which was a *Who's Who*. I asked the steward to get this out for me; and with fingers shaking a little I opened it.

'DESTER, family name of Baron Storrington.'

So? Turn to 'Storrington' then.

'STORRINGTON, 5th Baron (cr. 1760), William Colin Semple Dester, *s.* of 4th Baron and Cecilia, *d.* of Earl of Carshalton; 2 *s.* one *d.* Owns about 12,000 acres. *Heir: s.* Hon. Colin Semple Dester. *Address:* Castle Ivry, Brackmore, Sussex.'

It took that liner eleven days, steaming through the grey Atlantic and the blue Mediterranean, to come upon Alexandria, and most of that lazy time Colin and I spent together. If I was pleased to be a secret lover, he, beyond question, was happy with his new friend, one of his own age and regiment; even delighted with him. Because I was secretly flattered (and everything about this business was a secret in me) that he with his Castle Ivry and his Second in Greats should be so content with a Gerry Browning, my love was in part a humble and excited gratitude. Daily I walked the decks looking for him, and when I saw him in a deck chair, I would hang around, waiting to be seen by him and summoned.

'Come on, Gerry,' he would call. 'Come and talk.'

And how we talked, usually reclining in deck chairs high among the boats on the boat deck. And what a gay chatterer he was. To me an enthralling one, because he would unconsciously spread before me, speaking of Eton, Oxford, and Ivry, a pageant of gracious living in which wealthy or ennobled people moved among their stately homes and broad timbered parks; a life in which the whole of duty seemed to lie in caring for the workers and tenants 'on our few family acres', setting them an example by sitting in the family pew on Sunday, and governing the country, meanwhile, by socio-political activities. No, not the whole duty, because I could not help perceiving, as he rattled on, that duty for all the boys of his class meant donning the defence of Britain like a sword the moment she was attacked.

'But that goes for others of us too,' I told myself for my comfort.

He talked of his first pony, Heliogabalus, a roan with a tan muzzle (what did that mean?), an idle fat little beast who much preferred munching his feed to jumping a fence, and of that first hunter, Montegusto, who went over all fences like a greyhound. 'It was like flying to be on Monty,' he said, 'but I never had my young brother's easy seat or perfect hands.' 'No?' I said as if surprised. He talked of 'Pop' at Eton—I still don't quite know what Pop is—and of the Union at Oxford. He spoke of shooting on Scottish moors, of a sister finishing her education abroad, and much—very much—of 'Grandma', the Dowager Lady Storrington. 'She's an incredibly beautiful old piece, Gerry; all lace and pearls and aigrettes. She used to love me because I knew how to treat her. I treated her as infallible on all matters social, moral, religious, and literary. She thinks she is. I laughed heartily at all her stories, even when I didn't understand them, and I feigned an affection for her spaniel which stank. But then she got wind of my Socialist activities at Oxford and, oh God, she almost turned from me to die. She only recovered a little when she decided I must be mad.'

For Colin had rebelled against the High Tory traditions of his family and joined the Independent Labour Party, partly in youthful showmanship, but very certainly too from a desire, as he grew older, to take the side of the exploited or the oppressed. 'All the women of my family were shocked but not so Papa. He was only amused; he said he "enjoyed this period" and he bought me huge books on Socialism, "that dismal gospel", as he called it.'

'But are you still a Socialist?' I asked, for I too was rather shocked.

'No. *Hardly*! I withdrew from the Party when its paper attacked all the landed gentry, and my father by name, at the time of my sister's marriage. She married the Master of Strathcannon, and they chose to be funny about it. I wasn't taking that, so I contented myself with Liberalism. Whereupon Papa was amused again, and Grandma slightly relieved—though not much—and Papa got me made a member of the Reform Club just as war broke out. Yes, I'm really and truly a member of the Reform, so now I fear not what any man can do unto me.'

There was little flavour of braggartry in all this; it was rather his joy in the tranquil and sunny past now dropping behind us; in the memory of things probably lost for ever.

I listened and talked little, for I could see little to tell about life in my Baron's Court Road. I was partly ashamed of it too, since I was by far the more class-conscious. Once when expounding his radicalism he said, 'It's no good, Gerry: if *noblesse oblige* means anything at all, it means that you and I who haven't done too badly out of life ought to do what we can to lift up the plebs,' and I was delighted because he manifestly didn't count me among the plebs but held that *noblesse* obliged me too.

But never did his home life seem more different from mine than on an evening when we were a day out from Malta, steaming fast to Alex, and he began to talk of butlers and wines. Again I listened and laughed and said little, not wanting him to see that these were waters in which I had never even paddled and would certainly sink now. He spoke of the wine at some lord's house where 'the shooting was good but the butler ought to spend a month or so at Oxford to learn how champagne should be handled'. That butler was better at singing hymns, he said, than serving wines. 'You should have heard him in the chapel at Easter. Most of the footmen and grooms on whom we usually depended for Alleluias were away that hols and the butler and I had to lend all our aid to the women. We did well. I nearly burst a blood-vessel, supporting them as a gentleman should. I sing better than you, Gerry, old boy. Or louder, at any rate.'

But now, thank Heaven, he was back in waters where I could swim as well as he, and probably better, so I protested that he needn't be so sure of *that*. Trying to balance his fun, I said I could do a very powerful 'Hark, hark, my soul' in our church at home.

What church was that? he asked carelessly.

I told him, and by this narrow and frivolous channel we arrived at talk about religion: about the origins and meaning, if any, of life, and the purpose of man's poor struggling spirit on a wheeling and watery planet; whereafter, inevitably, and with thoughts that could not be disclosed, we had some conversation about death, its dark, utter mystery, and the likelihood, small but possible, of a life beyond it.

So we talked the days round, continuing often into the deep of the night, under the stars, and all the time the Mediterranean swept by our beam and formed the long wake behind us—a wake written in water and ever vanishing, like our youth and all these lost, long, careless, happy days. Our black ship went ever eastward towards Alex, and the sun would drop behind it into an empty sea, just as now it was falling behind our grey sweeper, *Guelder Rose,* as she ploughed on towards the tall-hilled isle of Tenedos. Before that voyage ended Colin's face and slim figure housed for me most of the delight that could be got from life, most of the spiritual emotions that I longed for —because I wished to have it so.

Tenedos was now right ahead of us, spread upon the sea under its conical hill, Mount Elias, and clothing itself in violet hues, as all these Aegean islands did, when a bright sun went down.

CHAPTER FOUR

IN the open roadstead of Tenedos it seemed that all the ships which had sailed out of Lemnos were lying in wait. We of the Koslis were transhipped from our sweeper to the *Marathon,* the cruiser from which we had practised going down rope-ladders to open boats. The moon, which had been haloed, sailed out into the clear, and the sea went calm. Praise be to God.

For a while that night we lay about the *Marathon's* decks, and while we slept—if sleep we did—all these ships from Tenedos moved out. Northward. The moon went down at three o'clock into a sea of great stillness, and then a bugle sounded Reveille.

We woke from our broken dozes to see a dark night pierced with stars, and that calm sea. A *flat* calm. Could it be that God was on our side?

Three-thirty, and the sailors brought us a breakfast of hot rolls and steaming coffee. 'These naval johnnies are gents,' said Colin at my side; and indeed it seemed they couldn't do too much for us. They waited on us and jollied us and comforted us, almost as if ashamed that they must stay in the shelter of their armour plates while we went ashore.

'Fall in. Get to your squares.' Our Company S.M. 'And for Gawd's sake stop that chattering. This is a parade, not a mother's meeting. All of you got everything? Rations? Ammo? Trenching tools? Water-bottle, all? No more water for years.'

We looked to our equipment and ammunition. All of us had laden packs, even the officers. Some of the officers had rifles.

'All okay? Good. Because you're not coming back here.

Next stop, Constantinople. May be able to fill your bottles again there. All present and correct, sir.'

'Thank you, Sergeant-Major.' Bill Drewer nodded and curled his golden moustache.

By the great cruiser's side lay a string of four ship's boats towed there by a steam pinnace.

Now A Company moved. B moved. I put my hand on my revolver holster, where it trembled.

The laden men went down the ladders and crammed into the boats, where already the bluejackets were waiting for us. Their oars stood erect like a coppice of masts. They must row us ashore when the steam pinnace, having got us as near to the beach as it could, cast off its tows.

Just before Colin stepped on to the rope-ladder he turned to me—a thing I have never forgotten—and asked, 'Coming, Gerry?'

The appeal gave me a moment of happiness. It seemed that he wanted me to be with him. It was as if he had need of me.

'Sure!' I assented, and stepped on to the rung immediately above him, while Bill Drewer, watching his men, said 'Good luck, old thing' and curled the moustache. He must have felt like a real Viking now. A Viking about to land.

'Aye, aye, sir,' I answered, trying to sound jovially nautical at the summit of a ship's ladder, and to appear unafraid. But probably I spoiled this second aim by repeating, 'Aye, aye, sir.'

'Pirrie and I are coming in the first boat of the next string because it'll touch ground first. See you ashore, old cock-a-hoop.'

'Yes . . . yes . . . sure,' I stuttered. 'Right-ho, Drewer. Yes. . . . So long.' And I went down the rungs slowly and clumsily, in spite of our recent practice.

At the bottom of the ladder, in the crowded and rocking boat, Colin deliberately and forcefully made a place for me at his side, saying, 'Come on, Gerry.'

The sailors in our boat were jollying us, even though they too must come to the beach. 'Come on, lads. Trips round the harbour. All free. Hey, steady, you lubbers! Don't rock the boat. Thought you'd been training for this lark. Mind where you put your foot, sir. We want to reach the shore—at least, I suppose we do. Gentlemen . . . gentlemen . . . kindly keep your seats; keep still.'

An unnecessary injunction, since we were crammed into the boat more tightly and immovably than in a cup-tie jam—but I'll not say that the crush of my neighbours' shoulders was not a comfort.

The darkness was paling now but not enough to give us sight of our landfall. Only a searchlight swung suddenly from a headland, and died.

'Christ!' murmured Colin; and just then the pinnace began drawing us away. 'Here we go,' he whispered.

When six strings of boats were filled they found their stations abreast of the *Marathon,* three strings on each side of her, with some hundred yards between string and string.

From somewhere unheard came the order to move and we went through the twilight with our great mother ship in the midst of us like an eagle with her newly hatched young beside her.

Jokingly Colin grimaced at me and said, 'Oh lord! I was happy on that nice sweeper. Don't want to discourage anybody, but wouldn't you say, Gerry, that we're being cast to the wolves so that the others can land safely?'

My heart took a sick fall. Death? Was it but a few minutes away? Jammed here between Colin and another, was I like a prisoner being taken to the firing squad?

Colin went on—perhaps he felt a need to talk: 'Do you feel rather like live cattle being taken to the Continent for slaughter? Must say I do. Well, there it is . . . here we are . . . two poor "towaways". . . . Gerry, would you *still* rather be here than anywhere else?'

'I suppose so,' I said, with a suitable grimace.

'I'm not sure.'

After that he went silent; and I was comforted to know that

he, like me, was secretly doubting and quaking, though resolved to hide fear behind laughter.

A few minutes to live? I couldn't believe it. Not to us would the bullets come.

But the boat moved on through the still grey night, and I have to tell (because I have always believed it) that in these minutes I knew something of a last cleansing and of a gift of grace. With my simple Anglican upbringing I had no doubt about my duty today. 'I must do this thing properly,' I told myself. 'And, oh God, the only way to do it is to be done with all my beastly self-centredness and to be ready to give up all. I want to do it properly.'

Mercilessly, the pinnace towed us on, and I thought of all the other boats going to the other beaches with the men who had gone cheering and singing out of Mudros Bay. I thought of the gigantic Australians and New Zealanders who were going to a beach far away from any of us. Each of these men, I thought, though jammed against his neighbours, is in a desert without parents or brothers or past friends. Are they all thinking the same as I?

'I will do it properly. I do really believe in what we've been set to do, and, if I must, I'll die for it. Never mind if I'm killed and never see Colin again . . . never see Mother again. I don't matter. I mustn't matter. I—I *don't*.' Secretly I asked my Anglican God to help me not to matter. To strengthen this desire I recalled the Special Order of the Day from our Brigadier. 'Fusiliers, Koslis, our brigade is to have the honour to be the first to land and to cover the disembarkation of the rest of our division. Let us carry it through in a way worthy of the traditions of all our regiments; in such a way that the men of Albuera and Minden, of Delhi and Lucknow, may know us for their equals in valour, and that history may hail us. Wesborough, Brigadier-General commanding.'

'Oh, yes, I will—I *will* be done with myself—I must—there's nothing else for me now. I *am* done with myself . . . I *am*. I can do this.'

And I have to report that though I doubted whether, should

I survive the battle, this self-abandonment would last, and though I was still afraid, I have never in my life known a sweeter happiness, a sharper joy in conquest, than in that towed boat. I knew then for a while the peace, the exultation, that comes when all one's selfishness is torn away, and one sits clothed in one's right mind (as I must think it) with fear at one's side, perhaps, but with no desire but to do all duties well.

The boat went on; the twilight changed into a pale grey haze over the breathless day.

CHAPTER FIVE

THE day an April Sunday; the year 1915. Not a sound in sea or sky except the sibilant run of our bows through the water. Sea and sky a picture of peace.

'There she is!' said a voice. 'Gawd, I didn't know she was that near.'

Yes, yonder was a headland, visible now like a waiting ghost. Gallipoli. Every head turned to greet it, and someone said, 'There's a little bay. I can see a bay.'

'Gentlemen, *if* you please! Keep still. You'll see plenty of it in time.'

So that was Cape Helles, guarding the Hellespont; that bay our V Beach; that grey village on its eastern arm Sedd-el-Bahr. Our shadowy Gallipoli Peninsula was becoming clear, like a picture developing on a slow grey film.

'There's another bay.'

'That's W. Cape Helles is between 'em.'

'Where are X and Y?'

'Round the blasted corner.'

'And S?'

'I dunno. Search me. Round the other bloody corner, I think.'

'But I can't see anyone on V or W. Isn't Johnny Turk expecting us?'

'Hope not. Hope he's gone for a shave. Or for a bint.' The voice stammered as it joked. A breaking breath had caught and tripped it.

'Where are the Australians?'

'Hell of a way from here.'

'Pity. We could do with a few of 'em here They're bigger than we are. Any nice bathing-machines on the beach?'

'Nothing there at all, so far as I can see. Just damn-all.'

'Now stop talking.'

'Quiet! Quiet!'

'No bandstand?'

'No.'

'Rotten place for our holiday.'

'Stop that talking. Stop it, I say! We're getting nearer. Not a word more.'

Look: on our port the *Swiftsure,* the *Euryalus,* and the flagship *Queen Elizabeth,* all with their twelve-inch, ten-inch, and fifteen-inch guns trained on the Peninsula. On our starboard, at the very gates of the Dardanelles, *Nelson, Cornwallis,* and *Basilisk.* Fourteen warships about the Peninsula's toe.

'Comforting,' Colin muttered, but his jaw was thrust to one side.

Suddenly, just before the sun lifted out of Asia across the Straits, the naval bombardment opened. It shocked our hearts and pounded on our eardrums. Shells crashed on beaches, slopes, capes, and hinterland. Shrapnel burst white on the sky; lyddite burst green, black and yellow on the ground; smoke clouded all.

'That's a village or something on the top.'

'It won't be there long.'

Unheeding the *Marathon* speeded us on, the six pinnaces keeping their tows beautifully dressed to left and right of her. She accompanied us till her anchor dragged; then the pinnaces slipped their tows; and the sailors rowed at speed towards the beach.

'Jesus Christ!' Colin's face was white, but he smiled when he felt I was looking.

Strange. Only about two hundred yards from the beach and not a movement there; not a sound. The beach was now clearly defined: an arc of sand embraced by scrub-patched and grassy hills. The ship's fire hammered all, but no answer came from that sickle of bay. Could it be that——

But no! When we, the Infidels, were about a hundred yards from Islam's wall, the Turks let loose their wrath at us. Every rifle and gun spoke. A cloud-burst of bullets stabbed the boats and tore the sea. I never knew what happened then. Sailors bowed over their oars, dead. Soldiers seized those oars and pulled—in terror and in courage, both. The soldier crushed against my right shoulder cried out as he took the bullets that might have killed me. His head drooped but, jammed between two of us, he could not fall. He cried out no more and was probably dead. Colin, on my other side, put a smile on his white face, and, for a second, I was glad that I screened him from some of the bullets. I lost sight of the other boats in our tow because men were dying around me with loud cries. They were lurching into death. But our rowers, madly pulling, got us within yards of the beach, and like others I got myself out of that boat. As I did so, the man on my right, no longer held up by the jam, pitched forward—dead, for all I ever knew. Colin was out ahead of me. We were in water above our waists, and I floundered on with no thought of bravery, only of shelter. Bravery could wait. I stumbled over a submerged rock and went under—which probably saved my life, because when I scrambled up again I saw some of those who had been near me lying under the water, dead, at peace, and weighted down upon their last couches by their sixty pounds of equipment. Colin was wildly plashing towards the shelter of a low sandbank. I rushed after him, not in love, because self-love alone was alive just then, but in need of a friend. I got through the sea's break and threw myself at his side under the bank.

Breathless, I looked around. Some hundred men were crouching beneath this long, low, broken parapet, a tiny fringe of Christians on an Islamic shore. There was perhaps eighteen feet of sand between the bank and the drowsy lap of the water.

'Bill Drewer's taken it,' were Colin's first words to me.

'Has he?' It seemed no very large incident amid all this din and slaughter.

'Yes. Look.' He pointed a shaking finger.

I looked, and there was Drewer. He must have received his bullet near the sand and slid down beneath the water. Weighted down by the harness of equipment which he'd donned like any private, he lay beneath the clear transparent water, with his cap washed away, his shaven head uncovered and his long yellow moustache uncurled and adrift like a weed. To what purpose had he bidden the ship's barber shave his head? There he lay, and it was hardly an hour since he had said to me, 'Good luck, old thing,' and grinned and curled his moustache. Near him lay the rifle he'd carried as an example to his men.

'Bill. Poor old Bill. Who else? Who else?'

Who of my platoon were here and alive? Of Colin's? I could count but seven of mine and eleven of Colin's. The only other officers ashore were Pirrie of D and Lippincott, who was wounded. Where were the rest of us? Under the water, on the sand, or drifting about Cape Helles in those boats manned only by the dead.

The other men beneath our bank were Dublin Fusiliers from other tows and——

Ah, but *yes*! The *Clyde*. The *River Clyde*, that old collier, stowed with men instead of coal, had grounded some three hundred yards away, and somehow or another the sailors, since their duty was to get the Army ashore, had dragged three decked-over lighters to make a pontoon bridge between her and the beach. Munsters and Hampshires had rushed out of holes in her hull, down some hanging gangplanks and along that tossed and straining bridge. So I could see because many lay on the lighters, dying or dead.

Another company of Munsters now rushed over this tottering pier, and perhaps a sixth of them reached our dead ground. We were now some two hundred under the bank.

'I take it,' roared Colin above the tumult, 'that the old Turk'll come haring down and bayonet us all.'

'I suppose so,' I said, my heart sickly shaking. I tried to recover my desire for self-abandonment, but to be soaked, shivering, and awaiting a knife through the lungs! Was Colin feeling like this? I hoped so, that we might still be akin to one another, and he want me with him. He jested, but did his voice shake?

'I reckon it's his job, Gerry, and there must be thousands of him up there. I shan't blame him. After all, we're kind of trespassers, aren't we? Definitely. Why doesn't the sportsman counter-attack and enjoy a little pig-sticking?'

But the old *Clyde* wasn't having that. From sandbagged casemates on her fo'c'sle and her bridge machine-guns poured her covering fire over us. Seeing us there, not once did they stop; they dared not stop. The Navy was to be 'father and mother' to the Army, and, God, she was our mother now! The old *Clyde* was her very spearhead, almost ashore with us; and behind her the great ships, moving slowly up and down, were bombarding trenches, village, fortress. *Queen Elizabeth* sent her roaring thunderbolts on to the hills behind. Let no reinforcement move.

Cheering from the *Clyde*. Cheering as of a football crowd. Turning, I saw that some men from W Beach had scaled the intervening hill, Cape Helles, and were trying to come to our rescue. An officer on the skyline waved to comfort us—and fell dead. The men behind him fell back. Some of our Munsters led by an officer waving a stick, tried to dash up the slope and effect a junction. All fell. A mad endeavour, but maybe we were all mad on V and W Beaches that morning.

One of the falling men blew up a mine and himself with it. Its detonation deafened me, and I was glad of this; the deafening seemed to dim one's apprehensions like a blow.

But now an unexpected thing. Two figures were running down the *Clyde*'s gangplank and on to the lighters. One was a chaplain in a pith helmet and a round white collar; the other a small man in a grey sweater, high top boots, and an Indian topee. On the first of the lighters the chaplain spun round and lifted a hand in pain as the blood spurted from his shattered wrist. But he came rushing on. So did Colonel Harby. I have never seen a little man in high encumbering boots run so fast. In those shining boots and that coarse sweater he appeared to symbolize glowing martial ardour in his lower half and honest homely labour up above. The civilian topee perhaps suggested the quiet and inoffensive elderly gentleman who dwelt within this battle array. He was not hit. Perhaps his very smallness saved him.

'The Colonel in fatigue dress,' said Colin.

Both men reached our bank. The Colonel, bent double, ran towards us, raising a hand in greeting and then plunging flat down beneath the bank beside us without a thought for dignity —rather like a little Rugby three-quarter racing through all opponents and wildly 'touching down'. Where we lay the bank was about five feet high, and he could rise again and stand there, crouching—after an anxious reconnaissance. 'Well done,' he said. 'Well done, all of you.' And he added 'Yes', as if he'd decided, after thought, that this was not putting it too high. 'Pirrie . . . Dester . . . Browning . . . is that all?'

'Lippincott is wounded, sir,' said Colin.

I had begun to rise, being more afraid of my colonel than of all the Turkish army above.

'Get down, you fool,' he snapped. 'D'you want to be killed?' I sat down, ashamed, and he went on, 'Look here, you chaps: no more nonsense; no attempts at going further. This isn't Balaclava.'

'No, sir,' said Pirrie and Colin at the same time, and I could see that, even under that bank, even on that narrow ribbon of life, each, thinking himself the senior, was proud of it and wished to assert it.

'The *Clyde*'s sending no more ashore,' explained the Colonel. 'The conditions aren't favourable.'

'No, sir,' said both of them.

The Colonel looked at the dead on the sand and in the sea. 'Yes,' he said, shaking his head. 'Good men.' He looked again at us survivors and said 'Yes', nodding as if convinced he was not exaggerating. 'Good fellahs.'

'Please sit down, sir,' recommended Colin.

'What?' But he sat down, slowly, as if he resented this humiliation. He sighed. 'The other fellahs'll come ashore as soon as it's dark.'

I was always dumb in his presence, but never so Colin, who'd been in the diplomatic service.

'You won't try to get back, sir, will you?' he said.

'Perhaps not. It may not be necessary. Major Wint is there. Thank God you chaps are still alive. It must have been pretty awful, wasn't it?'

'Very coarse,' said Colin.

'What did you say?' The Colonel's perception of young men's humour was always rather slow, and his laughter delayed till the fuse worked.

'I said it was rather coarse, sir.'

'Coarse?' But now the fuse reached the powder. '"Coarse", ha, ha, ha. That's good. "Coarse"; that's very good. Ha, ha. Yes, I'm glad the others are waiting for the dark.'

The Colonel saw me look at my wrist-watch, which the sea water had stopped.

'It's nine—but don't worry too much, boy. There are some ashore at W Beach. They've done better there than here, Dester. D'you know who that padre fellah is? He's the Dublins' and Munsters' chaplain: Father Finn, or some such name. I was with him in the bows of the *Clyde*, watching, and when he saw hundreds of his boys lying on the beach, he said "I can't stand this, Colonel. Dammit, my bloody place is out there"—or whatever it is padres say. And Irish padres at that. And he rushed out, though several tried to stop him. A pretty stout fellah, you know. But all these Irishmen are. All of 'em.'

The Colonel didn't seem to perceive that he'd done precisely the same. Perhaps he thought it a colonel's business but no part of a parson's to be as brave as that.

We looked towards the Padre. Some of his Dublins were bandaging his shattered wrist.

'Let's go and see if we can help. Dammit, I know my First Aid.' Rising, the Colonel hurried towards him, and we followed, crouching. The Colonel, I thought, though doing his duty, was as uneasy as any of us on the beach, and preferred action to waiting.

'Ah, be quick,' the Padre was gasping to the boys dressing his wound. 'Be quick.'

'How goes it, Padre?' asked the Colonel.

'Och, it's nothing much, Colonel.' But he was suffering from shock: his face white, his lips trembling, his eyes bright. 'A-ah, it's only a little thing.'

'Lie back and rest. You're white. Take it easy a bit.'

'Gracious God, no. I've got to get to those boys. Ah, be quick, son.'

'It's no use, Padre. You can't do it. It's just a killing ground out there.'

'That's why I've got to go. I must get to those who're dying. Of course, of course. I must give them their absolution. They must die at peace. Oh . . . gracious God . . .'

'But, Padre,' protested the Colonel. 'Don't they have to confess, or something, before you give 'em absolution? They've no time for that. That's no place for that.'

'Conditional absolution. Conditional absolution. Conditional——' stuttered the Padre.

'God'll do that for them, Padre,' said the Colonel, probably after a guess as to what conditional absolution might be. 'You stay and bless them from here.'

'No, no. They may want their priest. They are Catholics, all of them, and must have a priest if one's available. Sure. Is that finished, son?'

'Just ready, Father.'

'Padre, it's death out there.'

'That's what I mean. I must go to them before they die. Don't be asking me not to. I must go. Naturally.'

'But you too—what about you?'

'Oh, me? I'll make an Act of Contrition, and—and——' He shrugged off the rest.

I could see that the Colonel no more knew what an 'Act of Contrition' meant than I had known what Colin's 'Mods' and 'Greats' were; and that, like me, he hid his ignorance behind a silence.

'Thank you, boys,' said Father Finn. 'That's fine. Bless you all. Now . . .'

'Padre, don't—don't——'

He didn't listen. He looked towards his charges on the sand

and, trying to laugh, said, 'Here goes!' But he didn't go at once. It was not easy to go out there. He muttered something —his Act of Contrition, I suppose (and I have often wondered if the words were the traditional: 'I now begin and will endeavour to spend this day according to Thy will')—but still he did not move. Then he said, 'Oh, here goes!' again and crouched and ran out.

'Oh God . . . the fool!' said the Colonel. 'God save him.'

We watched. The Padre, crouched down, ran from one prostrate form to another, making a quick sign of the cross over the dead. Over the living he appeared to gabble his absolution. But between two men he pitched flat, pressing both hands to his hip, and he lay there, rolling his shoulders in an agony. Two of his Dublins, after only a moment of hesitation, ran out to him. One got him by the shoulders and, thrusting his mate aside, dragged him back into shelter. His Dublins then dressed his new hip wound while he gasped and groaned. This done, he lay there for a while in thought and then, seeing a man move on the sand, he whispered to himself, he waited, he said aloud, 'No, it's impossible; I must go.' He waited two moments more, and then, with a shake of the head as if to shake away the last of the will's infirmity, made a sign of the cross over face and breast and went crawling towards him as a reptile might. I felt myself praying for him passionately to my God of the distant Baron's Court Road. 'Oh God, in Thy mercy . . . spare him . . . Jesus, save him . . . oh *save*——' He reached the man before the Turks saw him, but only just. Even as the words formed behind my lips, and before he could speak to the man, the Turks killed him.

'Oh God!' said the Colonel. 'They got him. That's *it*.'

'It must be wonderful to be a Catholic,' said Colin.

And the Colonel said, 'At a time like this, yes. I haven't much use for 'em in peacetime.'

'Nor I, sir,' said Pirrie who was something of a sycophant in the Colonel's presence, like me.

'C. of E. myself,' explained the Colonel, glancing up

apprehensively at some shrapnel bursting above us. 'Take it you fellahs are too?'

'Yes, sir,' Pirrie assured him, though I'd often heard Pirrie maintain that all religion was bunk.'

I was pleased to be able to say 'Yes, sir' with some sincerity.

Colin kept silence.

'Still . . . a pretty grand chap, that, you *must* say.'

We were all staring at Father Finn's body lying out there on the burnished sand. Lying like a thrown sack beside his son in the Faith. That son was not dead yet for he turned his head once or twice towards his new companion, and I dare say the sight of his priest at his side helped him to die well too.

'Hope they keep off shrapnel,' said the Colonel, glancing up into the sky again, as if this episode of Father Finn were now over, and the battle had already thrust him into the past. 'We are badly placed here for shrapnel, if you ask me.'

'There's always the Navy to look after their shrapnel guns,' suggested Colin, gazing at the battleships disposed at distances around us like crouched beasts ready to snarl.

'Pray God they will, ha, ha, ha,' laughed the Colonel.

'Meantime what exactly do we do here, sir?'

'Stay. Stay till night somehow. What else? Hold this little bit with the help of the *Clyde*.'

'Yes. I see, sir.'

'And pray night comes quickly.'

Our bank was like one side of a broken trench, and the Colonel posted sentries where possible along it and made all the others rest as on a fire-step. The resting men cleaned the breeches and muzzles of their rifles where the sand had clogged them; then wiped and polished and fixed their bayonets, ready for a counter-attack. No further hint of rescue came from W Beach; no movement was visible on the *Clyde*. It was lonely under the bank.

But all day the Navy flung its shells crashing on to the braes above us, to keep our courage high. The *Queen Elizabeth* sent her messages of hope in the form of roars like those which fifty jet engines would make today, as her shells, demons heavy with death, flew over us. Queen Lizzie was fighting all out for us—was not the C.-in-C. aboard her? Her every gun spurted flame and her smoke wreathed her. Wonderful the comfort of her watching eyes and furious voice. The old *Clyde* too: she had only machine-guns, but did she use them for our comfort that day!

All day the sun blazed down upon us, drying our clothes (the day's one mercy), while shrapnel and shell fragments and bullets bespattered the world around us.

Leaning against the sandbank and looking out to sea, the Colonel chatted with us, as if reclining in a deck chair on a pleasure beach. What else was there to do?

'Can't understand why the damn fools didn't level out this sandbank. Then there wouldn't have been this ribbon of dead ground. What were their German advisers up to? It was the shatteringly obvious thing to do—in my humble opinion.'

Listening, not daring to say much, I perceived with wonder and interest that even a good man of fifty was not above 'showing off' before two young neighbours, though they might be dead any minute, and he—come to that—dead too.

'Murderers, they say, always make one mistake,' said Colin.

'Murderers—ha, ha, ha—murderers; that's good. But it was a mad plan this; from first to last I've said so. Landing us on six different beaches, all of 'em difficult, and all of 'em death-traps! I laid a very different plan before the C.-in-C. and I don't feel I was unqualified to do so. Dammit, I've been soldiering all my life; strategy and tactics have been my one great interest, and I may say I've made it my business to study the campaigns of the world's finest generals; I've walked over many of their battlefields.'

Curious, I thought, that he must not only uncover his little vanities before young men like us but never for a moment suspected that we could detect them for what they were.

'What was your plan, sir?' asked Pirrie, flattering him with a subaltern's interest.

'Why—simple, it seemed to me. But no one would listen

except old King-Reece—General King-Reece, you know—and of course he must go and die. The strategy of this campaign is wonderful: force the Dardanelles; send the Navy through to collar Constantinople and so shut the door to Egypt, Messpot, Persia, India; then join up with the Russkies and march over the Hungarian plain into Austria and Germany. Fine. Fine. But the tactics—damnable, in my humble opinion.'

'And your plan was, sir . . . ?' Colin encouraged.

'To attack with every man we've got at one point only, instead of splitting up our force like this, so that it can be destroyed in detail.'

'At the Bulair lines, do you mean, sir?' asked Pirrie, to give an impression of knowledge.

'No—good God, no. Anywhere but there.' (Pirrie looked abashed.) 'No, at the beach between Gaba Tepe and Ari Burnu—somewhere about where the Australians and New Zealanders are now—and God knows what's happening to them, poor fellahs. Not to stop there, by God, but to push through in enormous power right across the waist of the Peninsula—only five miles of it—to Eski Keui and Kalkmaz Dagh and Maidos.'

'I see, sir,' said Colin, to whom all these names were meaningless.

'From there we'd have dominated all their forts on the European side of the Narrows and at Kose Kalessi and Chanak on the Asiatic side.'

Colin nodded, as one who began to see that the route so named was the best way to victory. He nodded again, as if with increased understanding: 'Yes . . . yes . . . of course.'

'Of course; and up goes the Navy and we could have won this campaign in about twenty-four hours. As it is, the Lord knows what's going to happen. I don't like it. I don't like the situation at all.' He shook his head and gazed at the current from the Narrows sweeping around Cape Helles over the bodies of the dead.

'No, sir,' said Colin; and I managed an echoing 'No' too.

'Mind you, I'd have got the Navy to make a demonstration, possibly with a crowd of empty transports, against this damned useless toe of the Peninsula. That'd have contained the Turks here, and once we were across the waist we'd have penned them all up between us and the sea. As it is, we shall be penned between that old devil, Johnny Turk, and the deep blue sea.' He stared at the sun-sprinkled sea. Beyond the battle, it was a lapis lazuli blue. 'King-Reece agreed. He agreed absolutely. He said on what proved to be his death-bed, "Yours was the right plan, Harby."'

Colin glanced sideways at me, and winked. Kiss me, Harby.

'You look at the map, Dester, and you'll see what I mean.'

'I will, sir.'

'Mind you, I'm not suggesting anything against the C.-in-C.,' said the Colonel, so that I wondered what he *had* been suggesting. But of course his loyalty had just caught up with him and was upbraiding him. 'He's one of our finest soldiers, and a most charming man. I've the greatest admiration for him. A very fine general. And he writes poetry.'

'*What?*' Pirrie looked up astonished.

'Yes, extraordinary, isn't it? And it's quite good stuff, I'm told. It's been published, some of it, you know. "The Ballad of Something." Extraordinary. I've never heard of a reg'lar officer who wrote poetry before, but I suppose it's all right.'

'Sir Philip Sidney?' Colin suggested.

'Who? . . . Oh. . . .' But the Colonel went silent because he was now at sea. I felt sure that he didn't know why Colin had said 'Sir Philip Sidney', and didn't want to admit this. All that he could remember about Sir Philip was that he had laid his cloak before the Queen—or was that Sir Walter Raleigh?—and given his cup of water to a wounded man who needed it more. Both of these actions, beyond doubt, had the Colonel's strong approval; but on poetry he kept silent.

Sir Philip, in fact, silenced us all. Thereafter we lay or sat or crouched, thinking our own thoughts, as that day, all sunlight, gunfire and lyddite smoke, wore on. I remember thinking, I'm having a Turk's-eye view of one of the most extraordinary spectacles the world has known. Here at my feet lie the dead on the beach and in the sea. Look at their blood running in rivulets through the sand and lying sticky and crimson on reeds and rocks. The water itself is red. (Our pilots in those aeroplanes glittering overhead told us afterwards that the water fringing the beach was rose-coloured from the sky.) Look at those silent and heaving lighters with their cargo of dead men and those boats swaying away from sight, because dead men have no interest in rudder or oar. Farther out our splendid ships move to and fro with their gun-flames licking from their sides, their smoke billowing before them, and the water spouts dancing about them, where the Turkish shells fall short and over. In the farthest distance are the Isles of Greece, Tenedos and Lemnos—Isles of the Blest to us on this shore. And there, yonder, are the green plains of Troy reaching out from Asia towards us; behind them Mount Ida, which had been the seat of Zeus for the drama of Troy. Today she watches the opening scene of a later war, and a thousand ships again.

Somewhere about four o'clock Colin said, 'When do they bring us a cup of tea and a cake?'

The Colonel chuckled at this—chuckled more than once as he pondered it and found it funny.

'Browning's a hearty feeder, sir,' Colin explained.

'Ha, ha, ha. A hearty feeder, is he, Dester?' And the Colonel looked at me beside him. I only grinned because I liked being chaffed by Colin. Who chaffs you, loves you. Besides, in plain truth I *was* a large feeder and inclined, Lord knows why, to be rather proud of it.

'Yes, sir, he's a big robust type and needs his feed regular.'

'Ha, ha, ha.' And again, 'Ha, *ha*!'

Pirrie saw that the joke was going down well with the Colonel, and so carried it further. 'If only the man'd come along with the ice-cream cornets, sir.'

This too scored a bull. 'And nigger minstrels, eh, what, Pirrie. Ha, ha, ha.'

'Why don't they come, sir?' asked Colin.

'What, nigger minstrels, Dester?' Punjabi Harby was enjoying his joke.

'No, sir. The Turks.' For the day was quieter now, and the gunfire sporadic.

'I can think of several reasons,' said the Colonel, proud to be the expert with his young men. 'The Navy has silenced a lot of their guns and scuppered half their men. Dammit, the ships have been letting 'em have it for nearly ten hours. Then take a look at their wire.'

'Thank you, sir, but I'd rather not,' said Colin. And we all saw in imagination the Turkish wire straddling over slopes and hills.

'Their damn wire's more like steel cables than honest barbed wire. I doubt if they want to come through it with the old *Clyde* watching. She's got a double battery behind those sandbags.'

'Well, bless her,' said Colin; and we all looked at the grand old tub, aground and silent and angrily watching.

'Though, mind you,' continued the Colonel, 'I doubt if the naval guns have done all the damage they hoped. Their trajectory's too damn low for trenches. Said so all along. This idea that the Navy can sweep the Peninsula clear for us is just moonshine. Said so from the beginning.'

Since these words promised ill for our future we fell silent again. In the next hour, as I crouched or lay there, snapshots of memory came to me and faded in this bright sun. I saw our little house in Baron's Court Road with the black-beetles scurrying in the basement. I saw myself and my father travelling in a District Railway train to Blackfriars, and there on the Embankment my schoolmates making their way to school. How many of them were alive now, and to what end our training in Latin prose and Xenophon and Euripides? I saw our children's parties in neighbouring houses and the little girls in their party frocks, some astonishingly fat and all terrifyingly self-possessed and competent. How shy I was of asking them to dance, and how little shy were they. Why was I under this bank and not they, since in those days they were far less timid than I? A shell falling near dispersed these children of the past. Then I remembered a golden June day in Regent's Park on a green veld furnished with tall English trees and fringed with roses. The children chattered and shouted as they played amid the glades, while midges danced an infernal ballet and gently stung them all—but there were only stings in the air that day, not death. I saw the Thames bank above Barnes Bridge and myself waiting there to see whether a dark blue or light blue oar first flashed under the bridge, for who first shoots the bridge wins. Light blue—and how I yelled to heaven, for I was Cambridge that year. Where now were those young Greek gods who swept their oars before me that day?

The sun dropped towards the sea, and the shadow of Cape Helles fell across us. It was cold now. The sun went down beneath the water leaving a crimson sash along the sky and violet lights everywhere. Then, very quickly came the uneasy night; and the sky above Gallipoli, above the Turks and the ships—and above us on this shore—was a wide darkness of sapphire and inky dyes, hung with unheeding stars.

Much of that night on the cramped beach is confused in memory, but one thing remains clear and dominates all. For me, and I imagine for all who survived it, that night is the story of Doughty Wylie.

The night came down on to the beach like a relieving force—at first. In its darkness we could stand up and walk; we could search among the dead for men who were still alive. To our joy all the rest of the Dublins, Munsters, Hampshires, and Koslis came down the gangplanks of the *Clyde* to join us. We had friends now. Some joined us under the bank; others hid themselves around the cliff beneath the castle. Encouraged, we climbed with our wire-cutters to the Turkish wire and cut lanes through it in readiness for the morning.

Destroyers, anxiously watching, came close inshore and played their searchlights on the Turks above us. It is not good to play against an opponent with a blinding light in one's eyes. Nor good to be well lit with your foe in darkness. At any sign of movement among the Turks the *Clyde* opened up an indignant and insulted fire. I think no one slept on the *Clyde* that night. *Queen Elizabeth, Cornwallis,* and *Albion* watched over us too, bombarding on the slightest provocation trenches, village, fortress, and hills. Only once did the Turks attempt a sally, and we and the ships beat them back. Maybe they didn't know that we had now so many ashore.

But then, at about one o'clock, the moon came up and, standing high over Gallipoli, flooded our beach with a wan grey light. We had to take cover and stay still. It was too cold to sleep. We had groundsheets in our packs and covered ourselves with them. More, the dead on the sands gave up their groudsheets to us, and did not grudge them. Once again we were sitting cramped and crowded together under that bank. Colin said, 'Cold! Cold! Come close, Gerry. Poor Tom's a-cold,' and we got close, shoulder pressing shoulder, hip against hip, and this was pleasure to me, though a pleasure of the spirit only.

Three hours of cold and doubt and apprehensiveness. Some drowsed, twitching; some nodded heavily and dreamed of what? Others peered and listened. I did not sleep at all on this strangest of beds, but stared at the sands and the sliding water, and at the dead whose doubts and fears were done with; their sleep unbroken.

At what time the figure of Doughty Wylie appeared before my eyes I cannot remember. Other men told me that all that night he had been walking among the weary men to cheer them up and hold their spirits from sinking. It was he, they said, who with a grim smile had sent the men to cut the wire, ready for the morning. Colonel Doughty Wylie, of the General Staff, was a fine square column of a man, with a square-jawed face as kind as it was strong. I have seldom seen compassion so surely present in firm soldierly eyes. Doughty Wylie, after being wounded in many wars, had been British Consul at Adana where, it was said, the Armenians looked to him as a father because he would place his body between them and the massacring Turks. They loved him as they might have loved a priest or a king. It was said too that his great exemplar was

General Gordon. If so, then Gordon's influence stood at only one remove from me that night, for when I first saw the humour, the gravity, and the tenderness in Doughty Wylie's eyes, after hearing all these tales about him, I admired and even worshipped him at first sight. I chose him there and then, and with a private and excited joy, as my exemplar.

Now, wounds or not, he was back in the Army, and just before the grey dawn lifted out of Asia—promising what?—he came towards us. In the half-light I could see that his compassionate eyes were heavy with fatigue and the square chin duskily unshaven. 'Boys,' he said, not observing Colonel Harby at first, 'no, sit down, all of you; it'll be light soon. Listen, it'd be rather hopeless when the morning comes to sit here on the beach like a holiday crowd. It's plain what we've got to do. The lads on W Beach next door have made good their hold by capturing the hill above it. They suffered like hell, but they're there. I think you saw them for a moment; that's so, isn't it, Harby? Well, we're not going to be beaten by them. They're Lancashires, and I've never heard that Dublin boys couldn't do anything Lancashire lads could do——'

'Or Sussex lads either,' put in our Colonel, a Wiltshire man, late of the Indian Army.

'Of course. Naturally. Sussex and Hampshire—no one like 'em. Well, we've clearly got to take that village and the hill on its left and shake hands with those Lancashire lads. Agreed?'

None of us said 'Yes, sir' at once because he seemed to be asking the terrible, the impossible. We were weary, stiff, helpless with thirst, sleepless, and shivering.

Colonel Harby, however, spoke for all of us. He said, 'Agreed, Colonel. My men'll do it.'

'Quite. Thank you, Harby. I know they will. And the Navy's going to help us by pounding everything in sight with everything they've got; they'll reduce that village to stocks and stones, but, even so, it may be rough going, so look here, you Irish boys: just think of it as "the rocky road to Dublin"—what?'

The Dublin boys laughed—still a little apprehensively, perhaps; the Munsters too.

'And Dublin for us, gentlemen, is that hill just above us. Hill 141. I say we'll take it, don't you?'

'Yes, sir.'

'Yes, sir.'

'Good. Thank you. Good lord, the Lancashires are on Hill 138, and there's only 114 between us and them. They'll come to meet us, I bet. We'll shake their hands on 114. And listen, all: those splendid fellows, the Australians, are ashore at Z Beach, and fighting like the devil. I say we'll do the same. The old Home Country can't be beaten by these youngsters, however splendid. I'll tell you another thing. It's been whispered to me that because of their truly wonderful physique and toughness, they are a little—just a little—inclined to think themselves a cut above you Home troops. Got that? Fine. Well, get ready, all. Better than us? What the hell!'

He turned an eye towards Colonel Harby. 'Eh, what the hell, Colonel? Listen, men. We've got to allow that these Aussies and New Zealanders are as good as we, but when it comes to fighting, I have never heard that anyone in the world was better than an Irishman. One famous Scotch general, if he'd got a tough fight in front of him, used to say, "I shall need Highlanders for this", but for my part—and for Colonel Harby's too—we're inclined to say, "Good Lord, what we want just now is a few Irishmen . . ." with a nice stiffening of Sussex and Hampshire boys, of course. I'm an Irishman, you see, and Colonel Harby's a Sussex man—for tonight, at any rate. Just think again of those Lancashire lads round the corner. They've been sitting on their hill for hours, but what their flanks are like I can't imagine. Their left's on the sea, I hope, but their right must be in the air and waiting for us. God, what a welcome they'll give us when they see us coming. As they will, they will. Agreed? Agreed, all?'

A silence and then: "We'll try, sir."

'Do our best, sir.'

'Shure, sorr. Do our best, sorr.'

'And, my God, if you do that, we'll get there. I swear we will. Australia's there and Lancashire's there and, my God, so will we be. Thank you. Thank you, men.'

With a shy smile for us all he walked on through the quickening dusk to say similar things to other men.

'And yon's the dawn,' said a grim voice somewhere; and I felt fear then as I turned and saw the wan light lifting out of Asia.

But with all my heart I wanted to follow Doughty Wylie well in the terrible sally he proposed. I remembered my desire for self-offering in the towed boat and, telling myself that I had not done much with it yet, I called it up again and held on tight to it. 'I will do this properly.' I was very happy with it—but I wished the orders to advance would come quickly. It was not easy to hold it firm. I prayed and prayed to my childhood's God: 'Oh God, help me hold. Help me to do this well.'

The dawn was now a scarf of grey, and I think it was just before the long scarf dissolved into the full flush of day that Doughty Wylie came again. With his swagger-cane under his arm and his sad, tired face wearing a half-smile he said an extraordinary word. He just said, 'Come, my children.'

It was a word that no other officer on that beach could have used. Probably he had been accustomed to speak like this to the Armenians he was comforting, but I am persuaded that, with its humour and tenderness, his fatherly word did more for our weary men than any other could have done. Colonel Harby echoed him, but, having no original genius like his, could only call, 'Come, men.' Colin and Pirrie, each sure that he was the senior and had the right to lead the remnants, shouted cheerily, 'Come, boys.' And with Doughty Wylie leading, and his swagger-cane waving above his head like a fiery cross, and with the Navy supporting him with all its fire, till it must lift the barrage, we rushed up the slope, over a Turkish trench, and into the ruined Sedd-el-Bahr village, shouting and yelling, shooting from the hip, dropping our sweat, and massacring, some screaming as they fell but being left there to gasp and curse and roll and moan.

Colin raced after Doughty Wylie, with all a boy's imitation of an admired senior; I followed Colin as I had followed him ashore, because he was my friend and I wanted to keep near him; at one time I heard him laughing loudly instead of shouting as he ran; both of us ran faster than our colonel, who was small and hampered by his high boots, but he came as fast as he could, bellowing, 'Go on, men. Go on, men. Go on, men.' Whether he was junior or not to Doughty Wylie I don't know, but he was content to charge up after him like a subaltern, shouting in all directions, 'Move! Move! Don't stop! That's it. That's it.'

In that rush up the slope Pirrie was killed and it mattered no more whether or not he was senior to Colin. I got a bullet through an arm and felt nothing of it till later when I was extremely proud of it and eager to describe it in a letter home. At the time I felt only an exultant joy that I had left selfishness down there on the beach or in the sea and cared nothing, or little, what any man could do to me. We cleared the village and the castle ridge, and swung on to the hill above V Beach, the Lancashire boys in their captured trenches cheering us like madmen as we came and keeping up a joyous covering fire left and right of us. One of our superstitious Irish boys was waving Father Finn's helmet (which he'd gathered to himself as a souvenir) high above his head triumphantly, so well was its holy power working. We heard sounds of cheering from the *Clyde*. From one of the ships—*Queen Elizabeth, Cornwallis, Albion?*—who shall say now?—came what was apparently a *feu de joie* over our heads, as we bayoneted ourselves into the Turks' ruined trenches, and were there. We were there.

It was the most excited moment of my life. Our bridge-head was won; it was secure; we had a line right across the toe of the Peninsula. Soon the C.-in-C. from the *Queen Elizabeth* signalled, 'Well done, Fusiliers and Koslis. A superb effort. Stick to it and your names will be famous'; and Colonel Harby, now undoubtedly the senior Brigade officer ashore, signalled back, 'Thanks from all ranks to C.-in-C. We are here to stay.'

But Colonel Doughty Wylie lay dead on the stones of Sedd-el-Bahr.

PART TWO

THE HINTERLAND

So now the Greeks grow white with dust that flies
About them as the horse-hooves strike the ground
And drive the dust towards the brazen skies.
Battle is joined again; the chariots wheel round.

The *Iliad*, V. 502–505

CHAPTER ONE

Now while my wife and I stood on the shore, I telling her some of these things (though for the most part I could only gaze in silence), three young Turkish women, brown-skinned, black-eyed, and unveiled, came down that slope from Sedd-el-Bahr and sat upon the sandbank to enjoy the morning breeze. They reclined there in graceful attitudes and stared at us in their turn, silently. A little barefoot boy came running down after them, and he too stared at us and at our boat before footing it happily, playfully, along the tops of those rocks from which the rains or the seas had long washed all memory of sun-dried Irish blood.

'Ah, well,' I said, embarrassed by the women's eyes. 'Can't stay here for ever, though I feel I should like to. Come, my dear.' A last look at Cape Helles, tall and formidable, which rose between us and W Beach—and we went up that slope, our Turk following. Helles! Helles! This time I went slowly, for whether or not my youthful figure ever justified the nick-name 'Beety Browning', I am a heavy man now and, alas, I carry a protesting heel.

As I went I turned to the Turk and pointed inland, prodding the air vigorously, to imply that we desired to walk a couple of miles or more. He grinned as usual, but also shrugged in a gesture of mild despair. He was an N.C.O. of the Turkish Army and, like many such, he was not fond of walking.

'Not more than three miles,' I assured him loudly and distinctly, hoping he would understand and be comforted. After all, our front at its furthest was never much more than six thousand yards from the beaches.

Nodding, he loosed a power of incomprehensible words at me, which at first I thought might be a refusal to undertake such a journey, but at last I gathered (for I had picked up some Turkish at Çanakkale) that he was saying his grandfather had been killed up yonder.

'Oh, I'm sorry,' I said; and my wife said, 'Oh, dear,' putting sympathy into her eyes, but he only grinned at us, as if this were the most amusing fact that had yet emerged.

'By *you*,' he said, pointing at my wife first and then at me. 'You. Very plenty killed here.'

I apologized again as well as I could, but it seemed a work of supererogation, for he only nodded and laughed and said, 'Very plenty.'

We started again to ascend the slope, and he came a couple of yards behind us, ready to grin whenever we turned round. We had no cameras, and what he was instructed to watch us doing, or stop us doing, I have never to this day understood.

Hill 141. And 138 beyond. I could only halt and stare—and stare—and then walk on. I could not speak as we walked on through the scrub which lay like hirsute patches over so much of the rolling tableland. Any depression or trough amid this brushwood fleece, any grass-filled hollow, might once have been a mule trench, a Company Headquarters, or the dust of men; because all this tongue of land between coast and coast had been as reticulated with trenches as the leaf of a Turkey oak with veins. But now—strange, wounding sight—there were stretches of yellow arable among the scrub, and a few cypress-fringed gardens of fig and almond and mulberry, and away there towards the Dardanelles long terraces of olives and tended vines. And there—look, my dear!—there, no more than a hump on the skyline, its shoulders stretching from sea to sea, was Achi Baba, inviolate still, the grim old guardian of the Peninsula which had never yielded it to the Infidel.

Nowhere between the sea's three brinks and Achi Baba could I see anyone moving. There was nothing but quiet around me.

Coming out of my thoughts, I spoke to my wife of our children. 'Extraordinary to think that to Stephen and Margot, though they're both over thirty now, it must seem like some old costume war. Like Agincourt. Or Waterloo, perhaps. I know I never speak of Gallipoli to a National Service boy today without perceiving that he's thinking of me as a survival from the Dark Ages. Sometimes he seems quite interested to learn what it felt like to be alive in such simple-minded days.'

'Does it never begin to seem a bit like that to you?'

'Good heavens, no. Gallipoli—no, never.' To me so enduringly vivid; to them in their space-conquering age a vague name in a vanished phase of the human story. 'Time isn't doing its job on it for me. Is it for you?'

'No . . . no . . .' she answered hesitantly. 'No, I don't think so. . . .'

'Is it just what you've always imagined?'

'Not quite. Nothing ever is. It seems rather more beautiful than anything you've ever described.'

'It was rather beautiful when we first came, with spring flowers everywhere and a rash of scarlet poppies on Achi Baba. But after a week or two it was just a wilderness of sand and scrub, with no beauty anywhere but its changing light. You should have seen sunset here, and night.'

I don't think she heard this, for she went on, 'Everything else about the First War seems to be fading away from me, but not Gallipoli. How . . . how could it? Hardly more for me than for you.'

'Of course not,' I agreed; and because I knew of whom she was thinking I went silent.

We wandered on, and the north-east breeze played gently, pleasantly, on our faces, for we were walking straight into it. That old north-easter, our tireless, summer-long enemy! Old friend, I greet you.

I knew to what I was leading them. Before us, to the left of Achi Baba Nullah, stood a few stunted pines on the edge of a donga. These perhaps were they. I could not be certain because other groups of pines stood by shallow and shaggy dongas; but these could be mine . . . they *could* be . . . I went towards them, and there was certainly a depression in front of them that could well be a hollow long ago filled up and now growing its bent grass and yellow balsam, and filling with summer-dried sticks of asphodel. As I drew closer, there came on the north-east wind a scent as of pine dust and honey, and instantly a 'landscape with figures' built itself around me—entrancing me with an exquisite sense of recovery, sweet and sad. I am twenty-four again and sitting by a deep dug-out cut among pine roots, and Colin is with me, and Old Bailey, and poor Evverson; and Colonel Harby is coming towards us.

I stopped dead, halted by this sudden gift of the incense-bearing trees.

'What are we waiting for?' asked my wife.

'Is that a mulberry tree over there?'

'Yes. I think so. Yes, I'm sure it is.'

'There were mulberry trees near by. I can only see one now, but I suppose even mulberry trees can die in forty years. Can you see any other mulberry trees—not far from some pines?'

'No, my dear.'

'Not with a slight sinking of the ground in front of them?'

'Please: what are you thinking about? Tell me.'

'Eh? Thinking? I think I'm waiting for Cass.'

'I *beg* your pardon?' she inquired with a laugh.

'I'm waiting for Cass to rejoin the Company. It is his hour of deep disgrace. Poor Cassy; my heart bleeds for him still. You see, we lived somewhere here among the roots of pine trees, and this could be the place. The very place. It was the best dug-out we ever had. "No. 1, the Pines." We had fifty other dug-outs but never one like "No. 1, the Pines, Peckham Road". It became a sacred memory, not to be spoken of other than softly and with all the courtesy and affection due to the dead.'

'Was *he* with you then?' she asked. But she was not speaking of Cass.

'Of course he was. Naturally. Where else would he be?'

She gazed down at the sand and the grass and the asphodel. As for me, losing all sense of her there, I indulged the elegiac memory of friends and things enshrined in past time as in amber, and I vividly possessed them again, one after another, for a while.

CHAPTER TWO

It must have been about the 12th of May, because it had been found possible to withdraw us into rest from the eighteen days of battle. These battles after the Landing had been, less to capture Achi Baba and command the Narrows than to save our lives by seizing enough ground for guns, field ambulances, and stores. Achi Baba was still there ahead of us, its slopes a formidable array of trenches, wire, and gun-pits. Already men were saying it was impregnable.

Still, they had said V Beach was impregnable.

And now we were back in this so-called 'rest camp' in a grove of trees and our Company Headquarters was this admirable 'No. 1, the Pines'. I don't know if the French, who made much better dug-outs than we did, had built it, or some of our sappers, but it was excavated far under the roots and furnished with pine props to hold up the Peninsula above it. The mess table was 'out on the veranda' under a tarred blanket. The veranda, I should explain, was a square trench with a step cut all round it for seats and a square chunk of earth left in the middle for office desk and dining-table. From its floor a path sloped at an angle towards that long communication trench, Peckham Road.

It was round this table that we sat waiting for Cass. Four of us: Old Bailey, Colin, Evverson, and myself. All our battalions had been reorganized after their decimation in the boats and on the beaches, and Old Bailey, from the Hampshires, was our new O.C. Company. Cass and Evverson were fresh arrivals, and Colin and I, who'd been through the V Beach Landing, felt in their presence all the superiority of veterans and experts—and made a show of not showing it. I was also proud of having been wounded in that most famous affair and pleased that in the mad excitement of our final sally I had not even noticed the pain; nor had it hurt greatly afterwards. And, anyhow, my pride in it was worth the pain. I early conveyed information about this wound to Cass and Evverson by a show of making light of it.

It had kept me out of the first May battles, though I had insisted (secretly proud of my fine act, and 'act' was the word) on taking part in the later ones. For the most remarkable effect of that wound was this: failing to hurt much, it had lessened my fear. Men were even saying of me, 'Our Gerry doesn't seem to know what fear is. Bloody different from me'; which delighted me and increased my recklessness—if others were there to see. Oh, yes, I was extremely proud of my new reputation for fearlessness and would risk death for it before the eyes of chaps who in a few years wouldn't even remember my name.

You may have perceived, also, that this gentle bullet, by refusing to behave unkindly, had lessened my desire for self-conquest, so that I was back now among all the tricks of self-showmanship.

And yet in these seventeen days I had seen men destroyed by shells as summer midges by a finger's touch; I had seen them prone and scratching for cover, much as sparrows will dust themselves in the earth of a flower-bed on dry summer days; I had seen on the hot conquered land the bodies of our men black and aswarm with insects and loathly white worms, while flies buzzed above them; I had seen the criss-cross Turkish wire red in tooth and claw; and I had lived daily in the fetid breath of the Peninsula, that breath from blackened corpses, rotting lonely limbs, and fly-blown offal, a breath that travelled on the wind far out to sea.

And I still did not feel much fear. It was as if that bullet had been an intravenous injection that lowered the temperature of fear. Perhaps, too, the daily inoculation with excitements, and with the virus of sudden deaths all round me, produced anti-bodies against this epidemic of death, and an irrational belief in my luck?

I cannot say; but let me make clear at once that my new fearlessness was only of shells and bullets, not of colonels.

It was a tattered unshaven company, with uniforms still ripped and stained by battle, that sat around that earth table. But first I must introduce you to the new faces, and speak of the absentee, Cass, and of his arrival among us, before I come to the night when he returned to us in deep disgrace.

Captain Bailey-More was a regular officer and very conscious of this among his four New Army subalterns. Of tall, burly build and orangey hair, and being something of a dandy when possible, he was not unlike our late captain, Bill Drewer. Indeed Colin would say to me sometimes, 'It *isn't* Bill Drewer come back, is it, Gerry?' His jowl was as square as his shoulders and he prided himself on his hard-faced toughness. He said to us once, 'You know what they used to call me in the Hampshires?—"The Hun".'

'Dear me!' said Colin mischievously. 'And did they really? Go *on*!'

'Yes, my boy, and I was not ashamed of it. I reckon the Germans can teach us a thing or two about how to put the fear of God into our men and how to deal properly with all the traitors and slackers at home. They can call me a Thug, if they like; I shan't mind. I happen to believe in discipline, and no nonsense about it.'

Listening, I saw that he had cast himself for this picturesque role just as I would usually cast myself for a very different role: not a tough Hun, but someone whom all called nice and friendly and unjudging and sympathetic; and who in his own eyes was full of high principles but no small sinner, and therefore very ready to forgive. Colin declared that Bailey-More's nickname 'Old Bailey' was supremely appropriate because that grey palace in the City was a place full of discipline for the plebs, with whips and gallows at its disposal. But after a while we tired of calling him 'Old Bailey' and just called him 'Bay'. 'It'll save time,' Colin said, 'in a strenuous campaign.' Bay's father was a lord of the manor with a mansion and park in Hampshire, and it was obvious that he, Bay, thought Colin his only social equal. He looked down upon us others. I was no product of Wellington and Sandhurst, and Cass and Evverson came from schools that none of us had heard of.

How strange it seems to me now that with death flying round me every hour of the day, and no escape from it anywhere on that narrow sea-bound plateau; with the bullets of the snipers stalking us like footpads whichever way we went, my chief worry should have been that Bay had chosen Colin for his friend and might win his affection from me. My jealousy was no less painful than that of a man whose woman is suddenly approached by a rival more attractive than he. It was a sudden threat, and the pain of it put lead in my heart and tears near my eyes. And of course it quickened my hidden love, as a bellows with its sighs quickens the furnace in a smithy.

Colin being Bay's second-in-command, they shared a dug-out together when we were up in the Line, a square, narrow hole beneath the parados, and this seemed to make them inseparable. Often I would come along the trench and hear them talking and laughing together. I would stop near by, pretending to listen to the pad of bullets or the whirring of a mortar shell, but really listening for the pellets of pain in their talk, and almost craving the wound of them. There was pain in the fact that all their talk and laughter played about a social world strange to me. One day, while the bullets pinged and rapped, I heard Colin say (as I stood listening, leaning forward, spying, the pipe in my mouth a dead thing), 'Our place, Castle Ivry, would be perfect, if only the shooting were better.'

'Are you proposing to settle down in it when your old man pops off?'

'I don't know. I haven't yet made up my mind whether to spend the rest of my life as a serious-minded little landowner, and a popular master of hounds, or as a college don. There's a shocking fascination about the cloisters and the Common Rooms of Oxford. Which would you rather be?'

'There's no choice for me, Colin, old son. I haven't got the brains to be a don. No, I suppose I shall retire and settle down at Scrase Hall and just stare at the pictures over the port. Worse ways to live.'

'Have you never thought of going into politics?'

'Oh, yes I have—if only to hit these Socialist scabs as hard as I could. And I believe I could get adopted as a candidate. The old man's a power, not only in our constituency, but in the Party as a whole. What about you?'

'No. Somehow I don't like the idea of a political path made easy by a good income and limited by a seat in the Lords. If I'd had to make my own career it might have been different.'

'Oh, that's all highfalutin rot. You'd make a very nice little Tory peer.'

'But I shouldn't be a Tory, Bay. I should be a Liberal.'

'Good God! Good gracious me! No, no, no; talk sense, old boy.'

'I shouldn't be much good in the Lords. I was never a success at the Union at Oxford—always too nervous—sweating and gulping over my notes like a broken-winded horse. Then the Lord alone knows what the world'll be like after this war. Man's proving himself such an utter brute to man that I sometimes feel as if loneliness and isolation will be the only good things. I see myself as a quiet old gentleman strolling about the park and dreaming about Gallipoli and about all this time—which *is* a damned curious time, you must admit—and then in the evenings writing it all up, probably with the aid of my wife and the housekeeper.'

Bay said something which I could not hear.

Then Colin's clearer voice. 'But it'll be a comic sort of world after the war, with precious little money about to spend on fun. I wonder if I shall ever hunt again. Perhaps I shan't even have Ivry to live in. . . . Is Brother Turk annoyed about something? He seems to be sending a lot of extra stuff over. He's an extremely ghastly old gaffer sometimes. . . . No, I expect I'll have to keep a pub after the war.'

So they talked together about the future, with death plumping and thudding about their door.

A minute later Bay said, 'Yes, the old Turk seems a bit restless. I'd better go and look at the boys. Are you going to be a brave little soldier and come too?'

'No.'

'Not? Well, I don't blame you. Gerry's out there somewhere, isn't he? Where's our old Gerry, do you suppose?'

'Probably walking about in the open, as if there were no such things as snipers.'

'Yes, mad as a hatter, that boy. Seems to like bullets. But he'll stop one sooner or later. Jesus, I always thought I was a good shot but one of these bloody snipers can shoot the sights off a periscope rifle from a hundred yards away. Jack Welby swears that he stepped up into the open the other night with a fag and a sniper shot the ash off it. And the shot came from *behind* our lines! They're before us and behind us and all round us. Brave chappies, but I suppose every scalp they collect increases their chances of Paradise. *Saïda,* old dear.'

'*Saïda,* Bay.'

I slunk away, so that when Bay came out I was walking with a military air in the opposite direction. 'How's our Gerry,' he said, as he passed, for he was always genial. 'Everything in good order?'

'Everything's fine,' I said. Odd, I thought, that I should like him so when he's nice to me, and feel so grateful. I suppose it's just that he's really a very likeable tough, and Colin just can't help liking him, as I do . . . sometimes. I'm working all this jealousy up. Cut it out, Gerry, you besotted fool; rub it out. Mad as a hatter, that boy.

But this jealousy had now a life of its own, and wanted to live it without interference from reason.

'Everything fine, is it, Gerry lad? All the same, I'll put in my usual appearance. Never sure that you're tough enough with the boys, myself. So long.'

'So long, Bay.'

I looked at his back, and thought of his manor and his wine and tried to comfort myself by remembering how Colin had said on the ladder above the towed boat 'Coming, Gerry?' as if he wanted me beside him in that death-cart.

Sometimes, as in that death-cart, I considered whether to escape from the pain of jealousy (as then from the fear of pain) by a violent overthrow of my self-centredness; but I did not set about this conquest, partly, I think, because I really wanted to keep the sweet ache. Had I not always searched around me for a love with all its exquisite torments? And this time, so far from eschewing all egotism I even contemplated a withdrawal of myself from Colin and an ostentatious giving of my friendship to another as a means of igniting again his old affection for me.

But I was saved from this childishness by the unfortunate behaviour of Cass.

Cass arrived before Evverson. He came up with the mule transport and the rations. Bay and I were standing—or leaning—in the square, tumbled cavity in the support line, which served as Company Headquarters, when he appeared in its opening. Turning, we saw a neat little man with everything small and neat about him: small neat nose; small neat moustache, dark and crisp; and a small controlled nervous smile. Very trim he looked in that dusty and broken trench compared with us who were as unwashed as city tramps, the ration of water in the Line being about a pint per man per day. Our faces, though tanned, were made pale by earth and dust. His was pale too, but the paleness lay under the tan; it came from within, not from without: this was his first visit to a Line.

'Who,' said Bay, staring at him as if seeing a ghost out of the past, 'are you?'

'The Adjutant instructed me to report to you, sir.' A small neat correctitude in voice and words. And a shyness of all new faces.

'Oh! Aha! The new officer. Cass, is it, or Evverson?'

'Cass, sir.'

'Has the other bloke arrived too? Every-Man, or whatever his name is?'

'Not with me, sir.'

'You needn't call me "sir" except on parade.'

'Oh, pardon,' he apologized; and Bay shut his eyes in distress.

Opening them again, when he'd recovered, he asked, 'You're not a regular, are you?'

'Oh, no. . . . No,' he repeated, so certain he was about this.

'Territorial?'

'No. . I just enlisted when the war broke out.'

'In the ranks, you mean?'

'Yes. I was given a commission eight months later.'

I was instantly pleased to hear that he was many months junior to me. So pleased that I felt it my duty to comfort him. 'We're none of us regulars now except Bailey-More,' I said. 'Our regulars are all dead.'

'Is that so? Oh, I see. . . .'

'This is Gerry Browning,' Bay explained. 'No. 10 Platoon. He's afraid of nothing, which is strange since he offers quite a big surface to the enemy. Your platoon'll be No. 11.'

'I see. Thank you.'

A bullet winged into the parados behind him, unseating some earth. He winced, but, if flurried, he refused to show it. Evidently a little man who kept his feelings to himself. A shell went snoring over our heads, probably from one of our ships; it plonked without exploding far away. Something else sawed on the wind like a bow on a 'cello string. Like Prospero's island, our Peninsula was full of noises; often sounds, as of a thousand twangling instruments, did hum about our ears. Cass brought his eyes—gentle eyes—quickly back into the dug-out.

'You're older than I expected,' said Bay. 'Nearly as ancient as me. Thirty-odd?'

'Thirty-four.'

'So you must have been something before you joined up?'

'I was in a bank.'

Yes, one could frame that tidy little figure behind the bars in a banking hall. Gold on his counter for sweeping into a shovel, neat brass scales at his side. Prompt service to all, with nothing much said.

'Are you married?'

'Yes.'

Bay looked surprised, as if he didn't think bank clerks could afford to marry. 'Any chaps?'

'Pardon?'

Bay closed his eyes again. 'Any children?'

'Yes. Three.'

'Good lord!'

Colin came hurrying in, having heard that the new officer had come. So might an excited schoolboy come to study a new pupil, lately arrived in the entrance hall.

'Colin, this is Cass. He's got three children.'

'Good heavens!'

'And he's married.'

'I should hope so.'

'Colin Dester, Cass. My second-in-command. A thundering fine officer, but not quite the hero that our Gerry is—wouldn't you agree, Colin?'

'Like hell I would, and thank God for it.'

'Well, what do we do with Cass? Show him round the garden, I suppose, though it's not at its best just now. *Orderly!*'

An orderly appeared. 'Sir?'

'Britty, take Mr. Cass along to the Sergeant-Major. The S.M.'ll show you your bit of the herbaceous border, Cass. It's in charge of Sergeant Gale at present. But look: for Christ's sake, keep your head down in some places.'

'Yes, sir. I see, sir.'

When Cass was round the traverse and out of hearing, Bay said, 'Good God! Oh, my lord!'

'But why such dismay?' asked Colin. 'I thought him a pleasing little man.'

'You did?'

'Yes.'

'*Really*?'

'Yes.'

'Good lord!'

'He's so nice and proper in all his ways.'

'He's got three kids.'

'So you said. That, I confess, did surprise me. He looks too much the well-behaved little gentleman.'

'And he says "Pardon?".'

'Why not, if he's sorry?'

'But it's the way a draper's young lady talks.'

'Perhaps he's a draper's young gentleman.'

'No, he's a bank clerk.'

'Oh, is he? Yes, I feel sure you're right in that. I can see him twinkling along the High Street to his branch in a neat little dark suit and hanging up his neat little hat wherever bank clerks do hang up their little hats. Gee, I'm tired.' Colin threw himself down on an upturned box in the dug-out. 'I'm sure he's the most meritorious little clerk, with all his ledgers kept in copperplate style.'

Bay leaned back against the wall, filling a pipe and crossing one leg over the other, lazily. 'Yes . . . yes, but is he going to be any good to us? Shouldn't they have put him in the Army Pay Corps?'

'There may be more in him than meets the eye. After all, he's produced three children.'

'An accident, wouldn't you say?'

'No, I wouldn't. Everything about him suggests a quiet business efficiency in all things. That included.'

'Well, we shall see. Looked as though he'd got the wind up a bit.'

'Couldn't have it up more than I have. There's only one Gerry in this company.'

'Oh, call it off,' I said, though my pride always rose at such words, and my blush too—sometimes to my hair and all round my neck. 'What about giving it a rest?' I suggested, not at all wishing this. 'It's getting tedious.'

Fortunately for Cass we were withdrawn for rest the next

day and established in No. 1, the Pines, where he could more easily get acclimatized to our Peninsula.

Evverson joined us at No. 1, the Pines. He came to that grace-and-favour dug-out when we were all seated around our earthy table, taking tea: a meal which consisted of tinned apricot jam, thick army biscuits, and tea made brown as a floor-stain to defeat the flavour of chloride of lime.

Evverson, reporting, was a lanky, narrow figure, inexpertly dressed in more places than one. A large nose in a weak face seemed to pull his head forward so that his sloped shoulders bowed behind it. His step was oddly mincing and up-and-down, as if his brown boots had pneumatic heels. In his talk there was a kind of peering eagerness to please (which I could well understand, since I suffered from it myself). Like me, he felt insecure in the presence of his seniors. Conscious of this insecurity, he talked too much, too readily, and too rapidly, lest he appeared insecure. 'I understand. I quite understand,' he would say many times and fervently; usually interrupting us with this assurance before we'd finished. 'I understand perfectly.'

'These,' said Bay, sweeping his hand before our faces, 'are Colin Dester . . . Cassy'—Cass was so prim and proper that none of us ever managed to call him Harry: Cassy was the best we could do. 'And Gerry Browning. He's our hero. Afraid of nothing.'

'Oh, shut up!' I enjoined.

'Pleased to meet you all,' said Evverson.

Fascinated by this phrase, Bay stared at the face which had uttered it. Stared in a kind of momentary paralysis. It was worse than Cass's 'Pardon?'.

'Been gazetted long?' asked Colin; and I wondered whether he, like me, wanted to know if this new arrival was his senior: Evverson was certainly older; thirty at least.

'No. Only five months.'

Relief, I think, to both of us: he was senior to Cass; junior to us. I didn't mind Colin sharing my weak desire to be senior. Indeed I wanted him to.

'But I was in the cadet corps at school and in the Artists' Rifles,' Evverson quickly explained.

'What school was that?' asked Bay.

'St. Mark's Prebendal, Coldhampton.'

'Oh . . . Well . . . The Artists' Rifles are a fine crowd. Sit down and have some chlorinated tea.'

'Well, yes, I will, bless you.'

Bay blinked in dismay at these last two syllables, as Evverson sat himself down.

'Been on any other front?' Colin asked, while Bay apparently pondered deeply and not too happily.

'No. This is my baptism of fire.'

Momentary silence. We all felt embarrassed by this phrase. It belonged to the newspapers; not to an officers' mess.

'Well . . .' Bay was back in circulation again. 'I hope you enjoy it. Happy days to you.' He raised his mug. 'May we know what you were before you joined the Artists?'

'I was a'—he hesitated—'a local government officer.'

'Good God, what's that?'

'I was in the rating office in our Town Hall. Yes . . . I was the *senior* rating clerk,' he added, somewhat hurriedly.

'Can't pretend to know what that is, but it sounds respectable. Married? You're not going to tell us you're married and have three children?'

'Married? No.' He hesitated, and then hurriedly repeated, 'No, I'm not married . . . yet.' I observed the hesitation at once because it made the whole answer sound insincere, but only later did its full implication break upon me.

'Our Cassy here has three children.' Bay announced it proudly as if it were a credit to the Company.

'Good gracious me!'

'Yes, he's a vigorous old man.'

Cass only greeted this chaff, as always, with his mild smile. It was the small smile, obliging but well-controlled, of a bank clerk to a facetious customer.

'I see your initials are "M. A. Evverson". What does "M. A." stand for?'

'Maurice Alistair.'

'Good God! Well, don't imagine, Maurice, that this is the style in which we always live. This villa is only lent to us for a brief holiday by the sea. "Maurice *Alistair*!" Good lord! Usually we cower in fox-holes—all except Gerry who roams around, trying to get hit.'

'I understand. I quite understand.'

'He quite understands. Fine. Well, Cassy, if you've finished your biscuit you might show Mr. Evverson his dug-out. You'll actually have one to yourself, sir, in these luxury flats. Jump to it, Cassy.'

Evverson protested, 'No, *please*. Don't let me disturb you. I can wait. Please, please.'

Cass, however, wiped his neat little moustache with his handkerchief and rose.

'Oh, but I say!' begged Evverson. 'Please don't let me put you to any trouble.' He had risen too and was drooping towards Cass as if his doubts, and his desire to be no trouble, were weighting his shoulders forward. 'I can easily wait.'

'No trouble at all,' said Cass, the only words he'd spoken so far.

'It's most awfully kind of you. I . . . Oh, well, thank you so very much. . . . Bless you. . . .' He waited politely, or nervously, for Cass to take the lead; then followed behind him, feet springing and head advancing some inches in front of his breast.

When he was gone, Bay didn't content himself with a 'Good God!' He said 'Christ!'

Colin only grimaced.

'Did you ever?' Bay inquired.

Colin shrugged, not sure that he did ever.

'I thought he was quite a decent chap,' I said, feeling sympathy for Evverson, because in some ways, alas, he was so like me.

But Bay did not answer me or look at me; it was Colin who

was his equal and his friend. 'What's the Army coming to? It used to be a place for gentlemen.'

'There's a war on, Bay.'

'Yes, *but* . . . he says "Pleased to meet you".'

'Well, I'm glad he's pleased. Aren't you?'

'And "Bless you". Did you hear it? I was blessed, and so was poor Cassy.'

'Very benevolent of him.' Colin lit a cigarette.

Bay, having also finished his tea, began filling his pipe. 'Yes, but . . . I'm sure that, like Cassy, he calls children "kiddies".'

'He may do. Yes, I fear he does,' Colin deplored, blowing a smoke ring and following it with his eyes.

'And he probably says to his kiddies, "Don't say "What?" say "Pardon?".'

'He hasn't got any kids.'

'That's true . . . but I feel he'll say "Pardon?" to me, and I can't stand it.'

'It may not come to that.'

'And he's so damned apologetic. So damned ingratiating.'

'Only because he wants to be loved.'

'And, Colin, there's nothing he doesn't understand. He has a perfect grasp of everything.'

'But how satisfactory!'

'How damned irritating. "I quite understand . . . I understand perfectly. . . ." Saints above, I can't take it.'

Colin still followed the smoke rings with his eyes. 'He just wants to be a success with everybody; that's all.'

'Maybe, but the man's a fraud. I can tell it from the way he looks and smiles and speaks.' Bay filled his pipe rapidly, automatically, without looking at it. 'He's a hypocrite who's terrified to say anything but what you want to hear.'

'Aren't we all a bit like that sometimes?'

'*Yes,*' I interposed, both because this was so true and because I wanted my part in the talk. Neither heeded me.

'No, I'm damned if we are,' said Bay to Colin only. 'I pride myself on saying exactly what I think.'

'And that's the most fraudulent remark you've ever uttered.'

Colin now gave his eyes to Bay, as if he would gaze at a fact for a moment instead of at smoke. 'You'd never say exactly what you thought to the Colonel or the Brig. Nor should I. Too much sense.'

'Nor I. Not in a hundred years,' I declared, persisting in my attempt to be heard. But without success.

'Our Mr. Evverson's just a little afraid of you; that's all,' Colin summed up, and gave himself back to his cigarette.

This explanation so pleased Bay that for a time he said no more but buttoned up his lips, as if not wishing to deny or disturb it. He only unbuttoned the lips to say 'Well, well, we must take what the gods send', and to insert his pipe, now filled, between them.

A day or two more, and I observed that Evverson gravitated always to me for companionship and talk. He was happiest with me because he guessed that I was more 'his class' than Bay or Colin and more approachable than Cass. This approach pleased me since I always wanted to be liked and admired, and I suspected that he looked up a little even to me. Instantly I was as comfortable with him as I was ill-at-ease with Bay and all other officers who came from the regular army and high society. And within twenty-four hours he was as communicative with me as with none other; within fifty-four he was exuding such confidences as made me wonder whether there was something else, something 'different', in my personality that drew him to me.

Evverson was unlike any other officer I had met. He would come along the mule trench with his soft spring-heeled walk and his head drooping from his long neck like a chrysanthemum from its stalk. Seeing me, he would lift a palm head-high in a would-be humorous greeting. And one day, after giving me this jocular salutation, he invited me into his dug-out with the words 'Come and talk to the troops for a space'. *For a space* —where did he get such phrases from? In his dug-out we sat on his camp-bed and he said several things which seemed queer and out-of-place in that earthy hole. The first was when we were discussing our colleagues and I said that no one, at first glance, would have thought of Cass as a 'heavily married man'. This seemed to stir in him the confidential mood. He sat in thought and then proferred, 'Now, that's something I can never imagine myself becoming. I've no desire whatever to tie myself up to a woman for the whole of my life. But on the other hand I can quite imagine living most of my life with a congenial man friend. Do you sometimes feel like that?'

'Oh, no,' I said. And indeed I didn't, for it was not the conventional thing to think. 'I shall certainly marry some day if ever I can afford it.'

'I shouldn't have expected that,' he answered, and he appeared to take it down with him into some deep of thought, from which he emerged at last with the comment, 'Oh, well, you're different from me; that's all I can say.'

'I sure must be,' I said, pretending to laugh, but a little annoyed.

'The Greeks took the same view as I do. Exactly the same.'

'Oh, yes,' I agreed, but mainly to show that I knew as much about the Greeks as he did.

'By an ideal love they meant as a rule a partnership between men because this alone could become a full intellectual and spiritual union——'

'Maybe, maybe——' I interrupted, impatient to argue.

'They preferred what they called "spiritual parenthood" to physical, and held that this was only possible between men.'

'Maybe, but what you're forgetting is that women in those days were more or less slaves—except the hetairai.' That word I thought, should flatten him out, if it's the right one, and I think it is. In case he didn't know it I subjoined my translation. 'The tarts.'

'H'mm . . . I doubt if that's a sufficient explanation . . .' he parried weakly.

It was about five in the hot afternoon and his batman, Arthur Binns, appeared in the dug-out entrance with two mugs of stewed tea from the men's field-kitchen.

'I know the officers have already had their tea, sir,' he said, 'but I thought that perhaps you and Mr. Browning might like a cup.'

This was just the sort of thing that young Binns would do. He was a quiet, religious, well-mannered boy who obviously got a private pleasure from doing considerate, helpful, and unselfish actions. I suspected that behind his pleasant manner, and because of his religion, he was practising a self-discipline all the time. Nineteen years old, slight in body, soft in feature, notoriously pious, and something of a 'woman's boy', he was the natural stuff for a batman. In the Sergeant-Major's terms, he'd do less damage to the Company in that capacity than in any other.

'Oh thank you, Binnie,' said Evverson, taking the mugs. 'Thank you ever so much. Bless you a thousand times.'

I thought it either very democratic or very friendly of him to give the boy his nickname, and then felt uncomfortable about it. And while I was wondering what I really did feel, Evverson, his eyes having followed the departed Binnie, said something which I felt certain he would not have uttered to anyone else.

'A nice kid, young Binnie,' he said. 'The sort of boy one could love.'

So unexpected was this word 'love', so close did it come to my own untold and untellable feeling for Colin, that I had no answer, and Evverson proceeded, as if his mind were running on the subject, 'The kind of boy men go wrong with—if you call it going wrong.'

'Why, goodness God!' I exclaimed. 'Don't *you* call it wrong?'

'Oh, yes, yes of course,' he insisted rather hastily. 'Good lord, man, my father was a Baptist minister. I'm no longer a Baptist, mind you; I was converted to your church, the C. of E., when I was about nineteen. What I meant was that the Greeks didn't think it wrong.'

'Oh, damn the Greeks,' I said.

'Wrong? Oh, undoubtedly—good gracious, yes—and

especially with anyone as young as Binnie, but that's not to say I can't understand, and sympathize a little, when both chaps are much of an age. I don't approve, mind you. Don't think that. How could I?'

'Ask Bay what he thinks,' I suggested, laughing.

'Oh . . . Bay . . .' he sneered. 'A very crude bit of work, *Bay!* A mere prize bull among men.' He stood up as if thereby he could get relief from fretting memories of Bay. 'Phew! it's hot. What on earth's it going to be like next month, and in July? We don't know what's coming to us.' Flinging off his tunic, he undid all the buttons of his shirt, and this uncovered a little black crucifix hanging against his skin on a black cord. He saw my eyes fix on it and, not displeased that I should have seen it, explained with a smile, 'Yes, the Vicar blessed it and gave it to me when he said good-bye. I promised him I'd wear it always.'

'You're High Church then, are you?' I asked.

'Undoubtedly. Good heavens, yes. Only I hate that term. Let's say Anglo-Catholic. I'm a sidesman at our church, St. Magnus East.'

'Golly, are you really?'

'Indeed I am.'

Yes, I could imagine his soft springy walk up the aisle and his friendly smile as he accepted the collection plate. Then he steps forward to the next pew soundlessly, and as if on pneumatic shoes. Evverson a soft-footed sidesman—here on Gallipoli!

Still, it rather pleased me to know this. His churchmanship meant another point of contact between us, since I was one who throughout an unrebellious childhood had been regularly led to church to be shaped and pickled as my mother wanted me. And though a renegade now, I still had my memories of, and a deep funded interest in, the things of the Church.

That same evening I was doing my turn of duty among the men, and some time after eight I slipped into No. 1, the Pines, for a drink. Bay, Colin, and Cass were seated round two hurricane lanterns on the table. Colin with a foot on the earth step was leaning back against the scrub-roots and reading a small black book. Cass was writing on the table, probably to his wife and children to tell them with pride that he was now in the Front Line. Evverson came in after me, looked at Colin, and, eager as ever to say things that would show his perfect ease, asked, 'Reading?'

'Yes, this is a book,' said Colin.

Bay glanced towards it: a small volume bound in limp black leather. 'Holy smoke!' he said. 'Is Colin reading the Bible?'

'It looks like a missal,' I suggested, proud of the word.

'Looks like a *what*? Don't talk about missiles here.'

'A missal,' I explained, glad to air my ecclesiastical knowledge. 'It contains the Canon of the Mass.' This sounded good, but I was not sure that it was the right description or that Evverson at my side wouldn't correct me.

Bay said, 'Don't talk about cannons, either. D'you mean he's saying his prayers? He can't do that there here.'

'This,' said Colin, enacting patience with fools and talkers, 'is a pocket Homer.'

Bay snatched it from him. 'Lord help us, it's in Greek. The lad's reading it in Greek. Or he's pretending to. You can't really read this muck, can you, Colin?'

'Well, I can . . . yes,' Colin admitted. I don't think he had produced the book to parade his knowledge of Greek, but I fancy he was glad to have it discovered.

'Is it the *Iliad*?' I inquired, to show that I too had some acquaintance with Greek and, moreover, knew that Homer had written *two* epics. 'I did a bit of Euripides at school and a bit of Plato, but never enough, really, to be able to read Greek easily.' Thus I contrived to sound modest and yet to imply much more than the truth.

Bay only commented in his self-satisfied way, 'Well, I don't know one Greek letter from another but I seem to have managed all right.'

Now it was not surprising that Cass had contributed nothing to these exchanges: he made no pretensions to high literacy and moreover he was concentrating, with ever and anon a touching of his trim moustache, on his letter home. The remarkable thing was that Evverson, though listening carefully and swinging his eyes from Bay's face to Colin's, said never a word. And I will tell you why.

The next afternoon I had to go to his dug-out to recover a book which I had lent him. He was not there but on the wooden case that served him as a bedside table lay a small pile of books, and mine was the one on top. I did not content myself with taking it back. Always inquisitive about my friends, I looked at the one below it: a book of Anglo-Catholic prayers. And the one under that: a small privately bound volume, *Poems. By M. A. Evverson.*

'Golly!' Evverson wrote poetry! Poetry! A pity that I could not chaff him about it, and make fun of it with the others, because this would reveal that I'd been prying among his books. I glanced through some of the poems and thought them not bad. One even seemed good: 'A Sonnet at Mass.'

Stay. Means it nothing to our handicraft
That God has chosen for His earthly throne
No pure and lovely output of His Own,
That Fire and Wind and Water do not waft
Down to our waiting eyes His kingly shape,
But rather He has deigned to set His feet
In Bread which men have fashioned from the wheat
And Wine which they have garnered from the grape?
So prospers He our handicraft. . . .

And so on.

'There's much that we don't know yet about this Evverson,' I thought; and just as I was thinking this I saw that the two bottom books, unlike any of the others, were veiled in brown paper. Wondering if they'd been placed beneath the others and wrapped in paper because he was ashamed of them, I hastily drew them forth. The upper one was an illustrated uvenile, *Homer for Boys, His Iliad and Odyssey Retold;* and nstantly I knew why Evverson had kept silence about Colin's Homer. Posing as an intellectual, he didn't wish to confess that he'd had to learn his *Iliad* in this elementary way. And yet he'd studied carefully in this book, knowing that he was bound for Homeric waters and a sight of Troy; his enthusiastic scorings were on every page.

The lower book was a translation of Plato's *Symposium.* Knowing nothing of this book, I couldn't understand why he'd chosen to disguise it also in an ascetic brown habit like a monk's.

Not for me to condemn his furtiveness because I was now tempted to snatch the Homer away for an hour or two, read it in some private place, and so be able to discuss the *Iliad* with Colin on apparently equal terms. And what I did was far more shameful than any secretiveness of Evverson's. That afternoon, when he was in charge of a working party on W Beach, and I was free, I told Bailey-More that I was going for a bathe; a thing which we were encouraged to do on coming out of the Line, where our clothes could not be taken off for days on end. I slipped away, slunk into Evverson's dug-out, snatched both the Homer and the Plato, and walked rapidly away with them under my arm.

To bathe we could go westward to the Aegean cliffs between Tekke Burnu and Saghir Dere or eastward to the blue water of Morto Bay at the very opening of the Straits. I went eastward because my 'bathe' was to be but a spiritual immersion in the ancient Hellespont of Homer and an imagining of his 'windy Ilium' just beyond. I climbed a ridge which so far had hidden the Dardanelles from us, and there below me, set in margins of beauty, with cypress and olive and vines on this side, and the green plain of Troy on the other, and the shadowy mountains of Asia far behind, lay the royal-blue sheet of Morto Bay and the narrowing blue sash of the Dardanelles. In bays where the water was shadowed it lay like cobalt-blue steel.

I sat down in a place of rock-rose and myrtle and gazed at the Hellespont and at Troy. At the world's most famous water; and at a battlefield first in legend, where Agamemnon and his long-haired Acheans had beached their hollow ships. In this hour before sunset, our bathing hour, a hush would lie on the Peninsula till the 'Evening Hate' began; and truly this picture of the reedy Morto Bay and the grey Asian mountains beyond, glistening here and there beneath an apricot sky, seemed the picture of a world outspread in beauty and peace. The Hellespont slept with a sapphire glaze and empty of all but its dreams.

Seated among the myrtle, I read an *Iliad* made easy for me by simple language and coloured pictures. The old north-east wind, not yet our vicious enemy, played gently on my cheek as I read. Sometimes I raised my eyes from the book to see over yonder the battlemented walls of Priam's city, or the blue sea thrashed by the oars of Agamemnon's ships, or the same waves parting for Thetis and her sister Nereids to come up from their 'salt sea depths'. She is come to comfort Achilles, her son, who lies drenching the sand with tears, and burying his face in the earth and rending his hair, because Patroclus, his lover, is slain.

'I have lost Patroclus,' he bewails to his mother, 'and I loved him as my life.'

I was sitting up, tensed as I read this part, because of all the stories in Homer's pageant this of Achilles and Patroclus was gripping me most. Achilles had no shame or silence for his ardent love of Patroclus. His mother might tell him that if he now killed Hector who had killed Patroclus, he would die too, but he only rose from the ground and vowed, 'I will avenge his death on Hector and all the Trojans, though I know it means that I shall never return home nor see again my father, the old charioteer.' And of course, as I read these things and dreamed over them, I was Achilles, and one came to me with news that Colin was killed. A fine scene followed, whose contemplation, as I sat there, I enjoyed. In it I did not speak my grief aloud like Achilles but, masking it like an Englishman, walked away to my tent while all the others watched, knowing that I had been his friend. I stood by his grave when they lowered him into the Gallipoli earth and vowed to myself, 'I'll bathe a bayonet in the blood of those that killed him, and die too.'

But almost at once, I am glad to think, the dreadful selfishness of this dream—killing Colin that I might luxuriate in grief and grandeur—shocked me, and I substituted for it a fine episode in which I died saving him; a scene which I was able to prefer when I remembered how he'd taken to going everywhere with Bay and leaving me outside.

It was pleasant to linger there in the amber-bright evening, so when I had taken my fill of the *Iliad* I picked up the *Symposium*. And if the *Iliad* had been a rich source of dreams, the *Symposium* was nothing less than a spring of revelation.

But I could understand why Evverson had covered it up.

In this delightful Dialogue, as gay as it was serious in its praises of Love, I found that my exact feeling for Colin—a love ardent but 'without physical manifestations'—was not only allowed but highly advocated and honoured, and this by a mind of Plato's calibre. To my astonishment he did not even condemn a love among men which still carried bodily desires—but here I could not endorse him and fled quickly from trying to. I found also that I need feel no shame because I had first been drawn to Colin by a beauty in his face and form; and I was astounded to read that, in the love of Achilles and Patroclus, Achilles must have been the junior partner, the 'beloved' rather than the 'lover', because he was the younger and the more beautiful. But most of all was I moved by the words of Socrates when he assured the company that Love, since it was the child of Poverty, was not beautiful or rich but poor and worn and for ever in want, sleeping only on thresholds and in the street.

I knew what he meant. And so, I thought, would anyone who was the lover rather than the beloved.

Plato or no Plato, it was certain that I could never tell a soul the real truth of my feeling for Colin; but now I could feel justified in it and released from shame. It was as if Plato, dead two thousand years, had just spoken to me on this old Thracian soil. And one effect of this sanction and approval from the greatest of the Greeks was to add its quota to my love.

I was sitting and dreaming like this, in a kind of untimely timelessness, looking down upon the haunted but sleeping face of the Dardanelles, when a flock of white seabirds rose from it and flew away in alarm. Twenty seconds, and a shell came over with a jet-roar from Asia. It burst among the reeds on the sea's brink, hurling up a gusher of pale sand and earth. I did not run or move, being proud of my new indifference. But a second shell came screaming and churning over and fell close to me. It was as if the Turks had seen me sitting there and were lengthening their fuse to get me. I turned and went homeward quickly but still declining to run, lest those French soldiers yonder, wandering about near Sedd-el-Bahr, should see me and laugh. I always had to cut a figure before people who neither knew who I was nor would ever see me again. Better to be shot dead than laughed at.

Back among the pines, I looked stealthily to see if Evverson or his batman was about and, seeing no one, slipped into his dug-out and replaced the books.

And so I come to the night when Bay, Colin, Evverson, and I sat waiting for Cass.

CHAPTER THREE

DURING our 'rest' among the pines we had to do fatigues every day and often at night: unloading on the beaches, carrying along the trenches, digging in the support lines, wiring or sapping in No-Man's-Land. This was the last night of our rest, and Cass had been sent forward with his platoon to reinforce a depleted company of the Hampshires in a small night-assault. This assault was to straighten out a sag in the line between the Hampshires and the French. Our guess was that the Colonel had detailed Cass because he had his doubts about him and wanted him to get experience with seasoned troops. We did not think it a serious business, the May battles having now fought themselves to a standstill.

So that night we ate our dinner (bully rissoles and a 'trifle' made of army biscuits soaked in hot apricot jam, a foul mess) while the cool darkness came down upon the Peninsula; then sat around the hurricane lanterns, smoking our pipes, listening to the preliminary bombardment, and worrying not at all about Cass.

The bombardment seemed almost entirely the work of the French seventy-fives, for we had few guns ashore and little ammunition. But the French seventy-fives, lovely swift guns, well-supplied and gaily manned, were a joy to us all, a song in the heart when they sounded. We loved them like a beauty chorus.

They stopped. For a little there was silence; we could not understand why.

Usually this was our happiest hour on the Peninsula, with the angry sun in its bed, and the velvet darkness covering us, and the whole sky from east to west, from Mount Ida to Mount Athos, a world of stars. The men would sing in their dug-outs, the crickets chirp under the stones, and the frogs in the nullah give us the chorus from Aristophanes.

It was like this now for a time, and then the small-arm fire raged, the counter-batteries joined in, and we knew the battle was in being.

An hour of this exasperated fire—and we wondered when it would diminish. It didn't; it grew angrier; and while we listened in some mistrust, voices spoke outside. 'Is Captain Bailey-More there?' 'Yes, sir.'

'Christ! The Colonel!' said Bay. 'Colin, it's Puss-in-Boots.'

He said it in front of a batman, who grinned.

The Colonel's steps came down the trench path to our veranda. We rose to him so far as we could under the tarred blanket.

'Good evening, gentlemen,' he said. 'Do sit down.'

Tonight he was not in his grey sweater but in an Indian sun-proof tunic. He laid his topee on our table.

'Sit down too, sir,' Bay invited. 'A whisky, sir.'

'No. No thanks.' He sat down on the earth-cut seat. 'An unpleasant thing has happened. Damned unpleasant.'

We left it to Bay, our O.C., to say 'Yes, sir?' inquiringly, when the Colonel stayed silent.

'To put it crudely, Cass has turned and run.'

'Good God! You mean, sir——?'

'I mean, Bailey, he's led his men gloriously, but backwards.' Our Colonel was not a witty man, and therefore enjoyed reproducing the antique wit of the army. 'Led 'em into safety.'

'Oh, my God!' Bay said this as if in despair of the human race. As if sick that it should be one of his officers who had so disgraced humanity. 'God . . . !'

'And dammit, he left a great gap in the line.'

'But to hell, sir: that's a shooting matter, isn't it?' Plainly Bay was out to impress the Colonel.

'It could be a court-martial business,' said the Colonel, as if impatient with all questions whatever on an unsavoury topic. 'Yes. Dammit.'

'He's very new, sir,' said Colin softly, his face down.

'I know, I know. Dammit.'

I felt it desirable that I should speak and appear intelligent, so after much inward preparation and rehearsal, I said, 'What happened, sir?'

'It seems,' said the Colonel addressing the table rather than me, 'that the Turk put up a far greater resistance than anyone expected. The bombardment was nothing like heavy enough. Ship's guns are no good for this sort of work. Told 'em so from the beginning. The seventy-fives were all right but as a whole the bombardment failed. The Hampshires and the French had a terrible reception.'

'It sounded pretty hot,' Bay agreed. A big sycophant's agreement.

'The French white troops did absolutely superbly'—the Colonel, a romantic, loved extravagant praises—'but the black fellahs, the Senegalese, broke. And as chance would have it, Cass was next the Senegalese.'

'All the more reason why he should have held firm and enfiladed the Turks if they tried to get through.'

'Exactly. Of course.'

'Or tried to extend and fill the gap himself.' Bay was doing well.

'Yes, yes—naturally—but he was in a stretch of difficult country full of unforeseen pits and he was out of touch. He was out of sight of all in the dark till he saw the Senegalese tearing for home. The fire was awful, so he used his discretion and retired too—at the double.'

'Oh, dear . . . oh, dear. . . .' Poor words of Bay's, but they travelled on a tremendous sigh.

'And, if you please, he came home by the nullah where it was safer. I had gone up to the Hampshires' H.Q. in the nullah, to learn how things were going and all I learned was that Colonel Norris had rung up Brigade to know why the hell his right was in the air. Seems the French reserves filled the gap.'

An even greater sigh from Bay. That French should have to amend a British failure! Insupportable.

'I hurried up the nullah, and met Mr. Cass and all his men running like terrified hares towards me. Just now I said that he led his men back, but—devil take it—their doubling was better than his, and he was leading 'em from behind.'

'I think it's a too ghastly disgrace,' said Bay. 'It's a disgrace to the whole nation.'

'He's very new,' Colin murmured.

I said nothing. I wasn't going to endorse Bay's easy condemnation. Evverson said nothing either. He stared at the Colonel and I felt sure he was thinking he might have done the same as Cass. For my part, I was so conceited about my fearlessness that I was hoping I would have done just what Bay and the Colonel said ought to have been done. In this moment's silence I flung my men into the gap, saved the whole line, and next morning received the commendations of the French.

'Is he under arrest, sir?' asked Bay.

'No.' The Colonel snapped this out sharply. 'No, of course not. I don't even know at the moment if he's alive.'

'*Alive,* sir?'

'I want no court martials in my battalion. A fellah must be allowed a failure or two, I suppose. By God, if every officer who uses his discretion and retreats is to be shot, we shall be doing the Turks' job for them.'

Bay kept silence. I could see that he didn't agree but didn't want to say so to a colonel.

'I stopped 'em all in the nullah and gave 'em such a strafing that they obviously wished they were back in front of the Turks' fire instead of mine. After my brief talk poor Cass's face was whiter than when he first came in sight. I led 'em back to B.H.Q., and there, as luck would have it, there was an urgent demand for ammunition up in the Line. So I said, "Here's your chance, men. You take this ammunition up. It'll mean about three journeys over foul country and through heavy fire but if you do the job I'll see that everything else is forgotten." And, d'you know, they all said "Yes, sir". Just "Yes, sir", one after another. Good fellahs, really.'

We nodded, silently.

'I didn't like sending 'em back at once, but those flying fellahs have got the right idea: if one of their fellahs crashes, they send him up again at once, so that his last memory can be one of success. Sensible, what?'

'Yes, sir.'

'Yes, and the dump was quite near so they loaded up with boxes of ammo and bombs. And I noticed one thing: Cass never says much but he knows as well as I do that the men carrying bombs would be in the greatest danger, and he went straight—without a word—to collect a case of bombs. I let him see that I'd noticed this, as he was a bit down; I said, "That's the way, Cass"; and I think it pleased him and he'll go through hell now if he has to. Quite a stout fellah, really.'

Evverson suddenly said 'Yes, sir', eager for his Colonel to hear him agreeing with him. Evverson was by nature a window-dresser. Let Colonel or Major be in the mess, and he dressed his window to please these customers. He listened to them and then furnished window and counter with whatever provisions were clearly in season. Behind his counter, he waited in a suitably stainless white jacket and apron. I did not condemn him for this because I could remember times when I'd thought it wise to don garments of a similar whiteness. Indeed, nearly always in my youth I said what the big people liked to hear, and so walked the world in garments of unreality.

'I think so,' said the Colonel after a surprised and doubting glance at Evverson. 'Well, I came to tell you fellahs all this so that you'll understand if he comes back sooner than you expected. If he comes back at all it'll mean he's done his job properly, so—what I mean is—I shouldn't say anything about—well, about anything.'

'I will not, sir,' said Bay.

And Evverson said 'No, sir', emphatically agreeing with his seniors again.

'Won't you really have a whisky, sir?' Bay asked.

'Well, thank you . . . yes, perhaps. A small one. What's that you're writing, Dester?'

Colin's little black Homer was on the table before him, and he'd been playing his pencil on an Army Book 152 (Field

Service) at its side. 'Oh lord, sir,' he laughed. 'I'm afraid I'm using Army stationery for an illegitimate purpose.'

'What illegitimate purpose, ha, ha, ha?' To the Colonel our weakest jokes were a delight.

'I'm trying to make a verse translation of some parts of this.'

'But what is it?'

'Homer's *Iliad*, sir.'

'Good God!' He took the book from Colin's hand and looked at a page of Greek. 'Good heavens! You can read this?'

'Yes, sir.'

'Good lord . . . good gracious . . . well, well. . . .' One felt that he was in some doubt whether it was altogether right for these New Army officers to be able to read Greek. 'The *Iliad*. I know it all happened just over there. Just by Kum Kale, wasn't it? You must tell me all about it sometime. I should like to know. Perhaps you'd read me some of it—in *English*, of course, ha, ha, ha. Major Reid, who knows about Achilles and all that, says that that damned gun, Asiatic Annie, fires at us from Chamlar Tepe, near Achilles' tomb. Is he right, Dester?'

'I wouldn't know, sir.'

'He says that Xerxes built a bridge across the Dardanelles but that the current swept it away so that he had to transport his army back into Asia by boats and he was so damned angry with the current that he ordered three hundred lashes to be inflicted on it as a punishment. Is that true?'

'I think so, sir. It's what I've always heard.'

'Well, well, well,' said the Colonel, in surprise perhaps at such un-English behaviour.

He looked at the book again. 'And you're translating this stuff into poetry?'

'Into verse, sir,' Colin corrected.

'Good God!' Further digesting of this answer produced a further 'Good Lord!' He turned to another New Army officer. 'Can *you* read this stuff, Browning?'

'I learned Greek at school,' I said, 'but I'm not so good at it as Dester'—which implied that, in my own way, I was quite hot stuff at it, but modest withal.

'And you, Bailey?'

'Lord, no!' Bay could not have said No with more emphasis had the Colonel asked him if he were a Buddhist or a Mormon. He sounded as if he were glad that nothing so odd could be attributed to him.

'Well, I think we must all get together, and Dester must give us some lessons, ha, ha, ha.' A quiet examination of this thought showed him that it was extremely humorous. 'Ha, ha, ha,' he laughed. 'Let's see your verse, Dester.'

'Oh, no, sir,' Colin expostulated.

'Come, come. You can't disobey your colonel. That really *is* a court-martial business.'

Colin handed over his Field Service book, and the Colonel read in it, frowning a little.

'Read it aloud, sir,' urged Bay.

'No, *please,*' objected Colin.

'Go on, sir.'

'Oh, I can't read poetry. No good at poetry, Bailey.' All the same he tried to read it. '"The day is coming, dear, which thou shalt see, My heart foresees it well, the dark dread day When Troy falls, and thou, Andromache, Thy Hector slain, Art weeping led away. . . ." Who's Andromache, Dester?'

'His wife, sir. It's Hector speaking to Andromache.'

'Oh yes. His wife. Fancy it all happening just over there.' He read on—two more lines. '"Oh, let me die, oh, let me buried be, Before I hear thy dear voice weep for me. . . ." Well, I don't know anything about poetry, but I should have thought that was damned good. "Before I hear thy dear voice weep for me. . . ." Was Homer really as good as that? Poor Andromache. I'm glad he was fond of her, ha, ha, ha. Well, I've really learnt something tonight, gentlemen; thank you.'

When the Colonel was gone, feeling all the better for having been witty, we stared at one another. Bay spoke first. 'I told the Colonel I wouldn't say anything, and how right I was! I simply won't speak to the man.'

'Have some sense, Bay,' Colin recommended, always on these astoundingly easy terms with his captain.

'He let my Company down. He disgraced us all. Doubling away in the face of the enemy.'

'But he doubled back again. Like a sportsman.'

'The Turkish officers have orders to shoot all those who ever *look* back.'

'They have far more men than we have and can afford to shoot 'em in heaps. Let 'em; it helps us like fun.'

'But are we to have less discipline than bloody Turks?'

'No. Only more sense.'

'It *is* good sense. Let one platoon turn tail and the whole line's endangered.'

'He didn't know what was happening. My Christ, I can imagine it all. Now listen, you old fool.' Colin leaned back against a corner and put a leg along the earth seat to deliver his counsel in comfort. 'A small job turns into a major show. And there's our Cassy out of touch with everyone in the black night —far away from helpful friends like us—heaps of hardware dropping around him—and all of a sudden he sees what looks like the whole line withering away in this hellish fire. Probably chaps are yelling "They're going back, sir,"; and since he's much too reserved a little man to ask his sergeant what to do, he uses his discretion and comes home—rather too fast, I admit. In fact, legging it like hell. You must remember that he's much more used to crossing the High Street with his umbrella, and dodging the buses to get to his bank. I'm sure that at home he always crosses a road with commendable caution.'

'Well, I wish they wouldn't send officers like that to my company. The standard in my company, let me tell you, is going to be Regular Army *Plus*. Holy Peter, this pipe's foul.' He was cleaning his pipe with a feather—furiously, as if it were the soul of his company that he was purifying. 'Why didn't he stop in his bank?'

'Because he wanted to help us.'

'And ran the first time he went into action.'

'Nonsense, Bay. He just thought the war was over and had a

mind to get back as quickly as possible to Mrs. Cass and the kids. There are three of them.'

'I don't think it's a funny business. Not at all.'

'I do. Our Cassy absconded, but hurried back with the money when he saw the Colonel. God damn it, the lad was brave after his first tumble; he was brave with the bombs.'

'Only because he was frightened of the Colonel.' Bay never listened to arguments that would disturb an assertion of his. Having started an attack, he didn't abandon it like Cass, however hot the opposing fire. 'You read that letter found on the Turk: it said, "These British are the best fighters in the world. We chose the wrong allies." Well, what now? Would Germans turn and run?'

'I must say I think there's something in what Bay says,' Evverson put in surprisingly. No doubt he wanted his captain to hear him agreeing with him.

'Oh, *do* you?' Colin was now getting irritable. 'Well, what do you want? Do you want Cass to be shot?'

'Oh, no. No, of course not. But usually you have to make an example of an officer——"

'Of course,' mumbled Bay, doubtless to Evverson's satisfaction——

'—because it's ten times worse in an officer. He leads.'

Colin's temper was now gone. He had been nursing his pipe on his lap and now shoved it between his teeth. 'Oh, you both make me sick. The fellow's nearly forty but he joins up at once and comes out here and tries to do his best. To hell with you all!'

He rose to get away from them, but thought better of it and, sitting down again, gave himself to his Greek, with his head in his hands. I loved him for his generous wrath. And my jealousy was relieved to see him at odds with Bay.

We were all silent now and noticed that the Peninsula was silent too. The battle had died. Perhaps ten minutes later, as we sat there, we heard like King David 'the sound of a going in the mulberry trees' and Bay looked towards it, saying nothing. Evverson said, 'That's them. That's Cass and his boys.'

Colin said, 'What does he do now, poor devil? Come in and tell us? It's damned awkward for him.'

Bay grumbled, 'I care nothing for his awkwardness. I reckon he ought to feel awkward.'

Colin pretended not to hear. He went to the dug-out entry and waited there. I rose and joined him, and presently, there in the dark trench we saw Cass looking towards the dug-out but hesitating about coming into it.

Colin spoke. 'Hallo, Cassy, old boy. Come and have a drink. You must have had a hell of a night of it.'

And I added (having guilt in my own heart, I loved the idea of mercy), 'Yes, come in, old cock, and tell us all about it. We heard you'd done wonderful things, getting up the bombs. Come and drink.'

'Thank you,' his voice said. He came closer and we saw that his face, as he got nearer to his captain, was as white as it had been before the Colonel. But we led him in, and as he entered he threw a sick glance at Bay. Bay stared down at the table and said nothing, thus undoing all that we'd tried to do.

It was then that Evverson, eagerly agreeing with a senior (for a majority of two-to-one is a senior) but meaning a kindness too, said jovially, 'Yes, come and tell the troops all about it. The Colonel came and said good words about you.'

'The Colonel?' asked Cass anxiously. It would not be easy to rebuild what Bay had thrown down.

Colin, discerning that Evverson's words had been unwise, instantly lied, but not without stuttering. 'Yes, he said that getting the ammo and what-not up was almost worth a decoration—didn't he, Gerry?'

'He did. He certainly did. And by Golly I agree with him.'

But Bay's silence was like Contempt Itself sitting at a table, and I don't know if Cass believed us.

One more incident before the 'great change' came. We were again seated round a table in the evening light but this time our home was but a square hole in a support trench called

Sackville Street, and the table was but a cube of boxes. It was after sundown, and cool; the flies were all at rest, and the Turks too—or they were at their orisons, bowing towards Mecca.

We had watched the sun go down because we were still new to this nightly aureole when the sky was a glory of clear sea-green light broad-based in a glow of fire, and traversed by pure bright rays; this nightly gift to the Greeks of old which bred in them, perhaps, their clarity of thought and their devotion to beauty. As the sun sank it ran a flood of tinted light into every trench and dug-out so that when we went back to our table to drink and argue we seemed to step into a tank of violet air.

Argument raged across the table that night. It flared up in the end like a dry-scrub fire.

'Very pleasant. Very peaceful,' said Bay. And to shock Cass and me whom he regarded as patterns of a timid and standardized suburban morality, and Evverson who, as he would say, 'looked as if he wouldn't know what to do with a woman if he had one', he suggested, thumbing the tobacco into the bowl of his pipe and lighting it, 'All one wants now is a woman. One's earned it, what? It's more than a month since I——'

'A brief intermission'll do you good,' interrupted Colin.

'On the contrary, it's getting me down. In Alex I had my woman at least once a week——'

'Have some lime juice instead.' Colin pushed a bottle of the Government lime juice, a free issue, towards Bay's enamel mug.

Bay stared at the deep yellow liquid, wrinkling his nose. 'Would you say it looked like——'

'Yes, I would,' said Colin.

'Still, it was nice of the Government to think of it. They pretend it's to quench our thirst in the heat, *but*——'

'But what?' demanded Evverson, suddenly interested.

'My dear lad, it's to quench our appetites; not our thirst.'

'How do you mean?'

'It's something you don't need. You've got no vices. He only drinks that whisky, Colin, to be like us. It's the same when he tries to talk smut. Oh, I can see through our Evvy as I can through that bottle. Strong lime juice, Evv dear, is an anaphrodisiac. The Goverment can't send us on leave so they send us lime juice.'

'It's damned thoughtful of the D.A.Q.M.G.,' said Colin.

'He probably needs it himself. Would you say, Colin, that our Cassy needs it?'

'Who can tell?' Colin looked at the reserved Cass as if in despair of ever knowing *that* answer.

Cass only smiled. Since his shameful flight he had been more quiet than ever. An unsubtle little man, he imagined that this disgrace would follow him to the end of his days. And so he stayed alone with it and with his sadness. He didn't perceive that he need only wait and wait, and the days would fade into years, and all would be forgotten, even the campaign in which he once took fright and fled.

'What really worries me,' continued Bay, 'is all those poor Frenchies around Sedd-el-Bahr. How *do* they manage? I mean *l'amour* is their national sport. *Monsieur le Général,* what does *he* do?'

'Perhaps,' Colin propounded, 'that was why General d'Amade went home. Old General Gouraud is over seventy.'

'That's nothing to Frenchmen. They're in their prime then.' He drank a sip or two of the acid drink, and waited. 'No, it's not working. Give me the whisky. It's whisky alone that'll win this war. There's nothing else. Oh, dear . . . I could do with a visit to the Maison Meurice. That would help. There was some luscious stuff there. Especially one little bint, as brown as a berry, and with a little round bum——'

There followed a tale of his dusky adventures in the Red Lamp district of Alexandria. Colin, while not boasting like Bay, seemed to know of the places which he was describing, and at first I was shocked. I sat there, wondering what his secret life was, and determining that none of his private sins should modify my love. Soon I could not doubt that he had sometimes been with women in Alexandria, but I could feel no jealousy of them; they were irrelevant. Such jealousy as I felt was all for Bay.

After much of this talk Bay turned towards Evverson. 'I

doubt if our Evv approves. I've a suspicion—I don't like to ask him—that he's a virgin.'

'I certainly am,' said Evverson with a curious ardour, 'and I'm not ashamed of it.'

I listened in silence, knowing that I was a virgin too and would be ashamed to admit it.

'Oh, well, there's no accounting for tastes,' sighed Bay. 'Cassy's shocked too; we're making him blush.' Bay's native heartiness had not allowed him to continue for long his overt contempt of Cass. 'Do look, everybody, how he's blushing.'

Cass only provided another good-humoured smile.

At that moment the Turks' rapid fire spread like some crackling fuse across the breadth of the Peninsula from the Aegean to the Straits. Always they opened their 'Evening Hate' as the sun drained its violet glow into the darkening sea. What purpose it served was hard to say, since they knew well enough that all our men, at sundown and sunrise, stood to arms in the Line.

'Here comes the Turkish Delight,' said Colin.

Bay paid no heed to it: it seldom lasted long. Resolved to provoke Evverson, he thumbed again the tobacco in his pipe and went on, 'I should have thought that Evv as a Socialist believed in Free Love.'

'You seem to, anyway,' retorted Evverson.

'He got you there,' Colin laughed.

Bay didn't like being 'got' anywhere, and certainly not by Evverson. 'Oh, no, he didn't,' he declared without explaining why, because, try as he would, he couldn't see why. So he shifted to a stronger fire-point. 'I shall never forgive your Socialists, Evv, for opposing conscription. Look at our position here. We want men. Thousands of 'em. And we shall probably all be scuppered for want of 'em. I'd conscript the lot and fairly put them through the drill and make men of 'em.'

'And that's the way to make men, is it?' asked Evverson, whose lips had been moving, impatient to speak.

'Yes.'

'Men?'

'Certainly.'

'Not sour rebels?'

'Christ, let 'em rebel, and we'd shoot 'em.' He seemed to think this a retort both crushing and humorous. He smiled triumphantly as he repeated it. 'No nonsense. Shoot 'em.'

'And a lot of use they'd be then. . . . *Pfoo*!'

That contemptuous '*Pfoo*!' set Bay on fire. 'There's no blasted *pfoo* about it. Discipline is what the loafers need, and what they've never had. My old man taught me what discipline was from the moment I had a bum to beat; and I'm glad of it. Any disobedience, any lies, any slackness at school, any dirty games with the girls, and I got the tanning of my life. And if I funked it, I got it worse.'

'And it worked?' sneered Evverson. 'You've never told a lie since?'

'Not often.'

'And you're not afraid of anything?'

'I try not to be. I'm not a Gerry Browning, but——'

'It's true, Evv,' said Colin. 'He's not afraid of much. Or if he is, he hides it.'

'And you never muck about with the girls?'

Silence.

'*Touché*, Bay,' said Colin. 'What about all those knocking shops in Alex?'

'That's different.'

'Why? *Why*?' demanded Evverson.

Again Bay didn't immediately perceive why, so he said it was obvious.

'But *why*?' Evverson persisted.

'Because a man can do what boys cannot.'

'I see. One need only behave decently while one's small enough for a father to beat and bully. When one's big enough to hit back——'

'Don't you call my father a bully. He's a grand man. I'll give you an instance of the old man's wisdom, Colin. Once I and another boy climbed the steeple of East Hadly church and the vicar complained. What did the old man do? Gave me a sovereign for pluck and six of the best on the seat of my pants. Don't you think that was bloody clever?'

'Rather bloody confusing,' Colin submitted.

'Good *God*,' sighed Evverson and, as if unable to take any more, got up and walked out.

This contemptuous exit fired Bay yet further. 'Did he dare to do that to show that he despised me? That he thought I was talking nonsense? Great devils in hell! *He!* He of all people! Do you mean to tell me that a spot of my father's medicine isn't what *that* creature needed? Not that anyone could ever have made a man of him. That poor weed.'

His head was now heated too high for further talk. Muttering, he rose, knocked out his pipe, whose bowl was probably as hot as his head, and went out into the night. Bay, for all his toughness, had his poetry like the rest of us and could stand and gaze at the beauty of the Gallipoli night. Beneath the crowding stars the Turkish flares would leap along the whole length of the Line and dawdle suspiciously down, laying a silvery light on grey olive trees. Intermittent rifle-fire under these flares seemed to heighten their brilliance and their sweet spice of danger. From where he stood in Sackville Street the star-shells and Very lights would appear to be behind him as well as in front, so jagged and zigzag the Line.

At such a time as this the guns, great and small, from sea to sea, laid their quick fitful flashes on the sky. The glow-worms sparkled in the scrub. The men in their dug-outs sang gently 'Who . . . who . . . who's your lady friend?' or perhaps 'You called me Baby Doll a year ago'. And here and there candlelight glowed above the lips of a trench, while wood fires played on brushwood thickets or on the boles of slaughtered trees.

I think Bay got some healing for his anger as he stood there alone. Alone with the nervous Gallipoli night which lay around him like a poem pulsing and flickering with hidden life. Beautiful it was, but as a sombre poem whose subject is death.

CHAPTER FOUR

MAY was still with us when, suddenly, the great change came. The change which turned our eyes ever and again to the sea.

The ships were gone. Yesterday a chain of great warships lay around our narrow tableland; now—none. Only this empty sea—placid and sparkling and apparently innocent, but empty. Yesterday the Navy, 'father and mother to the Army', had stood there like a frowning mother indeed: ready, even eager, to loose off a virulent indignation whenever the Turk tried to bully her little boy; now—we looked at the sea in dismay and said, 'Mother's *gawn*!'

We soon knew why. German submarines had crept round by Gibraltar and were on the prowl beside us, between Anzac and Helles. And instantly the lords of the Admiralty had ordered all their most valuable ships back behind the boom of Mudros Harbour. *Queen Elizabeth*, greatest of all, the Queen Mother, our comfort and our glory, was steaming home to England.

The Navy had tried not to withdraw, but on March 25th the battleship, *Triumph*, lying off Anzac with a cordon of destroyers to guard her, went down while the Australians on their hills watched in a stricken silence and the Turks above them cheered to their skies. She had watched over the Australians so well that all their hearts sank with her; and every man of them offered a month's pay towards the cost of raising her; but her bed was too deep. Two days later the *Majestic*, lying off Helles with small craft around her, turned over like a beach ball on the waves and sank, while British and French in their hundreds watched from the sloping amphitheatres of W Beach and V Beach. Her keel showed above the water for the rest of the campaign, to remind us of other of the Navy's ships lying dead around the tip of our long forefinger of land.

What now?

Apart from the hospital ships, inviolable in their white paint and red crosses, only ships of light draught, trawlers, tugs and sweepers—and, later, monitors—dared approach us. On our narrow cape we felt like a lost people. And since the ravaging of the guns had turned it into a dry landscape of flying dust and faded scrub, we might have been (or so we said) on another planet lately discharged from the spinning Earth.

And yet, as Colin said when we were back in the Line, we needn't really feel lonely. The Turks were there. Didn't we hear them talking sometimes or chanting monotonous hymns to Allah? And old Achi Baba was still there, a hill alive with nameless men. There she was, stretching her shoulders right across the Peninsula and (one could imagine) smiling sardonically at us.

The ships went and the plagues came.

The sun was the first of them and father of all. Now, if the Turks did not fire at us, the sun did; nor for a moment did it hold its fire. It shrivelled heath and thyme and asphodel; it roasted the sandy ground so that a heat haze lifted from it like an insect hum made visible. Thirst burned on that tongue of land, cracking it deep, and since our water, brought from Alexandria, was now rationed to a quart of tepid liquid a day for all purposes, thirst burned on every human tongue, cracking spirit and will.

Then dust. The dust flew on that north-east wind and stung our eyeballs and caked on our sweating cheeks. It flew far out to sea like a yellow smoke, and like the travelling smell of our dead. At this time our Peninsula, lying slope-shouldered on the sea, sent forth its smell with the dust as if it were a single rotting corpse. And it always seems to me now that the whole heated, stinking place was often vocal too with the shrilling of the cicadas in that hot shallow lifting dust.

Worst of all, the flies. They came fresh from putrefying food in tins cast into no-man's-land; from the blackened bodies in the scrub or on the wire; and from the excrement in the Turkish trenches—for mostly the Turk's latrine was where he stood. These bloated flies, thirsty after a meal perhaps, alighted in the moisture on your lips, your eyes, your nostrils. They dropped on each morsel of your food and, unbeatable, pursued it into your mouth and down your throat, two or more at a time, like a pot-holing club inspecting an underground cave. The dysentery, I imagine, was the gift of the flies, and of the dust prowling ever around us.

This was a form of dysentery that raked and rent at your bowels and sent you rushing to a latrine abuzz with enthusiastic and anticipating flies. The men called it the Gallipoli Gallop, because it was always a question whether they could get to the latrine on time. The officers, perhaps to preserve some of their dignity, if not much, called it the Gallipoli Trot. It drained us of life and vigour till we were like an army of yellow-skinned cadavers, the sickest of us looking like scarecrows or skeletons in ripped and dirtied uniforms. Weary and weak, we could hardly drag ourselves to the latrines, and the uniforms of many were fouled by their failures to get there. Colin assured me that Xerxes' army, when on this very ground two thousand years before, had had dysentery too, but I got little comfort out of that—though I must say I felt glad about it.

Maybe the Turks, accustomed to summer and filth, suffered less, but they suffered enough to stay still for most of the day. After their ceremonial 'Morning Hate' when they greeted the Infidels ashore with rapid fire—'Christians, Awake' we called it—they appeared to settle down to their hookahs, their siestas, or their prayers. Or, duty done, they turned from hate to friendliness and tossed Turkish cigarettes to us in lively hope of some interesting tinned food from the West. Willingly enough we tossed them some bully beef but, like us, they soon tired of this and sent over a message, "Bully beef, *non. Envoyez* milk." We found some milk for them and shot it over, for we were fond of Johnny Turk.

So all over that gashed and cloven land the British and Australians and New Zealanders lay in their plague-stricken shanty-cities. Like convicts or hermits, uniformed persons set apart from the rest of their kind, they made friends with the small animals who came on visits out of the earth or the brush. These had little fear of us because we lived like them in the soil and among the roots. I had a pet chameleon who, we thought, was like Evverson, since it changed its colour according to its company and had a damned long tongue. Colin had a charming little jerboa. Bay palled up with a staccato-moving lizard. And there was a praying mantis of whom we were all very fond. We were less fond of the centipedes, the scorpions, and the snakes. The snakes used to hiss and shoot away from us as sharply as we from them.

Like the Turks we had little desire to fight amid these plagues of dust, flies, and dysentery. We lay, if only our Generals and the Staff would allow us to, in trench or dug-out, sweating and suffocating, beneath handkerchiefs spread over our faces. Unable to sleep, we lay there listening to the broken patter of machine-guns or to the shrill ceaseless chatter of cicadas unworried and at peace beneath the foliage.

One day in a fire-trench I looked at Colin who stood talking to his sergeant. His face was yellow, and beneath its skin there was little left but the fine bones. Under his pith helmet (we were all in shorts and helmets now) I knew that his hair was cropped close, as Bill Drewer's had been for fear of 'Gallipoli cattle'. The laughing eyes were bloodshot. His slight shapely limbs were now angular and thin. And I felt a sharp pleasure to think that this devastation of his looks couldn't injure my love at all. By now my love seemed almost to exist independently of him, because I wanted its high-wrought interest and the luxury of its pains.

'God, he looks sick,' I thought, as he joked with the sergeant. 'He ought to go off as others have done. Surely, if I love him, I ought to persuade him to go, even though it might mean that I'd never see him again.'

I determined to be loyal to the love, and when the sergeant

had gone with a laugh, and the sketch of a salute, I said, 'Colin, old man, you look bloody awful.'

'Sorry about that. It's hard luck on you and the boys, I know, but I'm spared all sight of myself, thank God.'

'You ought to report sick. You know you ought.'

'Don't talk such bilge.' His bloodshot eyes swung to the trench parapet beyond which, not twenty yards away, were the Turks. 'One doesn't report sick.'

'Some do. They just have to in the end. How many of your platoon have gone?'

'I don't know, but there are still a few left, and some of them look a sight worse than I do. Devil fetch these flies! "They come not in single flies but in battalions." *Hamlet.* Has Cass gone? Has Evv gone? To hell then, why must I? And what about you, come to that?'

'Oh, I'm fine.'

'Yes, you look it. You used to be an enormous great brawny lad, and look at you now: you look like an old balloon from which most of the gas is escaping. Doesn't he, Bay?' Bay had just come into the trench. 'Send him off to Alex.'

'I'm not going off for anyone.' I had my reputation for fearlessness to sustain. 'Not for Bay or anybody else.'

'Mutinous type, isn't he, Bay? Use your authority on him and send him off under arrest.'

Bay, who remained in a state of repulsively irrelevant health, had now, I was sure, something like a love for Colin, though there was nothing in it that he need hide. It was just that he was happier with Colin than with anyone else and delighted in this new-found happiness. He seemed to want to be always with him. And Colin, since his nature was affectionate, could only take pleasure in such an obvious preference, and give much of his time to Bay that he might enjoy it. Often I felt left outside—or I chose to feel so, wanting the pain of it; and at one time I managed so to develop my sadness that it issued in a shameful deed. Where now was the selflessness that I had found in the boat as they towed me ashore? Or as I obeyed Doughty Wylie and charged up the hill? The removal of fear had long removed the need of it.

It was early evening, and we were in our dug-out behind the Eski Line. This was a roomy cavern cut deep in the white earth wall of Gully Ravine. Gully Ravine, or, simply, The Gully, was an astonishing canyon on the left of the Peninsula, winding up to the Line from its mouth by the sea. To all the other nullahs and dongas it was as Gulliver to the Lilliputians. Inevitably, its white cliff-walls, a hundred feet high, were infested with thousands of cliff-dwellers in their dug-outs, bivvies, and shanty homes; its floor with headquarters, dumps, and transport lines.

Our dug-out turned its back on the Gully and faced a high, hanging valley that led up into the Eski Line. Roomy as a chalk-cave gouged out by the sea, it had an honest-to-God table in it made of pine props and case wood; it had egg crates for chairs, shelves on the walls, and pinned-up pictures everywhere of magazine girls wearing little but their saucy Come-hither smiles.

We called it 'Whitehall Court'.

Bay, Colin, and I sat in this white cave sipping whisky or the strong lime juice and talking as usual of women. We all smoked pipes or cigarettes as a protection against the last of the day's flies. Outside the batmen were cooking our dinner on a sweet-smelling fire of ration-case wood. How they got this wood we didn't ask, because it was against orders to take it unless it was broken. But resourceful batmen always contrived that it was broken.

'Dysentery,' said Colin, pushing the lime juice from him, 'is a good enough anaphrodisiac.'

'But I ain't *got* dysentery,' Bay objected. 'And I can't go on much longer.' He looked up at the saucy Kirchner girls on the walls, with their breasts billowing above collapsing lingerie or hiding coyly behind inadequate lace. 'Oh dear no. More than two months now. Dysentery won't last for ever. What are you going to do then?'

'You forget I'm engaged.'

'And that has a similar effect to dysentery?'

'Up to a point, yes.' Up to a point, he had said: how much did that mean when he was in Alexandria?

'Tell us more about the lovely girl. She's a knockout, is she?'

'She pleases me.' He blew out smoke from his cigarette, bombarding the drowsy flies.

'Olwen. Where on earth did she get that name from?'

'From her godfathers and godmothers in her baptism, wherein she was made——'

'Yes, yes, but "Olwen". Scotch, is it? Who's her old man?'

'Old Mallaby.'

'What? *Lord* Mallaby?'

'That's the boy.'

Instantly Colin seemed wafted away far from my reach, and I was jealous, not of Olwen, but of the world that took him from me. As always, when he receded from me, he became the more desirable, and my love grew, fed by the sweet pain of loss.

'In luck, aren't you? There's money there.'

'Not for Olwen, I'm afraid.'

'But he's got a colossal place at Great Henty's. About thirty thousand acres.'

'And the place is pretty well sinking him. Just as Ivry is sinking us. What we shall all do after the war I don't know. Keep a pub, I should think.'

I felt happier at this suggestion that the world which held him might be destroyed.

'Let's see the lady again.' Bay stretched out a demanding hand. 'Go on. We all know she's in that pocket. Olwen . . . Mallaby. . . . Charming sounds. Pity to change them to Olwen Dester.'

Colin, proud enough of his Olwen, took the photograph from his pocket-book and passed it to Bay.

'Yesss . . .' said Bay with a rich hiss. '*Very* nice. Very nice indeed. Yes, perhaps if I had something like that, I should be a better boy. Doubt it, but you never know. "All my love always, Olwen." Isn't that fetching? When'll you marry, Colin?'

'Fairly soon, I hope, but she's only eighteen.'

'Eighteen. How very pleasant. How undeniably stirring. Oh dear, oh dear.' He passed the picture to me, and I looked again at Olwen's face. Her eyes looked straight into mine. 'What do you think of that, Gerry?'

'Beautiful,' was all I said. 'Terribly, troublingly beautiful.'

'And I suppose you're terribly in love with her, Colin?'

'Afraid so. A bad show, but there it is.' He was palpably pleased by our praises and the more in love with her for them. 'All I can say is that a lifetime without the creature seems something not worth having.'

Bay looked mischievously at him; paused before speaking; and then said, 'Have you had her yet, old boy?'

Colin did not answer; his lips locked together.

'I see. Sorry and pardon. That's something I may not ask.'

'Do you really think it's a question I should answer?'

'No, of course not. Not a gentlemanly question at all.'

'It was not. And now if you'll allow me, my dear fellow; I think I'll write to the girl. You've got me all hotted up about her.'

From a shelf behind him he took writing-pad and began to write.

And I, still looking at the photograph, knew that the true answer to the ungentlemanly question was 'Yes, Bay'. Had it been 'No', Colin must have said simply and angrily, 'No, of course not.' The true naked Colin had not shown himself in his answer; we had seen only the curtain which he would often drop between us and his secret self. With my Baron's Court innocence I was shaken, but I felt not the smallest jealousy. Nor could I blame him, when I, with the photograph in my hand, was pruriently imagining her lying naked and beautiful in bed . . . or turning and coupling with her lover. I stared and stared into the photograph indulging these thoughts, and her beauty became very desirable. Almost I felt a happy contact and unity with her because she was a possession of Colin's.

We were seated thus, Colin writing fluently, Bay turning the pages of an old magazine, and I puffing smoke at the flies and dwelling as ever with my secretive thoughts, when Bay looked up and exclaimed, 'What's that? Listen. What the hell . . .?'

Sounds of cheering and laughter were coming down the Gully below us, and getting nearer. Then the sound of a scuttle by the batmen outside.

'Is the war over?' Bay inquired.

Evverson, who'd been outside talking to the batmen, rushed in. 'Come quick and see. It's a sight for the gods.'

We ran out and down the slope that led from our hanging valley to the Gully. Hundreds stood at the mouths of their sepulchral dug-outs in the Gully's sloping walls. Hundreds more had come hurrying out from their huts or tents on its wide floor. Since this was the deepest and safest highway on the Peninsula half the traffic of the war swept up and down it: motor dispatch-riders, horse-drawn G.S. wagons, mule-drawn ambulances, 'walking wounded', limbers and guns and the long pack-trains of the Zion Mule Corps. But now for a moment all such stood still to watch.

Three men were approaching. Two were soldiers with fixed bayonets, and between them a figure who was half a man and half a tree. He was painted green all over, from face to boots and hands. From his head, shoulders and waist sprang branches of green foliage. He came between his guards like a tree walking; and all the more like a tree for being taller than either of them. Behind him came a soldier carrying a rifle painted green from barrel to butt.

'Guess what it is, and you can have it, sir,' a voice behind me offered.

'It's a sniper,' said another man, eager to expound.

'Lor' bless us, they've actually pinched a sniper,' said Bay. 'Damned good. Hope they shoot him.'

'Oh, Christ, no,' Colin protested. 'He's only been doing his duty, picking us off, one by one.'

'But he's probably shot heaps of our boys,' Bay grumbled.

'Yes, I'm thinking of joining the League against Cruel Sports after the war. This is the first time I've been at the wrong end of the sport.'

'He might have shot you. Or, worse still, me.'

'No, he'd never have shot you.'

'*Why?*' Bay turned to Colin and demanded this indignantly.

'Because you have all the look of a regular officer, and the Turks have instructions never to kill our regulars.'

'Poppycock! *Why?*'

'Because they regard them as fighting more or less on *their* side. I understand that if a Turk shoots one of our staff officers, his O.C. promptly shoots him.'

'*Very* funny. *Very* funny,' sneered Bay, but having no humorous retort to hand, could only insist after a time:

'I say that if he was behind our lines he should be shot. We're altogether too soft. This is war, and it won't be won by being soft. The Huns aren't soft. I'm for putting a holy terror into these blighters.'

'So am I,' Colin mocked. 'Let's torture them.'

Among the watching men there seemed no thought of shooting or torturing him. Rather was this a triumphal procession with the man-tree as its hero.

'*Saïda*, Johnny,' they called; and 'Bad luck, Mustapha; it's a fair cop'; and 'Feeling a bit green, old chap, are you? Never mind; we shan't hurt you'.

But the prisoner seemed less green with fear than happy to be done with the war and, as it were, among friends. 'Turk mafeesh', he called, lifting a royal hand to his welcomers. 'Germany no goot. England vehr goot.'

'That's right, cock. We win the war, see? Compree?'

His teeth in the green face gleamed an endorsement. 'Turk mafeesh.' And in case we didn't understand the word (which we did) he translated it for us, 'Turk feenish,' and grinned again. Not that he believed it, but that he thought we should like to hear it. 'Lor Kisshenair vine man.'

He's a sniper, sir,' explained a new man at my side, gratuitously.

'I know that. But how did they get him?'

'They found him in a tree.' It was Evverson who supplied the answer. 'The Cheshires saw some branches waving when there was no wind, and their scouts crawled out and got him.'

'Caught him green-handed, as you might say,' said Colin.

'And where are they taking him to?' I asked.

'To H.Q., of course.' Evverson knew all about it. 'He'll be much more use to them alive than dead. That's what they got him for.'

'Johnny *kaput*,' shouted a voice, jeering; but another man rushed forward to this guest with a cigarette. ''Ere, have a fag, Abdul.'

The sniper put out a green hand to take it, but his guards disallowed this courtesy; and some men cried indignantly, 'Oh, let him have it, poor bugger.'

Others yelled, '*Imshi iggry*, Johnny'; not because it was appropriate but because it was the only Arabic they knew; and they imagined a Turk would understand it. Roughly, in English, it meant, 'Hop along, and quickly.'

The friendly fellow turned towards them. 'It's a long vay to Teeperary,' he said, and went on his way with a smile.

I watched him, fascinated, as he passed by. So, I think, did all the others. A dispatch-rider stopped to study him. So did two mounted staff officers and their orderly. An Indian with his goats drew them to the side of the Gully till he should be out of sight. An ambulance drew up so sharply that the white dust smoked up into the air from its wheels. Seldom had we dared to walk on the plateau above us because there an Invisible Death lived and moved, and no one knew from which direction it might strike. All over the plateau, before and behind our trenches, the Turkish snipers lay in the tall scrub or sat among the branches of the ruined trees. And here at last was this Invisible Death made flesh and passing before us.

Not till he had disappeared round a cape in the winding Gully did we return up the slope to our valley and our cave.

After dinner that night Colin went on writing his letter by
e light of three smoking candles which drooped and bowed
the hot night air. How well I remember the tallow-grease
nell of those candles that night, blending with the aromatic
nell of the dying wood-fire outside. And the silence. Silence
own in the Gully. Silence in the darkness overhead. Silence
p in the Line, save for the occasional whip-crack of a rifle.
r was it, perhaps, a sniper's rifle on the plateau?

At about ten o'clock Cass went out to take a working party,
ow assembled in the Western Mule Trench, up to the Line.
hey were to do an easy piece of wiring by Half Moon Street
n the left brink of the Gully. Bay sat polishing his pipe-bowl
y rubbing it up and down the cavity between his nose and
is cheek, and bringing it away to see how its dark walnut
nts shone in the candlelight. After a time he said, 'There!
Vhat a shine. What a patina. That's the only way to polish
pipe. On the natural velvet of the cheek and the natural
ils of the body. God gave us that cavity for precisely that
urpose. Now I'll go and see what Cassy's doing. The Turk's
nly about a hundred yards from Half Moon Street, and I
on't want Cass chattering too loud. Besides, he's probably
orgotten to put out his covering parties.'

'Oh, no, he hasn't,' said Colin. 'Cassy does everything with
perfect technical accuracy. You'll find each covering party
t exactly the right place.'

'May be so; but look: if they start firing, he may abscond.'

'No, no. Not Cassy. Never again.'

'None the less, I think that as his bank manager I'd better
go and take a dekko at him.' He laid the pipe on the table, as
ne who'd be back soon.

Not a whole minute later Evverson, after apparently listen-
ng to Bay's departing steps, got up with a feigned naturalness
nd went out too. It was as if, like a schoolboy, he had waited
or the master to go. Evverson had friends among the men
nd liked to go and talk with them in their dug-outs, a famili-
rity of which Bay, as a regular officer and a disciplinarian,
idn't approve.

Then, a few minutes later, Colin sighed wearily, tosse down his pencil, and tilted back the ammo box which was h chair. 'That's done,' he said. 'And now who's got an enve lope?'

'I have.' I jumped up in my alacrity always to give hi anything he wanted and so win his liking. 'I'll go and get it

'Sit down, you fool. I'll go. Where is it?'

'There's a writing outfit under everything else in the bolste of my valise.'

'Good. Thanks awfully. I'll find it.'

He yawned and went out, lazily singing, 'I have no pai dear mother, now, But oh, I am so dry. Connect me to brewery And leave me there to die.'

The sheets of his letter lay on the table beside me. I felt sur he must have written things about Bay and me, and for only few seconds I resisted the temptation to see what he had saic In me was the hot thirst of a jealous man to read good word about himself or even, with pain, the praise of his rival. leaned towards the sheets knowing that my eye would trave quickly to my own name or Bay's, if they were there.

'Darling Olwen, I've just been blowing off about you i the Mess, and it made me feel terrible fond of you, so now . . . no, nothing on the top sheet. Nor on the second or third, a I gently uncovered them.

On the fourth: 'Bay, our prize bull, has asked me to giv you his love. So has Gerry. Poor old Bay: a monumenta idiot, but in some ways quite a well-meaning one; as a bul he'd be excellent, but as a man—well, what can you do wit someone who thinks that to be hard and tough to the point o ruthlessness is the top of manhood? I try to teach him that al that Hunnish nonsense is not really virile but puerile, and tha it takes twice the strength to be forgiving sometimes, but h isn't educable and so a lost soul. Sad to be a lost soul and no to know it, but to think you're fine. That's enough abou Brother Heavyweight. Evv and Cassy I've described to you Evv is too damned argumentative and in too superficial a way; he does everything he can to be loved and then spoils all by arguing. Cass never speaks at all. He's just said his rst word for three weeks to Gerry. But he smiles easily, like ıe Cheshire cat on his branch. Quite a nice fellah really, as ıe Colonel always says—of everybody. But the one I like ır and away the best is still our Gerry. He's as intelligent as 3ay is obtuse, and as quiet as Evv is talkative. He doesn't say nuch, but is a devil to think. A diffident bloke, on the whole —like most large chaps—and one who, I imagine, is a good leal cleverer than he knows. He staggers me sometimes with ıis perception into all our motives. Useless for me to try any of my little hypocrisies before him; he sees through them all. 3ut honestly, Olwen darling, I think I'm damned lucky to ıave a friend like him in the Company; I love him, and Olwen beloved) I get the impression that he's really fond of your Colin. Why, I don't know. A very ordinary bloke, Colin——'

A moment of exultation—recurring moments of exultation —as when a student who doubts if he has done well enough in ın exam learns that he has passed with distinction.

'Roll on the end of the war, and then I'll get him to Ivry so that you can meet him. You'll love him, I'm sure. And I'll tell you what: when I get my pub, to be called The Green Sniper, and with a wonderful inn-sign designed by me, I'll have him as a partner, and Olwen behind the bar. We must get him out of his silly old Civil Service and——'

But he was coming back. That was his voice singing, '"Hush! Here comes a whizz-bang, You soldiers, get down them stairs——"'

I slipped the pages back into position; myself into position too.

'"Down in your dug-outs and say your prayers. Hush! Here comes a——"'

'Found it?' I asked as he entered. A foolish question, since the envelope was in his hand.

'Yes.' "You'll see all the wonders of No-Man's-Land if a whizz-bang—BUMP—hits you".'

As he put the letter into the envelope, I was thinking of Bay

with all the kindliness one feels for an opponent whom one ha
knocked down for the count; one lays a friendly hand on hi
shoulder as he rises from the canvas.

When Colin had sealed the envelope and signed it in th
corner as his own censor, I said, 'Tell us more about Olwen,
and he was happy to do so, liking to speak of her, and I wa
happy to listen, feeling now as if I shared her with him.

So we sat in that white-earth sepulchre and talked by th
smoking candles. He talked on and on of Ivry, and of Grea
Henty's, Olwen's home, and I, listening, felt ever and agai
that exultation and had to stop listening to identify it. 'I lov
him,' the letter had undoubtedly said. How much, or hov
little, could that mean?—anyway, a memory to live with fo
a while. The night was silent. Not twice in an hour did a
rifle's whip-crack split the dark silence of the Line. Our tall
was so engrossing that we were still sitting there when, long
after midnight, we heard Cass's working party returning.
There was much talking outside, excited talking for that late
hour—and then Cass came in.

His small round face was colourless apart from its dulled
yellow, which was the gift of Gallipoli's sickness and sun.

His lips moved once before he spoke. 'Bay's killed,' he said.

'Lord God!' Colin exclaimed. 'No!'

Bay . . . dead. Bay who, minutes ago, as it seemed, had been
joking about Cass, or delighting in his pipe's appearance, or
craving a woman, so full of life was he . . . now—now he was
nothing. He who had wanted the sniper shot.

Shock, yes, and an irrational sense that this was my punishment for having eavesdropped on a letter about him; pity too, and the pity all the more because I had just triumphed over him; but among all these emotions a pleasure that was shame-filling: pleasure that a man in whose presence I had always been uncomfortable, and one who'd been my rival, was for ever removed. Pleasure in his death? Oh, *no*! There on the table lay his pipe with all his boyish pride shining from it. Polished and waiting for eyes that would savour its sheen no more. I stared at Cass and echoed Colin's 'No!'

'Yes. He came out to the tape where we were putting up the wire and watched us at work. Then he went back to have a drink with the Cheshires and about an hour later came out again to see how we were getting on. It all seemed very safe. No-Man's-Land is wide there and the Turk was sending up hardly any Very lights. But as Bay was talking to Sergeant Dawes they shot up a shockingly bright one and Bay shouted to us to keep still. Either he moved to see that we'd all frozen or he called too loud, but there was a shot and it got him.'

Those infrequent whip-cracks that we'd heard—was one of them the one that Bay never heard?

'It got him in the heart, and he must have died at once. Died at once. He never said a word.' Cass was shaken into rapid talk, but I detected also in his next words a desire to suggest that he could now be trusted and would not run again. 'We got him back, Sergeant Dawes and I, and then I decided we must first of all finish the job. We did so. There were a few more shots but we managed to do it properly.'

'Where is he now?' asked Colin.

'They're bringing him down the Mule Trench. The Adjutant said, "Take him back with you, and his second-in-command will tell you what to do." That's you, Dester.'

I looked at Colin, now in command. I remembered that I was now second-in-command. And I had to call up that pity again, lest I felt pleasure. But I did feel the pleasure as well as the pity.

'Tell them to take him to the B.H.Q.' Colin spoke gently. 'He's the Padre's business now. They'll bury him down there in the Gully.'

'Yes, sir,' said Cass smartly, for some men were standing round.

We went out into the valley to see our captain pass by. They brought him out of the trench, a blanketed shape on a blood-soaked stretcher, and all his men in the valley stood at attention as he went by.

CHAPTER FIVE

THE Colonel sat in our dug-out next day, after we'd laid Bay in a little wired cemetery on the Gully floor. His fly-swatter was in his hand—and in almost autonomous action—as he spoke.

'You, Dester, will take command of the Company, with the acting rank of captain.' Slap went the swatter on a fly foolish enough to alight on the table. 'Poor Bailey-More. A very fine officer. One of the best.'

'But I'm not a regular, sir. Won't Division want to send a regular?'

'No. I told the Brigadier that I thought you'd do the job very well indeed, and he agreed—though what he knows about it I don't know.' Another fly died—or two or three died together.

'Cass and Evverson are a lot older than Browning and me, sir.'

'Yes—Cass—quite a good fellah, but—damn—he ran away once, didn't he?'

'And he ran back, sir, directly you asked him to.'

'Yes—quite a decent fellah. You'll be in command, and I'll try and get you substantive rank. I've great faith in both you men. Dammit, weren't we on the beach together, ha. ha, ha? Waiting for the nigger minstrels, eh, ha, ha, ha. Well, good-bye, you fellahs.'

When he was gone, happy with his joke, so happy that he swatted every fly he saw, I turned to Colin. 'Pleased, Skipper?'

'Yes. Can't help it, can one? But I didn't want Bay killed. And yet—oh, hell, Gerry!—I *am* pleased to be O.C. And I think old Bay'd like me to be pleased.' Colin's was an easier and franker nature than mine because it was less vexed by secret shames. 'And, to hell, Gerry, I've every intention of being a superb O.C. The men will follow me to the death. I don't mind telling you I'm going to be very different from old Bay. It's going to be all the difference between Queen Victoria and Edward the Seventh.'

'Well, that's fine, Skipper.'

'And now, Mr. Second-in-Command, I must write home at once and tell the old man and Olwen. Old Bay wouldn't mind my wanting to do that.'

The Colonel was right, and Colin too: he made a splendid commander. On our narrow and wasted battlefield there could be none of the wide separation between officers and men that existed in the spacious fields of France. We were all huddled together in similar dug-outs and mostly ate the same dull food in the same dirtied uniforms. Common homes, common food, common sickness, common filth flung the ranks together much as they fused Castle Ivry and Baron's Court in the Officers' Mess. But while Bay had produced to its utmost such separation as there was, Colin narrowed it to its utmost. He sat on the fire-steps and talked to the men. He gathered them around him after sundown and told them about the war. He joked with every man he passed. He called them by their Christian names, 'Jim' and 'Harry' and 'Bert', unless he was speaking to them formally, when he always addressed them as 'Gentlemen'. And the odd thing was that both methods were equally successful. The men would have followed Bay because, if stern, he was brave and skilful; they would have followed Colin because he had won their hearts. And he—well, he loved them in the full sense of that word. 'Wonderful lot of boys, mine, Gerry. Wonderful.'

As an inveterate churchgoer in my youth (under compulsion) I likened him to a new vicar who changes all the methods of the old, and averring that his predecessor neglected to visit his parishioners, promptly does this duty vigorously. Colin's parish was a succession of fire-bays but he visited them frequently, bringing to his spiritual children comfort and encouragement and jokes.

He had a chance to show his quality in a small assault one July night. Our brigade attacked on a mile front and Colin led his 'boys', yelling joyously. The surprise was complete, and the task soon done, with five hundred yards gained and hardly any men wounded. Cass and I did our parts well enough, but the surprise of the outing was Evverson. All agreed that his behaviour was hardly to be expected from the senior rating clerk of a suburban borough. He was seen leaping with knees up into the enemy trench as one leaps into a swimming-bath, his pistol on high and firing apparently a *feu de joie*. He accepted the surrender of the Turks in the trench, including the one under his boots, whom he'd grounded as he arrived. Then he dashed round the traverse to collect some more Turks, as enthusiastically as a boy netting shrimps in a pool and putting them in a jam-jar. He sent back to Base some two dozen specimens, mostly in poor condition. Colin complimented him, though suggesting that in a moment of happy abstraction he'd thought he was collecting the rates. The Colonel came personally to commend him, and I was happy for old Evv, because he looked so pleased.

Later he revealed to me (always his confidant) the roots of this bewildering performance. It was morning in a trench called Sauchiehall Street, and after he'd posted his sentries on the fire-steps and distributed his men among the bays, all smart and ready for the C.O.'s inspection, because he was eager for more praise, he invited me into his cubby-hole under the parapet. And there he expounded his longing to win a medal before the war was over, so that all the boys in the Town Hall should hear of it, and all the borough read about it in the local paper.

'Funny, but it's become a fixed idea of late, and it'll drive me to do anything, especially if there's an audience. Comic, but I'll risk death for it cheerfully. It's not that I'm brave really—no one less so—but that I'm vain, and my vanity's stronger than my sense of self-preservation. The other night I dreamt that I was going up some white stone stairs to a top floor to receive the K.C.B. from the Colonel—absurd because the Military Cross is about all they'll give to subalterns. I was in a morning coat and top hat because the Colonel represented the King, and when it was over I hurried home to Mum and Dad to show myself and say "Behold Sir Maurice Evverson." Then I woke up, sickly disappointed to find myself in this hole.'

I knew all that he meant. It was a picture of myself and my desires.

Seven days in the Line; seven in Rest (but do not suppose that 'rest' on our Peninsula was the antonym for labour; it was a synonym for it, denoting fatigue parties all day and much of the night). This time while we were in rest the rumour came rushing upon us and in a twinkling was everywhere. Had the excited speculation about it been a visible thing it must have smoked above our thronged earth like the smoke from field-kitchens, woodfires, pipes, and fags. Certainly from every latrine. For the latrines behind their walls of canvas or sacking were the men's clubs; and their club chairs the wooden bar on which they hung their naked buttocks over the stinking hole in the ground.

New troops—a whole Army Corps—were massing in the islands. Mudros Harbour was as full of ships as it had been in the great April days. Monitors mounting each a twelve-inch gun were ready to lie around us where once the heavy grey battleships lay. (The Navy had not left its family fatherless and motherless for long.) Hospital ships waited among the men-of-war. All the hospitals in Lemnos and Alex stood in clean readiness with twenty thousand empty beds.

It seemed confirmation of all this when a glittering staff officer, a general, all red tabs and gold oak leaves, spotless khaki and trim laundered linen, came from the luxurious H.Q. ship, the *Aragon*, to look at our sector. Colin escorted him round, showing him everything, and declared afterwards that when he showed him the latrines behind their sacking, the great man stared at them and said, 'Oh, yes. I see. Excellent idea. Excellent idea.'

August, and the truth was manifest. Our Peninsula was shaped like an anvil, and on this anvil the smouldering war was to be hammered into a decision. Not our campaign only but the war.

The Colonel was full of it. Was it not what he'd always said? Proof that he'd always been right? He'd never doubted the aim of the Dardanelles campaign; only its handling—because the handling was different from what 'in his humble opinion' it ought to have been.

'All officers to the C.O. at eleven hundred.'

All converged upon Battalion Headquarters in the Gully. B.H.Q. consisted of two sandbag cabins and a bell tent on the Gully floor and several cubby-holes pocked into the white slope above. One of the cabins was the Mess, and as we walked towards it we passed the small cemetery called 'The Rest Camp', where Bailey-More lay. We entered the Mess, leaving him outside.

'Sit down, gentlemen, those who can,' said the Colonel from the top of his table. Colin and I, still feeling junior, remained standing against the sandbag wall.

'It's hardly a secret any more, gentlemen, that we shall shortly attack, and I have the Brigadier's permission to explain it all to you, because it is no ordinary attack. But not a word yet to anyone else; not even to your sergeants. This could be the decisive battle. It should force a decision here, and if the decision is in our favour, it should mean the beginning of the end of the war. Small though our battleground here is, it is the place, as I've always said, where we could decide the war at a blow. As the C.-in-C. always says, it's the heel of the German colossus.'

No battle front in the war threw such a spell over its advocates—I had almost said its lovers—as Gallipoli, and Colonel Harby had been spellbound by it from the first. He spoke again now, and with excitement, of its fine strategic purpose and the rich fruits that should drop from it.

'Once command the Narrows, gentlemen, so that the Navy can pour through the Dardanelles to Constantinople, and then—dammit—everything should happen. The Turkish Empire falls. Greece, Rumania, Serbia, Christians all, join us against their Moslem masters. The door to the East is slammed in the face of the damned Germans, and arms and ammunition pour through to the Rusians, so that we can put an iron ring round the enemy. See? We feel confident that Germany, menaced by a flood of well-armed men from the East, all ready to pour over the Hungarian plain and cut off her supplies, must sue for peace some time next year. Nothing anywhere else can achieve this result, gentlemen. Failing this, the war of attrition in France'll go on for years. Personally I've seen all this from the beginning, but we must be grateful that the War Office appears to have seen it at last. So far, instead of supporting us they've thrown all their men and money into France. But now—in God's good time—some light has broken upon the War House, ha, ha, ha. Dammit, I go so far as to say that this is not only the decisive battle of the war but a decisive battle in history. Agreed?'

We nodded. One does so when a colonel asks if you agree with him.

'Thank you, gentlemen. Now then: look at Achi Baba.'

All of us saw in imagination that low, wide-shouldered hump which for three months had resisted us and now looked down upon us, smoothly smiling.

'Achi Baba looks gentle enough, but, not having fallen to us at first, it's now an impregnable fortress. So the position resolves itself into this: if not Achi Baba opposite us, then Sari Bair opposite the Australians.'

He glanced around at us to see if we understood. We tried to look as if we did. Some of us nodded. Evverson to my surprise—and discomfort—spoke. Spoke out loud. I had no doubt that he wanted to draw attention to his sagacity and general competence, with a view to that medal one day. Probably he'd been preparing his words while the Colonel spoke. 'But I understand that the Sari Bair range, sir, is much higher than Achi Baba. Nearly a thousand feet high in places, is it not, sir?'

The Colonel looked towards this voice as if to identify it. Probably he too was surprised that anyone should proffer a comment so soon. 'It's higher, yes, and much more rugged. Yes.'

'And heavily fortified, I suppose, sir?' Good God, the man was going on with his blather! To my disgust. I looked down on the floor.

'Oh, no doubt . . . of course . . . naturally. . . .' If I was abashed, the Colonel was disorganized. 'Fortified, naturally. . . . But whatever it is, we must get over it.'

Simple as that. 'Yes, yes. Quite,' agreed Evverson.

'It has the enormous advantage, you see, that it sits on the narrowest part of the Peninsula, and once we stand on its spurs we are only four miles from the Narrows. One great drive and we are astride the Peninsula, and the whole Turkish Army here is bottled up. Some of you men may know that this was precisely the plan which, in my humble opinion, should have been adopted from the first. I advocated it steadily but nobody ever listened, except old General King-Reece. He said I was right. Almost the last thing he said before he died was——'

'"Kiss me, Harby",' murmured Colin.

And because of this irreverence and because of my efforts, as in a church service, to hold back laughter, I did not hear the full tale of what the General had said.

'However, as one who knows the East well, I hardly expected to be listened to. The High-ups decided otherwise, and it is for them to say. And for us, most certainly, to obey. Now at last, thank God, it is to be attempted. Our task at Helles will be to contain all the Turks here by fighting our damnedest, while a tremendous force is landed at Anzac and at Suvla Bay to the north of it, and a terrific attempt made to capture Sari Bair. And then—damn—then to sweep on to the Narrows. What it amounts to is this: just as, instead of battering against an impregnable wall in France we are trying a way round by Constantinople, so instead of battering against Achi Baba, we're going round by Suvla. You can see, I think—you can see the idea?'

Murmurs informed him that we could see.

'Well, gentlemen, I hope that when Brigade gives us the word you will explain to your men the—er—dammit, the as-you-might-say splendour of the idea. You must show them that there was never a battle better worth fighting. Perhaps you could put to them that, all things considered, there's nothing, at this moment in our lives, quite so well worth doing. That's what *I* feel. They are good fellahs, and I make no doubt they'll understand and fight it gallantly. Tell 'em I've promised the Corps Commander they will. You too, gentlemen: I know I can trust you. Thank you.'

Though we were not allowed as yet to tell the men, they knew, every man of them, from Aegean to Hellespont, that a battle on the great scale was being prepared. And this knowledge proved a better medicine for their sickness and exhaustion than anything the M.O.s could give them on Sick Parade. Not that they had a Homeric craving for martial glory but that they preferred violent activity to arid inertia, and, ever sanguine, chose to believe, on hearing talk of huge reinforcements, that this might be going to 'put the kibosh on the war'. The winning post was in sight, and, since this was August, they might be home by Christmas. The plagues of dust, heat, and flies were no less in these midsummer months, but other things were better on the Peninsula. Our homes were better; we'd had time to dig and build them. Food was better; the Powers on the seas behind us were getting more frozen meat and tepid water ashore. Bakeries above W Beach were making us good white bread. It is possible, too, that we were becoming nearly as acclimatized to the heat, dust, flies, and carrion-infested air as were our friends, the Turks, just over the road. So we on Helles were in very fair heart for the battle. Most of us, unable to believe that *we* should be killed, were impatient for the thing to begin.

CHAPTER SIX

I SHALL always think, nevertheless, that the plagues, still current among us, helped to kill one of our number, but in an unobvious way, so that, unlike others who died, he died in dishonour. You must hold in mind that we were largely an army of drawn and emptied vessels, impounded on a wasted headland where all normal comfort was lost to us, and where Death came reaping by day and by night, if you are to bear with what happened now.

Three days before we moved into position for the battle, Cass and I were sitting on petrol cans outside Whitehall Court, our white cavern in the high valley. We were waiting in the last of the sun for dinner and for Colin. He had been summoned to B.H.Q. by battalion runner, and we were excited to know what such a summons could mean.

Evverson was not with us. For several days he had been assisting the Adjutant at B.H.Q. Someone had discovered, after three months, that he'd been a rating clerk in a Town Hall and deduced from this that he should be good at office work in an Orderly Room.

Colin did not come. At last I got up and went a little way down the slope that led from valley to Gully. I doubt if I felt very different from a wife who works up a fear that her husband may have been killed in the road. It was a relief when I saw him in the Gully, dragging himself wearily towards us.

'What was it?' I asked, when he was on the slope.

'Oh, hell,' he muttered irritably. 'Leave me time for God's sake.'

'Okay,' I agreed, instantly hurt. A rebuke from Colin could hurt and sour me as nothing else. All the same I had to glance again at his face because it wore the strained look of one how carried heavy news.

He was often irritable now, his unavowed exhaustion causing it, or perhaps the cares of captaincy. I bore it well enough when he turned his heat on Evverson or Cass; but if he snapped at me, I went into a pique from which, sometimes, I could not dig myself out for many days, or until he'd said something really nice to me.

He went into the dug-out silently. I followed silently, having no intention of speaking again and being rebuked. Cass, discerning trouble, came too.

Colin dropped gloomily on to one of our egg-crate chairs, while we two stood waiting for him to speak. 'It's the prettiest piece of news. And a job for you.' He looked up at me. 'A sweet job.'

I wanted to say, 'For me?' but I didn't answer at all. And I was happy not to do so because there are few things so pleasant as a huffiness with someone you love.

'We shall be one officer short for this bloody show. And it looks as if Gerry might miss the fun too.'

Miss the show? It was a stabbing disappointment, because I, like Evverson, had a dream of winning distinction in it, a swelling dream that outweighed the fears. Curiosity forced me to come out of my hurt silence, but I did not speak more pleasantly than necessary. 'What *are* you talking about?'

'Evv's in close arrest.'

'*What?*' Cass gasped out.

'Arrest?' I echoed, forgetting all injuries. 'In the name of God, why?'

'And the Colonel says you're to be the officer responsible for him. At least till someone else escorts him off the Peninsula. Which may not happen for days. That's your pleasant job, just when all the fun of the fair is about to begin. You'd better go and do it.'

'But the other day he was a hero. What's he done? What's he charged with?'

'With what they call "disgraceful conduct of an unnatural kind". What *we* call'—and he provided a single word.

'Evverson?' And Cass too: 'Evverson?'

'Aye. Our Mr. Evverson.'

'But . . . with whom?'

Colin named a man in our company, Private Gottsched. And the astonishing, silencing thing was that Gottsched was nearly as old as Evverson himself and no very personable fellow either, though friendly and very intelligent. Nor was he even in Evverson's platoon. 'He of course is under arrest too.'

Silence, till my curiosity made me ask, 'But how did they find out?'

'Seems they'd been suspecting something and kept some sort of observation.'

'You mean they——'

'I don't mean that the R.S.M. looked into Evv's dug-out and said, "Ere! You can't do that there here." I imagine—but I don't know—that one doesn't talk to an officer like that, even in these circumstances. I mean that, after keeping their eyes open, they sounded Gottsched and he confessed. The M.O. says there's an ingrained tendency in these types to tell the truth directly they know their secret's out. Seems idiocy because it's on their own evidence that they're hanged, but the Adj, who's had experience as a barrister with these gentlemen, agreed with the M.O. Evverson's admitted it all too. What else could he do? He's not such a cad as to charge his partner with lying.' Colin lit himself a cigarette and exhaled its first smoke like a visible sigh. 'The Colonel's red with fury; off his head about it; strutting around like a gobbling turkey-cock. He said to me, "I've never heard anything like it, Dester. My men are clean-living fellahs, all of 'em." Nice for him if he thinks that, but he should have seen some of 'em in Alex. They may not be Evvs and Gottscheds, but they're not quite as pure as he thinks. At present he's getting his only comfort from the fact that Gottsched has a German name. Evverson he's ready to shoot. He thinks he's been 'un-English'. Old Bay—I wonder what he'd have said.'

'But what now? What do they do to him?'

'Cashiered by General Court Martial, and after that he'll

probably get two years. That's what the Adj says, and he knows all about the criminal law—or thinks he does. The maximum sentence could be penal servitude for life. Will you only believe it? The Adj says he'll get more than Gottsched because he's an officer.'

You have to make an example of an officer: Evverson on Cass, when Cassy erred. . . . 'And it'll all be published in G.R.O. for the whole army to see?' I asked.

'Oh, sure.'

I dream always of getting a Military Cross and of all the boys in the Town Hall reading about it.

'You'd better go, Gerry. They're waiting for you. Maybe it won't be for long. They'll try to get him away before the battle . . . and, Gerry . . .' He paused, frowned, and squared his mouth. 'Christ, it all passes my comprehension—it doesn't make sense to me'—as he said this, a barrier rose between him and me, because *I* could just understand it, and the barrier left me sad and alone on my side of it—'but poor old Evv, tell him . . . give him "all the best" from us, and tell him that if there's anything we can do for him, here we are. Eh, Cassy?'

Cass said 'Of course', in his quiet bank-counter voice.

Muttering my 'Of course' too, I went out into our hanging valley where the batmen were around the woodfire preparing the meal. It so happened that at this moment the Gallipoli sky had unrolled its sunset along the west, a glory of golden bands and rose-tipped clouds beneath a sea-green glow that, blending with the purples of the east, touched all our scrub and cliffs with violet hues. The sweet-smelling woodfire, hissing and spurting where the pine logs were damp, sent up a blue smoke-column into the still air. Sundown; and all our Line must be standing to arms in their trenches, but the Turks were as silent as they. Not yet had they rent the serenity with their evening hate.

But it was a pregnant silence, as if quick with something that must bring it to labour soon. Standing there, I thought how our slain and desecrated land lay so often in an ambience of lovely light and colour, and somehow this made me feel glad, that by an irony of fate, or by its mercy, I had been made poor Evverson's jailer. For I could understand much of his state. At least I could understand that he had sought to be beforehand with death and enjoy for a little the beauty and the pains of loving.

Telling my batman to pack my valise and follow me, I went down the Gully to Evverson. I felt embarrassed by the task before me but not wholly dismayed by it, because both the self-dramatizing and the self-offering side of me were pleased at this chance of playing the Samaritan.

I reported to Orderly Room, and the Adjutant, seeing me, said, 'Oh, good. Sticky business this, isn't it? A terrible creature, this man. . . . The Colonel wants to see you first. He's sitting in the Mess.'

I walked the five yards to the sandbag Mess and saw him sitting at the table-head, writing, while his idle hand held away from his eyes a cheroot so small that it might have been made to his measure.

Looking up, he said, 'Ah, good.' He put the cheroot in his mouth, and his pencil down. 'Sorry to give you this horrible job, Browning, but it'll only be for a day or two. You know what an escort has to do? Just be with him all the time. He must take some exercise, of course, but you just walk with him everywhere. I'm sure you'll be as decent to him as you can force yourself to be. It's difficult to have any sympathy, I know—the whole thing beats me . . . beats me . . . but, there you are: a lot of things are difficult just now. Division tells me there's been a similar case to this in the Loyal East Devons. And the officer there was a regular! A regular,' he repeated, as if he thought this sort of thing less unlikely in these strange New Armies. 'God, I wouldn't be in either of their boots for something.'

'What do I do, sir, at night?'

'Oh, you must get your sleep. He won't try to escape if only because there's nowhere to go to on this neck of land, with the sea on two sides of it, and the Turks mounting guard on the other.'

'Is there a guard outside his dug-out, sir?'

'Good God, no! He's an *officer*. No, no. And in any case I've no men to mount guards. Dammit, there's a battle coming off. Maybe the decisive battle of the war.'

'What if he want's to go to the latrine, sir?'

'You must damn well go with him. Everywhere. And you mustn't allow him to talk to anyone except yourself, the Padre and the M.O. God, I wish they'd take him off quickly. The sooner we're quit of the whole business, the better. One wants to get on with the war.'

While he spoke I heard behind his words the low symphony of sounds in the Gully outside: a throbbing of motor-cycles, the voice of the R.S.M. slanging a guard, the jingle and neigh of an officer's horse, and ever and again the echoing roll of unhurrying guns.

'Shall I be able to get back to the Company before the battle, sir?'

'I hope so, my boy. Young Dester begged that you might. He has a high opinion of you, it seems, and he says he'd like to have you there when the time comes.'

Why should I be given this shaft of happiness when poor old Evverson . . .? 'I'd like to be with him, sir.'

'Yes. He says you're afraid of nothing. Is that so?'

'Oh, no, sir.'

'I thought it couldn't be. I mean, for my part, I'm afraid of everything: shrapnel, machine-guns, trench mortars, high explosive—in fact I can't think of anything flying about the Peninsula that I really like. Bombs? No, if there are two things in the world that I hate above others, the first is bombs, and the second is bombs, ha, ha'—he stopped the laugh abruptly, as if he had remembered Evverson. 'Well, go to this wretched, miserable fellow. He's up there in his dug-out. Swinburn's with him and will hand you your orders. He'll already have seen that he's got no weapon or potential weapon anywhere.' Rising he went to the door where a runner waited. 'Butt, take Mr. Browning to Mr. Evverson's dug-out. And then bring candles for God's sake.'

Outside, in the Gully, a straggle of 'walking wounded' was

coming down from the Line, some merry and joking above their blood-sodden bandages, others quivering with shock and silent.

Evverson's dug-out was high up in the white cliff. It was but a wedge-shape cut in the slope, but I observed that its cover of interlaced groundsheets was ampler than those of others. A groundsheet hung in front of it for a curtain. Doubtless this curtain was a mercy granted by B.H.Q. below.

I lifted it. He was lying there on a sleeping valise with Jack Swinburn beside him. Swinburn wore belt and revolver; Evverson neither. By the light of a hurricane lantern on the ground between them I saw that Evverson's face was whiter, greener, than the sickest of those walking wounded who had just straggled by.

'Hallo, Evv, old boy,' I said.

He rose into a sitting position. 'Hallo, Gerry,' was all he could say.

Swinburn said, 'Don't come in, cock, till I get out. There's no room for three, especially if one of them's as big a lad as you.' He clambered on to his feet, so far as this was possible under the groundsheets. 'Yes, we heard you were coming. I've got to get back to my duties. Well, so long, Evverson old boy, and . . . good luck.'

'Thank you, Swin.'

'Yes . . . keep the old pecker up.' With bent head he got himself out of that dug-out and, once behind the curtain, slipped a paper into my hand. Glancing down at it, I saw, 'Orders for Escort of Officer in Close Arrest.' I shot it into my side pocket and clambered into the dug-out; taking my seat on Swin's valise till his batman should remove it.

Evv did not speak, so I managed to say, 'He's right, Evv: keep smiling. Nothing's as bad as it seems.'

'Oh, yes, it is, Gerry. That's just facile. It's quite possible to be at a point beyond which there's nothing worse.'

'Well, you're not there, old chap.'

'I *am*,' he declared, almost as if proud of it.

'The Colonel said you had his sympathy. So did Colin and

Cass.' This was not quite the truth, but I was ready to ease him with half-lies. 'They said they'd do all they could.'

'Nice of them, but there's nothing they can do. The Army's the Army, and it's waiting for my head somewhere.' He seemed proud of this metaphor: it was at least something to be proud of in the heart of disaster. 'And whatever they say, Gerry, I know they condemn me utterly. They can never understand. You chaps are all safe from temptation with no women on the Peninsula, but what about us?'

'Us?'

'Yes, those of us who feel it's no crime to choose whom we like to love, so long as we hurt no one else.'

'You mean . . .?'

'Yes, certainly. . . . Even if it's a man. So long as he's one of your own kind. Gotty was. I knew it at once. Gerry, you must know what it is to be worn out and tired and hungry for affection; everyone knows it; and what if the affection's available? Doesn't one take it?'

But what he really implied was so strange to me that I could not say 'Yes'. I could only mutter, 'I agree that most people want some affection. . . .' My orders were to avoid all conversation about his case, but I hadn't the courage to stop him and, anyhow, I was so interested that I wanted him to go on. He lay back on the valise, with his hands behind his head, while I sat on my haunches, or cross-legged and tailor-wise, listening to this other strange lover.

'Did the Adj tell you anything about Gotty?' he asked.

'How do you mean?'

'About any punishments he'd had in the past?'

'No. . . . No. . . .' To what could he be leading?

'The Padre—did he tell you anything about my first sight of Gotty?'

'No. Why should he?'

'No, of course not. *Sub sigillo*'—even in his extremity he could not resist parading this knowledge of an ecclesiastical term. 'Though I wasn't making my confession to him: only talking.'

Impossible for me to appear to encourage him further—nor necessary. He was obviously longing to say much to me, and in this masked bivouac, and he lying on the bottom of disgrace, his heart was ready to uncover things that most of us conceal from our fellows. He wanted to talk truth, and I had always been his confidant. But I was not prepared for his opening question.

'In the old days,' he said, 'would you have gone to a public execution?'

'No. Of course not,' I answered promptly, in no such need as he to ransack for unpalatable truths.

He shifted the hands from behind his head and linked them on his breast. 'Well, I should. I should have been drawn to it, fascinated. When we were in Alex, a Greek spy was sentenced to death and I heard they were going to hang him at dawn from the pylon of a suspension bridge as an example to other Greek traders. I wanted to go and watch—I almost did—but I was afraid of someone seeing me there.'

I said nothing in reply, but I was thinking (with my face towards my lap) that I too would have felt tempted—and equally ashamed of being recognized at such a dread entertainment.

'At school too, Gerry, when a boy was being whipped by the headmaster I always had to hurry to the Head's door and listen to the strokes. They stirred me, each of them. I know most people say this sort of thing is morbid and pretend they don't suffer from it, but I wonder, I wonder. It was certainly true of most of the boys at school.'

'Oh, yes,' I said, more ready, after his example, to talk truth. 'I think there's a little of that in most of us.'

'Well, the first time I saw Gotty, he was doing his Field Punishment No. 1.'

'F.P. No. 1. What on earth for?

'Refusing at first to obey a lawful order, and then showing "dumb insolence". He was a sensitive creature, and something must have got him on the raw.'

'A pretty savage punishment.'

'The Colonel can be pretty tough, we know, but in this case he said he gave it him to save him from worse: court martial, penal servitude, and what-not. Anyhow, I was walking along the Gully and saw Gotty lashed by his wrists and ankles to the wheel of a field-kitchen. I'd never seen F.P. No. 1 administered before and I couldn't keep away from it. It was like someone crucified—or waiting to be shot. Or waiting for the lash. I kept walking back to look. Easy enough because he was tied there before everyone's eyes for an hour. But honestly, Gerry, I didn't only feel an excited fascination; I felt a great pity for him; and when it was all over, after his second dose of it in the evening, I went and sympathized with him.... That was the beginning.... The funny thing is that I felt excitedly drawn to him from the very first moment, *because* he was publicly tied and exhibited like that. I tried to be particularly kind to him afterwards and ... he was grateful in his hurt ... and his shame ... and, well ... that was the beginning for him too.'

I only played with the buckle of my belt (which I'd undone) and looked down upon it, waiting for him to go on.

A weary sigh, followed by a small despairing shrug on the bed, and he went on. 'He's only a half-educated man of course, but I loved teaching him and lending him my books and so on. I taught him all about Troy and about Xerxes bridging the Dardanelles and Thermopylae and all that. He simply thrilled to the beauty of Simonides' epitaph on Thermopylae.' Poor Evv, still displaying, even in despair, a now useless culture. 'You know it, of course?'

'Oh yes,' I affirmed, wanting him to believe—even in his despair—that I'd known it for years, though I'd only recently heard it from Colin. 'Yes,' I repeated, ashamed.

'Yes ... yes ... of course ... and I lent him the *Symposium*, of which I've got a copy here. Have you ever read it? Actually it praises and exalts the sort of affection we were beginning to feel for each other; though I swear that wasn't why I lent it to him. He *had* a deep affection for me, I know.' One other thing of which to be proud. 'Affection breeds affection, you see, or rather—I'm damned if I'm going to be afraid to say it —love breeds love. It seems simple enough. You'd think we all had the right to live and love as we like, but no. . . . There's no place for us in this world. No place . . . no place. . . . Except prison. . . . It's penal servitude for me now, and disgrace for ever after. A priceless sensation it's going to be among the boys I worked with and the people who knew me. I was well known.'

'It may not come to that, Evv.'

'Of course it will, Gerry. You're just saying kind things which you don't believe. But it's nice of you to want to say them. Bless you. Did you know that I asked for you? Swin told me that I should have to have an officer from my battalion, so I said "Please ask that it may be Beefy Browning". I felt you'd be gentler than some. Decent of the Colonel to let me have you. No, I know what's coming to me, Gerry.'

'Well, even if it does, everything passes with time. Our worst memory fades till it can be almost a pleasant thing when we contrast it with our present happiness.'

'But public disgrace is not a thing that ever has an end. Ever, ever, ever.'

'Oh, yes, yes . . . surely.'

'No, Gerry. And, apart from that, prison is something I can't face the thought of, whether it's two years or twenty. It may be bearable by unimaginative types but—have you ever thought about it? I think about it all night, lying here. You're pushed into a cell, and the door slams; its spring-locks shoot into the wall and it becomes part of the wall—flush with it. You're walled in; you're bricked up; you're in a steel safe alone. Either you can stand it or you can't. I couldn't. One of my nightmares has always been that I'm in a narrow, hollow place from which there's no struggling out, and the horror of it has always been such that I've had to force myself to wake. But you can't do that in a prison cell. You're still there. Still there.'

The words conveyed their full terror to me; nevertheless I offered, 'One can get used to anything.'

'Not to that. You may bear it for two days—ten days—but if you've got two years, there are still seven hundred days to run —oh no, I should go raving mad. I should dash my head against the wall. And that wouldn't kill me; I should still be there.'

What could I say? I was glad of the interruption when my batman brought my valise. He crawled into the dug-out, and I saw his quick fascinated look at Evverson before he removed Swin's valise and arranged my bed for me.

When he'd finished, he said, 'I'll be outside, sir, if you want me. They've put me on the ration strength of H.Q.,' and I saw that he was proud of his present position.

'Right you are, Allen,' I said.

'And if there's anything I can do for Mr. Evverson . . .'

'We'll let you know,' I promised.

When he was gone Evverson continued the broken conversation, 'No, I don't want to live. Surely they could let you kill yourself if you're one whom prison . . . I wonder how Gotty'll stand it. . . . Gerry, have *you* ever felt that you could love another man as a man loves a woman?'

'Yes . . . yes . . . up to a point,' I stammered. 'But not . . . not . . .' There was no finishing the sentence in front of him.

'Then you don't know the whole love,' he said.

This statement was like an abrupt, unexpected blow of disappointment. I wanted to spring to the defence of my feeling for Colin, but of course I couldn't speak of that.

We argued no more.

That night, as we lay side by side, I was often awake because anxious and frightened by my responsibility. The Turk was restless too. I heard guns pounding the beaches where we must be embarking drafts and shells and stores. Asiatic guns, no doubt, because their shells were not whistling overhead. Was suspicion alive in Asia and around the slopes of Achi Baba? An aeroplane droned through the night.

Since Evverson was clearly awake, I said, 'Johnny's got the wind up,' trying to be friendly.

'Has he?' he replied, without interest, for his own trouble was far larger than the war.

Perceiving this, I did not speak again. I listened to the frequent typing tack-tack-tack of machine-guns and the slaps of rifle-fire. I heard spent bullets sigh into the Gully, and a horse scream. I heard working parties or relieving battalions marching past and away; but I don't think Evverson heard any of these things. He was shielded from them by his private and impenetrable wall. He slept sometimes, because once he called out 'Oh, Christ my God . . . Jesus . . . Jesus . . .' and later 'Holy Virgin, Mother of God . . .' which surprised me, till I remembered his little book of Anglo-Catholic prayers.

All the next day I lay with him in that cliff-side dug-out, seeing no one else, because no one came to him. Sometimes, to stretch my limbs I stood outside the dug-out curtain and looked down at all the pre-battle traffic in the dust-smoking Gully: new troops going forward to the Line, an eighteen-pounder battery rolling after them, a file of Zionists with their pack-mules stringing along to our hanging valley, whence they could thread with their supplies into the Western Mule Trench. Not once did Evverson come out and stand there; he could not bear to be seen by the men. It was a small torment for him to go to the latrine because he must pass their fascinated eyes, with his escort following behind.

'Is the coast pretty clear?' he would ask me, and I would wait till I could say, 'Not too bad now, Evv.'

And he would slip out, saying, 'Thank you, Gerry. Bless you.'

In the dug-out I tried to talk with him, but where was the subject that had no residue of pain? Most of the day he stayed silent while I read. About midday Colin's batman arrived with a tin of cigarettes and the words, 'The Captain sent these along, sir, to Mr. Evverson.' Thereafter Evverson smoked cigarette after cigarette, lying back and staring up at the groundsheet roof. I smoked too till we'd struck our last match, whereupon I imediately sent my batman to buy a box from the Mess, happy to be able, like Colin, to give Evverson something, however small. I tossed them on to his recumbent form saying, almost apologetically, 'Some matches for you, Evv'; and he accepted them with a 'Thanks, Gerry. Thanks very much. Bless you'.

Then it was night again, and we tried to sleep. It was difficult because the Turk's guns were noisier than the night before; so was his small-arm fire. No question but that he was nervous of something now.

I could see that Evverson was awake. He tossed from side to side, but whichever way he lay he faced his bedfellow, Despair. As for me, it was long after midnight when I fell asleep. My sleep of two hours must have been heavy after last night's wakefulness because Evverson was out of his sleeping-bag and partly dressed in tunic, breeches, and boots and bending to get out of the dug-out before his movements woke me. His every movement must have been stealthily silent till his head disturbed the groundsheet roof and his shoulder rustled the curtain so that it whispered in the night.

'What is it, Evv? What is it?' I asked in alarm 'Where are you going?'

'It's nothing,' he answered.

And next second he was out in the night.

For another second—two seconds—I did not move because only half awake and transfixed by doubt. Then indeed I woke to my responsibility and snatched myself out of my sleeping-bag. But to extract oneself from army blankets sewn together is not an instantaneous act like leaping off a bed; and when I got beyond the dug-out curtain I could not at first in the darkness see Evverson anywhere. Then I descried a figure near the top of the cliff-slope: Evverson had run along a high shelf-road and was climbing the ravine wall on to the plateau above.

Just as I was, in shirt, pants, and bare feet like a cross-country runner, I clambered and stumbled after him. What was he doing? Had misery driven him mad? My state was one of excited alarm, untroubled by despair. He could not kill himself; he had no weapon. 'Evverson!' I called. 'Hell, come back.'

But, hearing me, he began to run. He ran out of sight over

a brow. I ran over it, fell into a donga, and on rising could not see him. Then indeed—desperation. Ah, but there was his figure, fast lengthening the distance between us. I ran after him, the prickly scrub tearing at my feet and the stones in the sand cutting them. Had it been daylight up here, we must both have been shot down like loping hares by the snipers hidden in the brush. But the night was heavy and dark, its only light the quivering of gun-flashes along the Line as if it were blinking from a hundred eyes. I might not be afraid of bullets but I was scared by this wide lonely heath and the darkness and that mad shadowy figure ahead. A Very light shot up; and I froze, as instructed always to do; but not he: he ran on, seemingly straight towards the Line. What could he do there? He could only tumble into our reserve or support trenches. What was he doing? What wild purpose led him on?

As I asked myself this, a question leapt up: that green sniper; Evverson watching him; had he come out here to find one of that green man's colleagues who would kill him? To meet the Invisible Death which lived on the plateau? No weapon? He had a dozen weapons up here, fifty perhaps: the rifles of the snipers in the brushwood or on the high hidden tree-platforms behind the Turkish Line. Was he hoping that a Very light would illuminate a target for them? Great God, I could see, as I ran, the words on my sheet of orders '. . . allows to escape any person whom it is his duty to keep or guard . . . shall be liable to penal servitude or such less punishment . . .' 'Evverson, stop! Evverson. . . . Come back.'

He heard me. He stood still. He struck a match and held it trembling before his face. Shots. Bullets hissed towards him.

Then I understood: he *had* the 'potential weapon'; one which I had given him; a small present of matches.

'Put that *out*!' I screamed, and myself stood still, in horror of that light.

I don't think he put it out; either it burned out or the wind blew it out.

I went towards him more cautiously, not knowing what

was in the madman's mind to do; and in fact he lit another match and held it before him with shaking fingers.

'For Jesus' sake . . . Evverson. . . .'

But a sniper's bullet put that match out—one of several bullets—and all was dark again, but not so dark that I did not see him fall.

I got to him where he lay on his back with one arm outflung, one knee crooked up, and his head on its side. His unbuttoned tunic was outflung too, as if he'd bared his breast to the enemy—but the wound was not there. His untied boots were splayed apart, lying all too clearly on lifeless feet. Throwing myself down beside him, lest other bullets searched the area, I found myself gazing at his grey face in the darkness, and I saw there the neat puncture above the left eyebrow. The lustreless eyes, gazing into mine, picked up such light as there was, and were terrible. Rising warily, I looked at the back of his head; it was not neat. It was smashed. For a while I lay beside him in a sick fear, not of the snipers' bullets, for the whole plateau was silent again, but of the disgrace and punishment that must be coming to me. Yet was I wholly to blame? The Colonel had said, 'You must get your sleep.'

All quiet and dark. But was that a pale fringe of dawn beyond the Asian mountains? I must go back to get help and to take whatever reprobation and punishment awaited me. Down over the lip of the cliff I went, and terrible was the sight of his dug-out, still there but empty. I went to the Adjutant's sandbag hut and woke him. It was all that I could think of to do. The Adjutant, after staring and muttering curses and telling me that I was 'for it', went with a lantern to the Colonel's tent. I followed like a guilty dog.

The Colonel had a camp-bed in his own light Indian Army tent, and he sat up on it, eyes staring, as I told my story. With his sparse grey hairs awry and a bush of grey hairs peeping above the open neck of his pyjamas, he looked small and old and insignificant. I wanted to lie by making no mention of those matches and suggesting that a Very light had shown their path to the snipers, but where would have been the good? The matches must be lying at Evverson's side—oh, why had I left them there? I told him the truth, shaking.

For a time he did not speak, and I stood there, listening to the stretcher-bearers making ready to go up the cliff. I spoke first. 'I must go with them, sir, to show them where he is.'

'He is dead, you are sure?'

'Oh, yes, sir.'

More silence. And then, 'Oh, well, Browning, perhaps it's for the best. Yes, whether he intended to or not, he's done the best thing for the battalion. Saved us something we could well do without. And I don't honestly think it was your fault. Of course it wasn't. I told you you must have some sleep. I'll tell 'em I told you that. I don't know about those matches. They may strain at a gnat and say they were a potential weapon. . . . But oh lord—to hell!—let's forget the matches. I don't want any dammed court martials in my battalion. Evverson got out of his all right, and I don't see why he should hand it on to you. No, I know nothing about matches. You meant well, giving him them. I'll just tell 'em it was damned plucky of you to go chasing after him. Pity you didn't get a wound while you were about it. I shan't try to get you a medal, ha, ha, ha, but I'll see you don't get a G.C.M., "General Court Martial", what? That's all right. Don't worry, boy. Done your best. And, to tell the truth—it's sad, but I'm relieved.'

'Thank you, sir,' I said. And as I went out, I was ready to die for him in the coming battle, if he asked me to.

In the morning I climbed up to our hanging valley to tell Colin all about it. I found him standing outside Whitehall Court with the Padre.

Our Brigade Chaplain was a little round-faced middle-aged parson, as gallant and conscientious as he was pompous and professional. Colin, always impatient with him, styled him a 'pompous and hidebound little idiot', though he went often to his Communion services in ravine or tent, as an example to the men. Even so did his father, I imagine, attend the chapel in his park to set an example to workers and tenants. Bomb, rain, or shine the Padre visited his parishioners regularly, in fire-bay, support trench, or bivouacs. He staged little Communion services everywhere, and if shrapnel exploded above his earthy altar and his half-dozen worshippers, he did not lift his head from chalice and paten, nor turn it to see if any were slain—or if any were still there. The men respected him for his pluck and his sense of duty but once he was out of sight they would grin at his solemn objurgations and his innocent remoteness from the lives of licentious soldiery. They mimicked the dreadful singsong sanctimony which he held to be the only devout manner in which to read the Bible and prayers. Unlike other padres on the Peninsula he refused to discard his black stock and white clerical collar. 'They are the outward and visible sign of my spiritual function,' he would explain in his pompous way. 'They're all that's left to me of my Church's uniform, and if I have to minister to a dying man, I want him to know at once who I am.' In this, I think, he did not err.

But now uncomfortable words were shooting between him and Colin, as I came towards them.

'Hallo, Gerry,' Colin said. 'Look: I'm leaving the Company in charge of Cass because I want to be present at old Evv's funeral. I don't know what's the official thing to do in a case like this and I've no intention of finding out. The Padre here knows exactly what to do.'

'And I'm not ashamed of it,' snapped the Padre, for Colin's tone had sounded rude and, I fear, was intended to.

'He says he can't read the proper service over him.'

'Why in hell not?' I asked.

The Padre turned to me. 'In the eyes of the Church Lieutenant Evverson died in mortal sin.'

'Yes . . . but . . .' I began.

'And he committed mortal sin upon mortal sin. Directly I heard of his arrest I visited him, and he refused to repent. He said he had come to believe that what he did was no crime. A terrible thing to say. And to that he added suicide. I can only pronounce, then, that he was doubly guilty of mortal sin.' He seemed proud of these two words, mortal sin.

'Oh, but God above, Padre!' Colin interrupted. 'Surely whatever he did, it's done with now. What the hell is mortal sin, anyway?'

'Mortal sin is a complete violation of one of God's commandments with full knowledge and deliberation. That seems to fit this case exactly. Mortal sin extinguishes justifying grace in the soul and, unless remitted before death, entails the final separation from God.'

'I wonder . . .' was all Colin answered to this.

The Padre spread a fat and helpless feminine palm. 'I am merely a man under orders like you. And that's the position which my Church orders me to sustain at all costs.'

'What position?'

'That mortal sin is mortal sin.'

'And forgiveness is forgiveness, or am I wrong?' said Colin with averted face. 'And mercy mercy, or is that another mistaken idea?'

'With God all mercies are possible. I am only stating the position which the Church feels it imperative to uphold. What the Army's view is, I don't know, though I should have thought that suicide was a kind of desertion. Worse, far worse, than a self-inflicted wound.'

'Maybe, but he's dead now, and surely you don't want to pursue him with punishments. I'm just asking you; that's all. I just want instruction in the doctrines of the Church. I'm a little seeker after Truth, you see.'

'I only know what my orders are, Dester. *You* have to obey King's Regulations. So do I.'

'Yes, but are they your King's?'

'For me, yes; because I assume no right of private judgment. For me the Church is God's sole interpreter upon earth.'

Colin moved away and back again, in unconcealed impatience. 'Well, I don't know what *my* regulations say, and I thank God I don't. I was his O.C. and in my innocence I'm going to represent his company at the funeral——'

'So'm I,' I interposed.

'Damn it, I liked old Evv, and he served us well till this happened. I imagine he went rather mad, as I probably shall before we've finished here. You too, Padre. Lord knows what you'll be getting up to. God damn it—excuse me, Padre—it's not certain that he *did* commit suicide.'

The Padre could not accept this. Nor I. We shook our heads.

'Well, if he did, he was probably dippy.'

'And Padre,' I ventured, 'wasn't he one of your best parishioners, a High Churchman and all?'

'Exactly,' Colin endorsed. 'He used to blow off enough about his churchmanship. Almost he persuaded me to be a Christian. Poor old Evv. He wanted like nothing on earth to win a medal, and now Gerry says he's got a neat little circular hole in the middle of his forehead—the only decoration he'll ever get. I reckon that the least he should have is a gentleman's funeral.'

'Yes, he was a High Churchman,' agreed the Padre, 'and for that reason he'd expect me to honour the rubrics of our——'

'Oh, come, Padre,' Colin almost laughed. 'What? *Now?* Is he still C. of E.? Over there? I wonder what the Colonel's view is, Gerry.'

This offended the Padre. 'In any church parade I am in sole command, Dester. Even if the C.-in-C. himself is present.'

'Oh, quite. Absolutely. And the Colonel'd be a stickler for that. I wasn't thinking of what *you'll* do, but of what he'll do. Gerry, I tried to plead with him for poor old Evv. Not easy. But I couldn't help thinking of all those boys in the Town Hall before whom Evv wanted to appear as one of the war's young heroes. So I asked him if the truth couldn't be kept from them and his parents and everyone. I suggested that it was possible to be exhausted morally as well as physically. To be wounded in the soul as well as in the guts. It took him some time to accept this. Seems there's nothing in King's Regulations about it. I said Evv had fought well at one time, but the old boy shrugged that one away on to the Mess floor. He could only keep repeating, "I've absolutely no use for that kind of man; absolutely none"—which missed the point, really. Then I spoke of the old Peninsula's prison-like segregations of lads still young and when I'd explained 'segregations' to him, he seemed to see something. For the first time. And I think perhaps old Evv's suicide helped. He looks at it differently from the Padre.'

Resenting the sting in this, the Padre grumbled, 'I'm doing my very best for him. I shall commit him to the uncovenanted mercies of God.'

'To the how-much?' Colin inquired.

He repeated the grand phrase. 'The uncovenanted mercies of God.'

'Oh, that'll do for me,' said Colin. 'I have every confidence in them.'

The funeral was at noon that day. A burial party of a corporal and four men carried the blanket-shrouded body on its stretcher towards the little cemetery near the Gully wall, where our late captain lay. The Padre in surplice and scarf, which it was safe to wear down here, waited by the opening in the wire fence. Colin and I followed behind the bearers, and at first I thought we were the only mourners, but on looking round, I saw the Colonel and the Adjutant coming too, at some distance behind and, as it were, informally. Not so informally, however, that the Colonel still wore his workaday sweater; at least he had honoured a dead man with tunic and Sam Browne belt.

Strange soldiers standing about in the Gully, and including some turbaned Indians and a squat little Ghurka, sprang to attention as the procession went by. A company came marching up towards the Line with rifles slung, and its O.C., perceiving the business afoot, yelled, 'March to attention. Eyes LEFT!' A mounted officer stayed his horse and saluted. None of these strangers knew that the blanketed form was wrapped also in disgrace. He was just one more who had earned the last salute of honour.

In the little dusty cemetery the bearers stood about the grave with ropes under the body. The grave was on the opposite side of a path from Bay's, so Evverson would lie with his fcet towards his captain; these two who'd argued together so often. The Padre went to the grave's foot; Colin and I to its head. Colonel and Adjutant kept at a distance.

I had attended burials enough on the Peninsula to know that the Padre was omitting much of the usual service, but what he did read he uttered in a voice that sounded full of pity, song, honey, and sanctimony. All the time he was speaking—or singing—the traffic of the coming battle beat past our wired enclosure: dispatch-riders speeding and leap-frogging over the stones; a G.S. wagon drawn by four mules with riders astride; an officers' mess float; a fatigue party carrying timber and wire from a dump. A mile and a half away a nervous Front accompanied our service with the wood-pecker tapping of machine-guns.

When it came to the Committal the four bearers, at a glance from the Padre, lowered the body into the grey tumbling earth, and I heard the words, 'To His uncovenanted mercies we commit our brother here departed . . .' but no more. Nothing about a 'sure and certain hope'. Nor about a voice from heaven saying 'Write. From henceforth blessed are the dead. . . .' Only some collects and prayers and 'the grace of our Lord Jesus Christ . . .'

As the Padre stepped back, the Colonel came forward to the grave's foot, Colin and I moved two yards away. He stood and saluted the body down there. The Adjutant did the same, copying him. This duty performed, the Colonel turned to the Adjutant and began, 'Robertson . . .'

'Sir . . .?'

The Colonel looked down again at Evv's body. '"Killed in action",' he said 'Enter that up, won't you. . . . No . . . "Died of wounds", what? . . . Yes, I think so.'

CHAPTER SEVEN

THREE o'clock and I stood in the trench, with my men left and right of me. The Peninsula was quiet. Did the Turk suspect nothing in this August heat and the siesta hour? When I peeped above the parapet, I saw two doves and a solitary jay flying above the scattered remnants of an olive grove and alighting on it, unalarmed. In our trench no voice spoke: the only sounds were the whisper of a pull-through being drawn up a rifle barrel, and the rasp and click of bayonets being fixed for duty. I too had a rifle with its bayonet newly sharpened. It stood on the fire-step at my side.

I looked at the men. Some of them were marked for death in a matter of minutes. Which? You . . . or you . . .? Or perhaps myself. Colin? Oh no, *no*! Not Colin. God keep him safe.

All these men, like their officer, wore the proper mask of calm, but what thoughts moved behind their still faces? The fingers of some fumbled as they tried the bolts of their rifles. Were they thinking, as their officer was, that once again a time had come when one must try to break the chains of self and offer up all one's hopes in life, all one's dreams of a perfect lover or of ample wealth, or perhaps of dedicated service, one day.

'I will try,' I told myself; and indeed I tried to recover that peaceful consecration which I had felt in the towed boat, but I had small success, because I had left it too long in an atrophy.

The August sun burned the metal on our guns and the sand of the trench, so that both were hot to the touch. The heat on the plateau above drained into the trench—like heated water into a bath. As we breathed it it parched our throats till thirst dragged at them. Caparisoned in heavy equipment we dropped our sweat on the yellow marl, where it dried quickly.

The other side of death? What would it be like if one found oneself there? In minutes. If conscious, would one still be Gerry Browning? If so, how lonely! Would one think of Colin left behind and perhaps lost for ever?

I blinked to drive these thoughts away, and with my sergeant I walked along my sector of the Line. At our point of junction with No. 8 Platoon I encountered Cass. He gave me his shy smile but as always his thoughts stayed unspoken. Perhaps they were visiting his bank in the High Street or his small home and garden where the children would now be at play. His smile was as insincere as mine.

Returning to my place in the centre, I came upon Colin, who was at this same business of inspecting and heartening the men.

'Look here, boys,' he was saying to the men in this bay. 'You've got the grand idea, haven't you? You all understand —hallo, Gerry, old boy—you all understand what we're doing? It couldn't be more exciting or more important. We're holding the Turks from the boys at Suvla. If we fight like hell we may even draw heaps of the bastards away from Suvla. And if the Suvla boys can land in force and capture Sari Bair, the war is practically won. Don't you agree, Gerry? I don't say it'll all be over at once, but that we can, so to speak, begin to pack. Got it?'

'Yes, sir.'

'Yes, sir.'

'Have you all seen the C.-in-C.'s Special Order of the Day?' Some hadn't, so he drew it from his pocket and read. '"Soldiers of the Old Army and the New. Some of you have already won imperishable honour at our first landing"—that's me and Mr. Browning—"or have since built up our foothold on the Peninsula yard by yard with deeds of heroism and endurance"—that's all of us, by Golly. "You, soldiers of the new formations, are privileged to have the chance of playing a decisive part in events which may herald the birth of a new and happier world"—well, that's roughly what I was trying to say. A new and happier world after the war. That's what it's all about, really, even on this bloody spot. But the first step is to win the damned old war. Phew! Foully hot.' With a balled-up handkerchief he padded at ear and chin. 'New and happier. Great man, the C.-in-C.' He put the paper back in his pocket. 'In short, give 'em hell.'

'Yes, sir.'

'Hell, and a bit, sir.'

'Always supposin' they don't give it us first, sir.'

'Well, if they do that, sir, we hand 'em a bit more? Eh, sir?'

'That's the idea, gentlemen. We'll be the first wave. We grab our objective, and the second wave passes over us. Damn this north-east wind and the dust. Have you noticed, Gerry, that we've had the wind in our faces ever since this match started? Why can't we change sides with the Turk? Bring the boys over when you hear my whistle. Well, good luck, chaps.'

'Thank you, sir.'

'Good luck, Gerry.' A pat on my back. 'My blessing on you, old boy.'

He waved, smiled, and went. I knew no more of his thoughts this afternoon than of Cass's. Perhaps he was thinking of Olwen. 'She pleases me. A lifetime without the creature seems something not worth having.'

And now he was gone. Colin—don't get killed.

I was hardly back on my step when a sound that was both a heart-stopping hiss and a tearing of the air like a sheet of buckram announced the bombardment. There was a flash as of orange lightning in front of us, a crash like the fall of a house, and a cloud of black and ochreous smoke. The battle for Sari Bair had begun.

It began with this race (as it appeared) between our field guns ashore and our naval guns at sea. All were hammering the Turkish trench-system where it cut this narrow cape from shore to shore. The shells chased, pursued, overtook or flew abreast of one another. Smoke columns and tall flames sprang from the breast of Achi Baba. Dark chocolate eruptions, flushed with sulphur yellow, burst from every Turkish trench. Deafening; benumbing; if the Peninsula was really the anvil on which the war's destiny was being hammered, then our ears sang and beat with an 'Anvil Chorus'. And the earth beneath our feet, as in response to deep organ notes, vibrated.

It stops; all stops; we are ready with our 'white arms' fixed. I look at my wrist-watch. A minute to go. The minute hand ticks round heartlessly. Seconds. I have time to brush the running sweat from nape and neck. Fear is an aeration in my bowels, but I am two people: one emptied by fear, the other exalted by the wine of excitement. Colin's whistle—'Come, boys,' I cry and remember one who has been a hero in my mind ever since V Beach. I want to imitate him, but I certainly can't bring myself to say with his ease, 'Come, my children,' so I say 'Come, boys,'—and that with difficulty.

Our bayonets rise from the ground like a line of shining grass blades. We are out, rifles at the hip. We are running through the tufts of scrub, the cast-out ration tins, and the bomb-holes. Praise God, that second man in me, the exalted one, possesses me like a devil; it is the same with the others—or with most of them: we cheer and bellow and laugh. Not all. I glance along my advancing line and see Cass properly abreast of his men but his face is blanched and his lips grimly set as he goes forward steadfastly, rifle at the trail.

Why don't the Turks fire? Are they holding their fire? Are our racketing machine-guns, which cover us, keeping their heads down? We reach the forward trench. I see the Turks. Only four of them in this bay: youths with brown-leather faces above blue-grey uniforms faded and dirtied and torn. Two of them are ready for their Muslim Paradise: they fight shouting 'Allah Hu!' and 'Allah Din!' and are bayoneted. Two fling up their hands in surrender, and I do not allow Corporal Lodge to bayonet them.

The trench is ours. That is soon clear. I hear cheers on all sides. Good: I know my orders. 'All right. On to the next. Pass the word. Ready? *Okay!*'

We are out in the open again—in the eighty yards we must

cross. 'Keep extended. They may notice us this time.' How right: we have not gone six yards before the Turks, as on V Beach long ago, welcome us with everything they've got. The bullets fly towards us like dust on that north-east wind. No man could evade them any more than he could evade the sting of the dust. Cass? One look his way. I see him stop, stand still, gaze for a second into the unknown, and then bow before it as to his fate.

Even as he pitched my bullets find me; but they take me only in forearm and thigh. Sharp pain but not unbearable. The shock fells me, and I am down with the rest. I stay down. To rise up is to die.

'All back, sir.' A man has crawled out to me. 'All back. Captain Dester's orders.'

'All?' I scoff.

'Yes, sir. Captain's orders.'

Orders that many can no longer hear. I however can obey. Turning about, I see that we'd made but a few yards when the bullets reaped us down.

'Pass the word. All back.' Cass? Seems unkindly to leave him there. A discourtesy.

A few of us got back, crouching from scrub to scrub.

A big fellow, Tom Bax, with all the tenderness of an outsize man, was binding up my wounds when Colin came along the trench. 'Good, Gerry. Footling to go on through that. A coarse business. Very. Colonel tells me that by the bloodiest luck the old Turks were massed in that trench and about to attack *us*. Badly hit, old boy?'

'It's nothing.'

'Is it really nothing, Tommy?'

'Not much, sir.'

'Hurray! I didn't get a scratch, Gerry. I just lay down and pretended to be dead. Yelled to the men to do the same. Damned unheroic, I dare say, but hell! I'm no Gerry, and I believe in using some sense sometimes. The old Colonel seemed quite satisfied. Says he wants *some* officers and men left. I may say I feel much better with him in the trench beside me.

Ie's now inviting the artillery to have a go at that trench. Iow's Cassy?'

'Out there.'

'Dead?'

'I dunno. Looks bad.'

'God! Have they killed our Cassy——'

Instantly the avenging roar of our eighteen pounders and our-point-five howitzers not only smothered his words but drove him back to his place at the Colonel's side in search of orders. Almost at once the dried scrub behind the enemy rench took fire and blazed with a crackling that added its nusic to the percussion of the guns. The smoke lurched up in tilting column twenty feet high, and the north-east wind ent it across our front in an ash-blue travelling wall. Black moke gushed up into the ash-blue, with a high flame following, and it looked as though the shells or flames had reached and broached some oil drums. Quickly the fire spread; the wind bent the spires of flame to the west; sparks danced from he flame in spirals and sprays before changing into a black chaff and dying on the wind; the smoke darkened and thickened; and suddenly I saw, even as it stung my eyeballs and choked my breath, that we had now a perfect smoke-screen in which to dash out and bring Cass in.

Moreover our guns, bashing that trench, would cover a sortie.

Quick, let me do this. Yes! My sweet reputation for fearlessness—to dash out, when wounded myself, and rescue a friend—this would crown it. The smoke might clear, but who wouldn't risk death for a reputation so dear to him?

I thrust aside the big Samaritan who was binding up my wounds. 'Just a minute, Bax. Leave it. It can wait a mo——' And I scrambled over the parapet and went crouching through the smoke towards Cass. (That medal this time . . .?)

'Cass . . . Cassy.'

But he only moaned gently, his head on his arm, his body and buttocks quivering like the body of a rabbit dying in a gin.

'It's me, Cass. Gerry Browning. Where're you hit?' Bu
I could see: he'd been hit in front—in belly or breast, perhap
in both and more—and the blood ran in a pool from unde
him.

'Can we get him in, sir?' A man was crouching beside me
me: my Samaritan, Tom Bax.

'We'll try.'

'The kids,' Cass moaned to the ground beneath his head
'The kids.'

'They'll be all right, Cassy. Can you hear me? Gerry
Browning. We're going to get you in.'

'And Molly. . . .'

'Cass, old boy. . . . Take his feet, Bax. Now, how's this,
Cassy?'

'There's enough money. Just enough.'

'Come. We're going to get you back. Is it safe to move
him, Bax?'

'I don't hardly know, sir.'

'Pinkie. . . .'

'Now, easy, boy! We're taking you——'

'. . . and Pickles . . . Jesus, Jesus. . . .'

For a second, out there in the smoke, something of Cass's happy home life flashed before me. All so far away from him now.

'Jesus . . . God . . . dear Christ in heaven. . . .'

Bax shook his head, and his lips framed, 'He's for it, sir.'

I laid a hand on his shoulder, and the Turks chose that moment to search the smoke with machine-guns and mortars. Something seemed to shatter my right shoulder with an agony beyond anything I'd ever imagined. It hurled me to the hot sand. I tried to move the arm and found it was hanging loose like a rope with my hand on the end of it for a tassel. As I turned my face to look at it, a bullet shot through both my cheeks. Now the agony was in a molar nerve. I tried to lift my hand to it, and the agony was in the shoulder again. It crouched there, leaping like an animal. It rested, and leapt again, leapt higher. High above bearing. 'If only I could die

. . die.' The pain was larger than the campaign, than victory, than mercy, than the world, here or hereafter. 'Let me die . . . *Oh* . . . but I mustn't scream. . . . Hold; don't scream. Even dying, let me keep my name for courage. Bite. Bite hard.'

Oh, think: this insufferable pain—was it retribution? God's punishment for my having backslid from that vision in the towed boat—totally backslid, once all fear was removed? A stern discipline for having sought again little but my own glory? Whom God loves He chastens.

I could turn my head enough to see Cass and Bax. Cass was silent. Dead. Bax was lying still, but, catching my eyes, he gasped, 'I'm only hit in the leg somewhere, sir. Not bad. Only pretending to be dead. We'll do something soon, sir. Stick it out.'

'. . . die . . . die. . . . How to die. . . . How to will oneself dead.'

The scrub-fire was dwindling. Its travelling wall of smoke was now an evanescent wall. Soon the Turk would see us here. Do not move. I might cry for death, but not for more of these agonies. Lie frozen here.

My blood, pouring from me, sank into the sand like water. Where it flowed from my mouth the flies came down upon it. They massed over and about it on my cheek's side. Or they sizzed and hummed, spirally above it like motes in a sun-ray. Oh, lucky Cass. Dead.

I know not how long I lay there, shifting only my eyes to the many sleepers around me. I must have died from loss of blood had not sparks from that dwindling bonfire set new brush alight, and the north-east wind, lately our enemy, sent clouds of smoke to cover me. And then a voice: 'Gerry . . . Gerry, are you all right?' Colin. 'Are you all right? Oh, good! Here we are, then. Can't do without our Gerry. Take him that side, sergeant. Not you, Bax. You're hurt; you're bleeding like a pig. Go home. Boss's orders.'

'Morphia,' I said. 'Morphia. Please, please.'

'Yes. Buckets of it in a second. Just let us get you back; it'll only last seconds because we've only a few yards to go.

Where are you hit? Face and shoulder? Oh, well, that's fin
Neither of those'll kill you. We'll soon have you soled an
heeled.'

'The smoke is thinning, sir,' warned the sergeant.

'Yes. Quick. Can you walk, Gerry? That's it. Goll
sergeant, one half of him's a redcoat. Come—that's it. Pu
your good arm along my shoulder and I'll do the rest.'

'Thank you, Colin.'

'He come the minute he see you, sir,' said the sergeant b
way of comfort; and comfort in pain it was.

'So did the sergeant, Gerry. He thought, 'Can't do withou
our Mr. Browning. Best officer we've got, not excluding th
Captain.' That's what he thought, even if he didn't say it; an
he raced me to it. Got here first.'

'Only because I was afraid the smoke might clear away a
any moment, sir.'

'Thank you, sergeant,' I stammered. 'Water. . . . Any hop
of water . . .?'

In a trice Colin's free hand had dragged his water-bottle fron
his side and was putting it to my lips.

'No, Colin. You'll have none.'

'I'm not wounded. Take it, damn you, Gerry; I'm you
O.C. And we've no time to wait. Now then. Gently doe
it—yes, I know its agony, but it's only a few yards.'

'Morphia. . . .'

CHAPTER EIGHT

Above Cape Helles, fearlessly in view of Achi Baba, along that stretch of hill for which we'd fought on the morning after the landing, there stood now a camp of white tents like small marquees, with the Red Cross and Union Jack flying above them. Fearlessly this hospital, No. 17 Stationary, stood there because all agreed that Johnny Turk and his German officers were gentlemen and would never fire on sick and wounded men. Nor did they, though they occasionally requested us to shift our hospitals a little to one side, so that they could 'have the honour' of firing at our troops on the beaches.

In one of those tents, in the Officers' Lines, I lay on an iron bed with, if you will believe it, a mattress under me and sheets about me. And the tent had double walls, the inner one of some yellow stuff, so that the torrid August sun could not get at us. None the less our square canvas ward was filled with heat and heavy with the smells of ether and iodoform. There were sixteen of us, twelve in beds and four on stretchers between the beds. All our beds had a tilt because of the slope of the old battlefield beneath them.

Three days I lay there, waiting my turn to go on to one of the white hospital ships that stood off Cape Helles, and listening to the battle for Sari Bair, which drummed on and on through the days. On the evening of the third day, when the light was dimming and an orderly had lit the hurricane lamp that hung between the tent poles, Colin appeared in the entrance. He sought my bed, came to it, looked at its clean sheets and at the soft yellow wall behind it, and exclaimed, 'Such comfort! Why in hell wasn't I wounded?'

'How did you get here?' I asked.

'We've been pulled out, and we're back in the old Kuchu
Burnu Line.'

'I'm glad you came, because I've been lying here thinkin
that I never thanked you for all you did.'

For Colin, when they got me into the trench, had remove
the filthy field dressings on my arm and leg and, tearing hi
own from the lining of his tunic, had bound up these wound
again. He had rent my shirt and improvised tourniquets fo
them. As well as might be, he had bandaged my shoulder an
face; then grinned and lifted a hand in farewell. 'Good-by
for the present, Gerry boy. I must get on with the war.'

'Lord, that was nothing,' he now demurred. 'I'm gettin
quite a dab at this medical orderly stuff.'

'How goes the battle?'

His eyes evaded mine. 'I've been talking to the old M.O
outside, and he says yours is a three months' job. You'll go t
Alex or Mudros and probably miss the rest of the war.'

'How goes the old battle?'

'Oh, it goes on.'

'Yes, but how's it *going*?'

'Don't know. Bloodily at Suvla, I'm afraid. They've don
just what we did at V Beach: stormed up from the beaches bu
failedto get the main hill beyond. We failed to get Achi Bab
and they've failed to get Sari Bair. Or at any rate, to hold it.
Is this allowed?' He sat himself on the foot of my bed: no
room for chairs in that crowded tent. 'God—think of it!—
for a moment they stood on Sari Bair, and the war was won.
They stood on a col between Chunuk Bair and Koja Chemen
Tepe and looked down and saw the Narrows. The Narrows
themselves, all bright and shining and blue! It was dazzling
and they screamed and yelled with delight. They had all the
Turks here and at Anzac trapped—or so they thought—
but——'

'But what, Colin?'

'The usual. There was no one to support them—at least, no
one came—and they were driven back, those that were still
alive. They lost all sight of the Narrows, and no one'll see 'em

again now. The battle's petering out under Sari just as it did under Achi. The old Colonel said this would be a decisive battle and by God, it *is* a decision.'

'Oh, no, Colin.'

'Oh, yes.' Having started down a melancholy slope, he let himself slide the whole way. 'It's decisive, not only for this front but for the whole war. When they were driven off the Chunnuk Bair ridge, peace went out of sight for years. Or so everyone thinks.'

'Well, what do we do on Gallipoli now?'

'God alone knows. I should say you're lucky to be getting away from it.'

'I don't want to get away, Colin.' Lies. Lies.

'Don't be an ass. Go—and thank your stars. God, you're sweating, aren't you? Pain? Not much? Good. Poor old Cass. He's gone. He's missed whatever's coming to us.'

'Colin—*ssh!*—look.'

A small figure stood in the entrance of the tent, frowning as his eyes scanned the beds.

'Christ!' whispered Colin. 'The Colonel.'

'Is Lieutenant Browning here?' the Colonel asked of the first bed in a voice suited to the quiet and dimness of the tent, and to the pain of thoroughly good fellahs.

'Yes, sir. Over there. Last bed but one.'

'Thank you'—whispered.

And softly on the points of his Russian boots, he came towards me. As at Evverson's funeral, in honour of death, so now, out of respect to all hospitals everywhere, and to the R.A.M.C., and to the dignity of sickness, he'd put on his tunic and belt, and stepping among the stretchers, he held his Indian topee before his breast like a civilian in the corridors of a nursing home. He smiled as he met my eyes.

'Well, Browning, they tell me good news of you. Nothing desperate, they say. Good lord, there's Dester.' Colin had risen and gone to the far side of the bed.

'I was asking Dester how the battle was going, sir.'

'Well . . .' Not for him to raise despondency.

'I gather it was very nearly a success, sir.'

'It was—it was. Within an ace of everything. Within an ace. They were on Sari Bair and had the Turk at their mercy. It proved that the plan I'd always advocated was right. Absolutely.' He couldn't stop now. 'At their mercy. They had victory in their hands for us if only we could have driven on; and in April we could have done so because the Turks were less prepared and the weather was cooler and there was water in the springs after the rains. But, my God, in the blinding heat of August! The poor fellahs were exhausted and half mad with thirst. The Turks counter-attacked, perceiving that it was crucial to do so, and they drove those grand fellahs off. Down again on the wrong side, never to get back again. It'd have been different in April. That, at least, is my humble opinion.'

'I'm sure you're right, sir,' said Colin, though, as I knew, he was less sure than he said.

Then silence. The Colonel was not good at sick visiting. He stood there helpless, so I had to strengthen him. 'Thank you for coming to see me, sir,' I said.

'Not at all,' he stuttered. 'I wanted to see *one* of my officers who was still alive. Did you hear about the Adjutant?'

'I haven't told him that yet, sir,' said Colin.

'The Adjutant?' I stared at him.

'Yes, he volunteered to take the second wave over and—well——' I'll swear the Colonel gulped. 'Most of his men were shot down round him, and he was last seen going on, into the smoke, with Sergeant Russell a yard or two behind.'

'They're dead, sir?'

'Suppose so. 'Fraid so. Anyhow they went into the smoke together. And that's all.'

He was still in some difficulty about speaking, so I dropped my eyes from him, and Colin tried to ease us all by offering something that was almost humour.

'Yes; and poor Cass absconded again, sir, but in the right direction this time.'

'Absconded?' The Colonel, not good at metaphors, looked bewildered. 'Oh, I see. Ha'—but he decided not to laugh.

'Yes. Absconded. A good chap. Thoroughly good chap. They got him in, Browning, and buried him beside Bailey-More. And—and near to Evverson.'

'What'll happen now, sir, if Suvla's a failure?' I asked, to turn his thoughts from unhappy things.

'Try again, I suppose.'

Colin put in, 'Then there's nothing in this talk about evacuation, sir?'

'Good God, no! Don't listen to that sort of stuff. Clear out? No, we just don't clear out from a position that thousands of good fellahs have given their lives to win. No, no—that would make this the bloodiest tragedy in the world.'

'But what can we *do*, sir?'

'Dig in. Stick it out. Then try again.'

'Try what?'

'I dunno. But damned if we give in.'

'What about winter, sir?'

'Well, what about it?'

'They say the storms'll turn all the ravines into porridge, and that the old Gully'll be a roaring river of hogwash.'

'Perhaps. Can't help that.'

'And, worse still, that the seas'll wash away all our jetties. What do we do without harbours?'

'I dunno. Stand a siege. Ladysmith,' he mused, turning to old memories. 'Mafeking. Mafeking lasted seven months.'

Colin's eyes told me that he thought this kind of talk brave but hollow. He believed that winter must force the surrender of both the Suvla and the Helles armies or their destruction where they stood. And he was the wiser man.

Winter? Three months. August, September, October. Always wanting to stand well with the Colonel, as indeed with anybody I was talking to, I pretended a gallantry I did not feel. 'I shall hope to come back to the battalion before the winter, sir.'

'Do if you can, Browning. We shall need fellahs like you badly, I suspect. Your men know you and trust you now. I'm sure you will, if you can.'

But would I? Come back? Little doubt that, after my wounds, I should be offered a job at the Base, miles from the guns. And, remembering that agony, maddening, sickening, would I have the courage to resist the offer and fight my way back to a doomed peninsula?

Had Colin caught my thoughts? He chaffed, '*You* won't come back, Gerry. You'll be shipped to Alex and may even get to England. If by any chance it's England, you must get somehow to Great Henty's and give my love to Olwen. Only tell her I sent you, and she'll really spread the table for you.'

'Olwen? Who's Olwen?' asked the Colonel.

'His girl,' I explained, hastily and mischievously, though hurt at Colin's apparent easiness in the loss of me.

'Ah ha!' This was exactly the Colonel's level of facetiousness. 'His girl, what? I've never heard anything about this. Why have I never been told? Most important. What's she like, Dester?'

'She's all right, sir. A pleasing girl in her way.'

'All right! What a way to talk of one's fiancée. And a pleasing girl. Good heavens! I can't understand the modern generation. Pleasing *in her way*! I'm sure she deserves something very much better than you.'

'She does, sir.'

'She's very beautiful, I suppose?'

'She's terrific, sir,' I said. 'Absolutely.'

'Is she indeed? And how the deuce does Browning know, Dester? Has he met her?'

'Met her photograph, sir. That's all.'

'Ah! Her photograph. You have it?'

'Yes, sir. Somewhere.'

'Somewhere be hanged. Produce it for inspection at once. Come on. C.O.'s orders. From that breast pocket.'

Colin did no less, secretly pleased, I was sure, to do so, and the Colonel looked at the picture. 'Yes. Yes. Lovely. God bless her,' he said, with all the simple but deep goodwill which the elderly can feel for someone young and fresh and vulnerable. 'Much too good for any of you. Just you wait and see if I don't write and tell Miss Olwen how you——'

Would I come back? As the Colonel and Colin bandied their whimsies between them I was looking at both. 'October . . . early November . . . if Colin's still on the Peninsula, and the Colonel too—because I have a love for both of them now, in different ways—will I have the guts to struggle back to them and share their peril?' Weak and sick, I couldn't answer my question. And when the Colonel turned to go, with a shyly uplifted hand and a crisp (lest any unmilitary affection showed) 'Come back to us soon, Browning', the answer I gave him was true to the letter, but it was not heroic, as I wanted it to sound, and as he, ever a romantic, liked to think it. It was, on the contrary, an exact expression of fear and weakness. 'I'll come if I can, sir.'

It seemed an echo of what Colin had said when, next morning, the M.O. told me I would be taken in an ambulance to the French Pier at V Beach because a high sea had wrecked a jetty at W beach. They crammed some twenty of us into a horse ambulance, while the M.O., standing by, said, 'All aboard for Alex. Get to Alex, and that'll be the end of the war for you. Lucky stinkers.' The ambulance took us down a rough road between those hills, 138 and 141, where Colin and I had fought on an April morning months before. I stared at the scrub and sand, but my thoughts stood still; they would not reap for me the magic of this place. I stared down the hill at the piled stores, the bell tents, the huts, the horse lines; and everywhere among them the blue-clad Frenchmen active, gesticulating, laughing. And there where she had grounded was the old *River Clyde*, rusty and riddled, but still busy, with men passing in and out of those dreadful square exits in her hull.

Against the French Pier there stood—or, rather, tossed—an old trawler, salty and rusted. It would take us out to that beautiful white hospital ship lying far off shore. They got us on to the pier, where other 'walking wounded' waited, and as I stood there, I stared at the water sliding up the sand or slapping on to the rocks. There was the low sandbank. With bivvies and shanties under it where once we had lain, because it still offered shelter from inland guns. Men slept there now where men had died. There it was . . . and there it would always be. . . . I saw this forgetful strip of sand and water crimson-dyed again, and I dwelt for a while with Father Finn and Bill Drewer and others whose blood had flushed the wavelets and stained the sand.

The water was not calm today as it was then, and, looking out to sea, I watched the white-crested rollers making towards us, an advance guard, perhaps, of those winter breakers that would attack our frail jetties and be worth an army to our enemies.

'Come along, sir. Come along, all. No waiting, please.' The trawler's skipper, a grizzled and jerseyed veteran from Hull, perhaps, and the North Sea beds, was standing by his gangway with his peaked cap on the back of his head and offering a running exhortation as we got aboard. The grins, puckering his wind-etched face, uncovered a row of teeth too perfect to be true. 'Come along, gents. This place is dangerous. Annie's sent over two of her coal-boxes already. I never care how soon I get away. I'm no Nelson; my name's not Nelson; it's MacHasty. Move along, please. Thank you. My knees are all bruised from knocking together which is odd, like, because my legs were bandy at the beginning of the war.' He was inclined, as each man stepped on to his gangway, to rest a hand on the visitor's back, partly in a captain's welcome to his vessel and partly to speed the incoming guest. 'Hurry, gents. We don't want a massacre. War I 'old with, but not with murder. Step right in, sir. Pleased to see you. "Wash me in the water That you washed your dirty daughter——"' he was now singing to himself, without enthusiasm—'"And I shall be whiter than the whitewash on the wall. . . ." Lemme give you a hand, mate. There y'are. Just like that, see? . . . Not at all. It's a pleasure. . . . Come along, sir. Don't know about you, sir, but I've got to consider my old woman, and she'd rather have her old man in the kitchen than his V.C. in the parlour. Maybe you're not married yet, sir, but, my God, you'll know all about it when you are. Not 'alf you won't! Sometimes you'll wish you was back on Gallipoli. Some peace and quiet there. Shift along to the bows, please, gents. Thank you.'

Many were older and sicker and senior to me, so I let them get first into the trawler and stayed myself in its stern. As it moved out, breaking for me all contact with the Peninsula, I did not know, was my heart happy at an escape or very heavy at a parting? Watching the Peninsula recede, I found some relief and comfort in composing letters I would write to Colin. Their words would half reveal all that I felt for him. In the first I would write, 'I will come back if I can'—no, 'I will come back to you if I can.' Many such words did I put together as the boat chugged away, because I was, as it were, pleased with the melancholy of this parting and sinking myself deep in it.

The whole pointed shape of the Peninsula, a Land's End of rocky slopes and seaward ravines, was now visible; a terrible land suspended in a vehicle of limpid Aegean beauty. It's two hill-grasped beaches, on either side of Cape Helles, were fading into shadows. The old *Clyde* looked but a child's discarded toy. Deadly and dreaded and hated it might be, that Peninsula which was now slowly becoming a mere spectre on a broad sea; it was foul with death from brink to brink, a theatre of scattered illusions and blasted hopes; and yet it was sacred too and wonderful and somehow loved.

PART THREE

THE SEDD-EL-BAHR ROAD

What hope is ours, Patroclus, when no more
Comes any to our call? The Greeks must now
Seek safety in their long black ships ashore,
For all that were our bravest, all lie low,
By Trojan arrows, Trojan spears, o'erthrown
And Troy's power mounts, and hers alone. . . .

The *Iliad*, XI. 823–827.

CHAPTER ONE

I REMEMBER that when I was on the hospital ship, watching the Peninsula fade, I knew that, whether or not I came back to it before the campaign ended, it would call to me always with that lodestone quality which invests some scenes in a long-dead past. And now, forty years afterwards, I had obeyed that call and come back to it, an ageing—no, let me take refuge in the world 'elderly'—an elderly man. Elderly, to be sure, because, incredible as it seemed, I was now many years older than the Colonel had been, and stranger still, even older than our great and famous C.-in-C., who was sixty or so in those days. The Colonel must have been long dead now; the C.-in-C. had died some ten years since (I remembered the obituaries, and the outbursts of tragic praise, ardent loyalty and silent-till-now regrets); and here was I, with a wife beside me and a Turk behind me for my orderly (or detective), wandering along the old Krithia Nullah in search of the place where our company fought its last fight of all. I wanted to be able to say to my wife, for it was this more than anything else that she had come to see, 'It must have been somewhere here.'

The September afternoon was mellow, and the country around us as empty and tranquil as any wide heath in the Sussex Weald. The nullah had its summer dryness yet, so that the dust of Gallipoli smoked away from our feet, just as it used to do, on the old north-east wind. And I limped on through scrub and scented pines, with an excited expectation gripping at my heart, and my eyes peering into the landscape, and peering again.

I knew I could come near my place because it had been about five hundred yards north-east of Twelve Tree Copse, and Twelve Tree Copse was now a war cemetery enclosed in a white wall and made sombre and beautiful with cypress, arbutus, and juniper.

I kept those dark trees on my left and, walking on for a few hundred yards, stopped.

'It was here,' I said.

'Sure?' she asked; and trembled a little.

'Fairly sure. It must have happened just about here. But, dear God, how different. How different it all is.'

I was standing in a field of stubble. Stubble that stretched for miles.

For, while on other parts of the Peninsula the depressions in sand and scrub marked where the trenches had been, just as on our South Downs the Roman fosses can still be discerned, here, near the feet of Achi Baba, a new generation of Turks, stout, toiling peasants, had turned over all the land, right across the Peninsula, and made of it a fertile soil, so that, standing here, we saw little but this thick creamy stubble flushed with rose and faint purple hues. Of could it be, I wondered, that the thousands of invaders digging here, and dying here, had given this soil its new fertility?

I took my bearings again from Twelve Tree Copse. Hardly a doubt about the place, and I repeated 'Dear God', because these acres of tinted stubble, with a lark above them in full autumn song, were the extreme opposite of the No-Man's-Land which I was imagining, with its dead lying tossed about beyond the wire and in the dust.

'Still, this can only be it, my dear.'

My wife, unable to speak, gazed down at the stubble, and I said no more—nor moved—because I did not want to break in upon her thoughts. For my part I thought of Evverson and Cass and other officers and men, whose names I could no longer remember. Evverson, if only he had chosen to live on till his disgrace was a forgotten thing, might now be a happy old man like me——

This wayward thought of mine was dispelled by the sight of a Turkish peasant riding a donkey along the green bank that was the wheatfield's boundary. He was frighteningly tall and lean, his feet almost touching the ground on either side of his mount, so that I felt he might with advantage get off occasionally and carry the donkey for a spell. He wore a stockinet pointed cap and tattered garments much as we used to find the Turkish soldiers wearing when we came on a visit to their trenches. His main difference from them was that when he saw us, he grinned with surprise, delight, and curiosity and, straightway dismounting, came towards us, leaving his thin and patient beast to stand untethered and alone.

He stopped opposite us: a grey bristled, wrinkled man all my age and more, and so tall and narrow-shouldered that he made me think of a menhir from prehistory standing in an open field. And yet there was that in his face which suggested a Mongol ancestor who had come out of Asia with Genghis Khan or Tamerlane: high bones, slit eyes. So pleasantly did he smile, and so polite was his continuing silence, that I felt his curiosity must be gratified. Pointing a finger to my breastbone and then to the ground, I said in that baby language which one supposes suitable to Turks, 'Me—fought—*here*.'

He got this, and, delighted, poured forth a spate of words which I couldn't understand but took to be a longer version of 'Me too'.

I called forward my orderly (or detective) to see if he could interpret and, between us, we gathered that the delighted fellow was saying, 'All of my age were here and most of them were killed.'

'Here exactly?' I pointed to the stubble.

'Yes, yes,' he said; and made a show of firing a rifle. Bang! Emptying the breach and firing again—Bang!

See? When he'd done smiling at me he turned and gave a brilliant smile to my wife, that she might not feel left out of these amicable exchanges. No doubt he'd been told that the English took their women seriously, and he had enough of Oriental hospitality in him to believe that all visitors to his land must be humoured in their eccentricities.

So tall was he that for a second the wild notion seized me that he might actually be the green sniper who'd been brought down the Gully. 'Ever a prisoner?' I contrived to ask with words and pantomime and help from my private Turk, who was enjoying with many supporting smiles and much loud talk this sudden diversion in a dull and empty day.

'No, no'; and he fired again and bayoneted several persons, left, right and centre. Nevertheless: 'German no goot; English vehr goot,' he said, and grinned in his happy conviction that this remained true, a fact of nature.

The words called up other Turco-British courtesies that were current in our day and, smiling as happily as he, I tried, 'Bully beef *non? Envoyez* milk?'

He recognized the words with uproarious joy and assured us 'Bully beef *non, non, non.*' His opinion hadn't changed with the years. '*Non, non, non.*'

Couldn't agree more, I expounded, my hand waving bully aside as untouchable.

'Wounded,' he said in his own language, and he placed his right palm horizontally before his brow, and his left before his chin and smiled proudly. I soon gathered that he was implying that because his head had shown above a trench he had been wounded in it. At once and with pride I showed him the scar in my cheek, at which he stared with lifted eyebrows and shrugged as if he would say, 'Things happen like that in war. You. Me. All the same. Strange that we're here to talk of it. We ought to be under this earth instead of on top of it. No?'

It was almost a family joke between us.

As a fellow causalty I offered him a cigarette which he took from my case after wiping an earthy hand on his baggy trousers. I lit it for him, and when it was drawing, put out my hand to shake his.

Again he wiped the grimed hand on a buttock; then took mine and shook it vigorously and painfully as if this were the best joke of the afternoon.

It was only later that I thought, What a symbol we made, there in the stubble.

I said '*Allah Din!* and *Allah Hu!*' though I'd long forgotten what exactly the words conveyed; but he accepted them in the spirit in which they were offered—with boisterous laughter.

'God zave ze King,' he supplied, trying to sing it since he supposed it to be the English equivalent. 'Long leave our noble King'; and he added for my further entertainment, '*Saïda,* Johnny, *imshi iggry, backsheesh.*'

I was quite sorry when this convivial affair was over and he left us to return to his beast parked against the bank and dutifully waiting. As he went I apprehended for the first time an extraordinary thing: his approach to us had been almost without sound; and his departure was the same. I looked at his feet, and, absurd as it must sound, those feet called up to life again, with a strange piercing sweetness, nearly all that I had forgotten about the end of the Gallipoli story. They were wrapped in sacking.

CHAPTER TWO

THE hospital ship did not take me to Alexandria but to Mudros East on Lemnos Island, and there I was led to another hospital of square white tents on a dried-up hill. I had merely exchanged No. 17 Stationary on Helles for No. 16 Stationary at Mudros.

The huge wind-blown harbour between the burnt hills seemed nearly as full of warships as on that April day when the great armada sailed, but they were not now waiting to go out to battle amid a storm of cheering; they were lying anchored in safety, and some of them had lain there ever since a submarine mortally stung the *Triumph* off Anzac and the *Majestic* off Helles. Greek yachts and bum boats plied among them, while the monitors served as their deputies off Helles and Suvla.

On the hills there were far more tents and hutments; Mudros East and Mudros West, two sickly villages till History came and sat down beside them, had now vast suburbs of canvas and wood all over the sweeping hills: tents and huts to house Communications, Transport, Canteens, Depots, Dumps, the Y.M.C.A., and the men in rest or transit or prison. The tents, one and all, were more yellow than white because of the blowing of the yellow dust, after ten thousand feet had eroded the soil.

I often think of those parched hills as they must be today: empty except for the thistles and stones, and a few lean goats. The Intermediate Base we called Mudros then, and certainly it was an Intermediate Base for me, where I was held between Cowardice and Courage, whose other names were Alexandria and Helles.

Three months I dawdled there. There was talk of sending me to Alex, and I strove against it—but I did not fight to get back to the Peninsula. Just as I would be sour with Colin, and wander off alone, if he rebuked me, so now I was sour with God, and kept myself to myself, because He had hit me so brutally (as I half believed) for having failed Him on Helles.

This dawdling at Mudros was easy; everything favoured it; most of the M.O.s were young men, hampered by hesitations and doubts, and it was a commonplace among us to say, 'On the Peninsula the M.O.s won't let you get off it; and at the Base they won't let you get back to it. Once off it you can dodge the rest of the war forever.'

So the weeks became months and I was still at Mudros. I kept my thoughts away from this idling and delay, but I was not very happy in my hospital tents. My first tent was an E.P. tent like the one on Helles and again I shared it with eleven officers. Our beds were comfortable; we actually had bedside tables; we drank bottled soda water instead of the vilely chlorinated water from the Mudros wells or the Nile; but we had no mosquito nets, and the flies were as bad here as on the Peninsula, and the heat seemed worse. It stood in the tent like a silence made visible; it waited outside like an angry power.

One broiler of an afternoon the hospital—heat or no heat—was electrified into nervous, hurrying life by four syllables: 'The C.-in-C.' Promptly all the white stones that marked the avenues between the tents were painted a fresher white; our orderlies cleaned every corner of our tent and even made the beds of some of us a second time; if we protested, they said 'The C.-in-C.' and we leapt out of bed. The Commander-in-Chief was this day visiting every hospital on the island.

I was eager to see this legendary man, for in our battalions which had taken part in the First Landing we chose to admire him in his far-off gandeur much as the British people like to worship a monarch whom they have seldom seen and never spoken to. Our Colonel Punjabi Kiss-me Harby, who had served under him in South Africa, swore that he was one of the greatest of soldiers—always subject to the proviso that he should have landed all his forces above Gaba Tepe instead of on six different beaches. But since the great man had done precisely this three months later the Colonel was able to speak of him now in near-superlatives, which, I am sure, was what Punjabi Harby wanted to do. That so fine a soldier should also write poetry the Colonel left on one side as something beyond his understanding.

Not all agreed with the Colonel and with us who served on Gallipoli under this famous Commander. From the beginning, at home, at Gib, in Malta, and in Egypt, there were many who decried him as far too much the artist, the contemplative, the delicate-mannered gentleman, for a great leader in furious modern war. And now that the landing at Suvla had apparently repeated the failure at Helles, his detractors (as a hospital orderly with a liking for language put it to me) were 'as the stars in the sky for multitude. Only run lame for a little, sir, and the dogs leap on to you'.

Colin would have none of this detraction; he chose to admire; and I followed Colin. In Colin's view our C.-in-C. was like what Sir Philip Sidney would have been if he'd lived to be sixty-two. Or like Marcus Aurelius who, even as he rode to his wars with the Marcomanni, would compose apothegms about the duty of living tranquilly rather than happily, with wisdom, justice, and fortitude for one's guides.

But if I was impatient to look upon so famous and controversial a figure I was not a little frightened lest he spoke to me. How could one who was afraid of colonels be other than abject before a C.-in-C.? And it was all too likely that he *would* speak to me, because one of the miracles attributed to him was that, on these tours among the wounded, he 'found something new to say to every bloody man he visited'. No matter if the bloody man was brown, black or yellow; he said his bit, as the occasion demanded, in Hindustani, Swahili, or Japanese. Merciful heavens, would he speak to me?

It was now late afternoon and we heard movements outside. The O.C. Hospital's voice: 'Officers' Ward again, sir. All wounded.' Another voice, quiet, of pleasing quality but edged now with the slight wiry hoarseness that comes with years: 'Lead on, Major.'

Silence rushed into the tent ahead of these voices and possessed it. Not a movement in any bed, nor by either of the orderlies. In our yellow-lined tent the silence and the heat were as one.

'Mostly from Suvla, sir. And some overflow from the Australian Hospital. There's one lad from Helles.'

Oh, *no*! That must be me. Don't single me out. Let me be inconspicuous. I don't want to be spoken to. At least I don't think I——

I had no time to decide what I wanted. Out of the broiling sun, into the soft yellowed light of our tent came the O.C., the C.-in-C., and our young doctor.

The orderlies sprang to attention.

From my bed I gazed at one figure only. By the side of our solid square-built major he hardly looked a soldier; he seemed a frail and slender aristocrat dressed for the war in a uniform of old-fashioned cut which was now a little loose for a shrunken figure. One saw in the narrow face and spare limbs the booklover rather than the soldier. But his left hand told another story: some old battle had left it misshapen and gnarled and stiff.

'That's the uniform he wore at the relief of Mafeking,' my neighbour, a gigantic Australian, whispered. But I was too nervous to laugh, with the Presence now standing among us.

And too interested. That face was kind, its lips humorous beneath the small shapely grey moustache, its eyes bright with intelligence and filling with compassion as he scanned our bandages. You saw he could but love us because we were men who had obeyed his orders and suffered. When I saw the kindness in those wrinkle-framed eyes I felt less afraid. But not much less.

When he came close and was talking to the man two beds from mine I saw more in those eyes and experienced a surge of compassion. Ever adept at reading people's thoughts, I could see behind his friendly smile and laughing words all the sorrow of a man whose fine plans had miscarried; plans which now lay dead on the hither sides of Achi Baba and Sari Bair. He must be thinking, as all we on Helles thought too, that they had not failed through fault of his. We believed with him (and I believe still) that if the powers at home had not starved him of guns, shells, mortars, bombs, and men, in favour of France, he would have carried Achi Baba in the first weeks of May, held Sari Bair within hours of the Suvla landing. As I watched him laughing with the man two beds from mine I guessed he must be feeling like an artist whose *chef d'œuvre*, on which he has laboured greatly, and for which he has hoped all things, fails in a hostile market and earns him disfavour rather than acclaim.

Now he came to the Australian next to me and inquired about his wounds (the enormous man was largely bound up) and talked to him gaily about Melbourne and Sydney, which he had visited. The Australian, to my relief, answered him with some respect and did not call him 'Cock' or 'Chum'. There was nothing in the man's talk to worry me at first except that he called him 'General' instead of 'sir'.

Now he was at my bed and smiling down at me, while the young doctor said, 'Lieutenant Browning, sir, King's Own Sussex Light Infantry.'

'The *Koslis*?' he exclaimed. 'A fine crowd. What a fine crowd. But you were not there in the Landing, I suppose?'

'Yes, sir, I was.'

'You *were*? At V Beach?'

'Yes, sir.'

'My God!' He turned to the O.C. behind him. 'Major, here's a comrade of the First Landing.'

The whole tent was looking at us. It was one of the proudest and pleasantest moments of my life. No one else in that tent had been on V Beach on the great day. For a while I was Number One in that tent.

'And you were not killed?'

'No, sir.'

'Nor wounded?'

'Not on the beach, sir.'

'Well, you must be almost unique. How did you manage it?'

'I fell over a rock and pitched into the sea, sir.'

'Excellent. And they thought you were dead and left you alone. What then?'

'I ran straight to that little sandbank.' Ashamed of not having been wounded at once, I said, 'I was wounded later on,' and then, ashamed of having boasted (or, more truly, of sounding like a boaster) I added, 'But only slightly.'

He didn't seem to hear. He was staring down at me. '*You* were one of those under the sandbank. I watched you all from the deck of the *Queen Elizabeth*, and there didn't seem anything I could do to help you. It was a bitter feeling. Commodore Keyes, who's the least soft commodore I know, said he couldn't bear the sight of it any more. And all that the Admiral could do was to order Queen Lizzie to fight all out for you. And did she? My dear lad, she gave you all she'd got. From every gun. The great ship shook from stem to stern in a kind of passionate desire to do something to help you.'

'We saw it, sir,'

'We were simply deafened by her roars and almost scorched by her flames. But it did us good. It helped us.'

'It did *us* good too, sir.'

'*You* under that bank! What a tale you'll have to tell your children. Are you married?'

'Good heavens, no, sir.'

'Well, you must certainly get married so that you can have children and tell them. Do you mean you were with Doughty Wylie when he led that attack?'

'Yes, sir.'

'Well, now listen: I shall always say that that attack of Doughty Wylie's was one of the finest things in the war. Or in any war. To have called up the courage of exhausted men who'd been lying chilled and hungry under that bank all night, and to lead them up a hill to a victory that secured our line for us—d'you know: I wrote home and called it the Miracle of V Beach. Doughty Wylie's Miracle. I mean: you can only achieve that sort of thing if you're standing on the very summit of yourself. And Doughty Wylie was, I think. I suspect he knew he must die.'

'He was wonderful, sir.'

'Everybody must have been wonderful on that beach.' He seemed to muse a moment, silently. 'It must be quite good to die when you're standing on the very summit of yourself. Let's think that about him. And I want you to know this: I've been in all too many wars—the Afghan War, the two Boer Wars, and—oh, well, the Lord only knows what else—if *He* hasn't forgotten—but I rate the storming of the two Helles beaches from the open sea as the finest feat I ever saw. Even our friend here, who was at Anzac'—he turned to the big Australian—'will allow that.'

'I certainly will, General,' said the Australian with his extreme and embarrassing ease.

'I thought you would. Hundreds of Aussies and New Zealanders have said so to me.'

'Yes the boys at Anzac had a sticky time but they're ready, one and all, to hand it to the old Twenty-Ninth at Helles. You're right there, General.'

'You see?' He was looking at me again. 'You can tell your children I said that, and that Australia agreed. You've had a part in something you can always be proud of.'

Silence in the tent for the Commander-in-Chief and me. I was a glory in the tent; or, at least, like the King's daughter in the psalm, I was all glorious within.

'The Koslis. Then young Colin Dester is one of your officers?'

Sweet to hear that name suddenly spoken. 'Yes, sir. He's in command of my company now.'

'Well, you've got a pretty good O.C., I imagine?'

'He's wonderful, sir.'

'A nice lad. I know his father well, Lord Storrington. Do you?'

'No, sir.' I saw the Baron's Court Road.

'I've shot with him once or twice. It was at Lord Storrington's request that I got young Colin out here, and when he arrived, I offered him a place on my personal staff. Did you know that?'

'No, sir.' How surely I should have contrived to let Colin know of such an honour. But not to me, his most intimate friend, had he mentioned it. Seemingly, to him and his kind, in their high security, it was as easy to refrain from boasting as it was difficult for me. Or could it be that he didn't conceive of this as an outstanding honour to one of his class and attainments?

'But of course he refused. Said he wanted to "do the landing" side by side with the rest of his crowd. The proper thing to say, no doubt.'

And how surely I should have let Colin know of my handsome refusal—always supposing there'd been such a thing. I stayed silent, leaving it to my C.-in-C. to talk.

'I saw him the other day when I went round the Kosli trenches. He's still as thin as a rake, but who isn't? We're an army of skeletons, aren't we? I don't think any insurance office'd look at us twice. *You're* a lot depleted, you know. Are they going to let you get back to the Peninsula?'

'Oh, I *hope* so, sir,' I said. An actor's line to please him.

'Yes, try to, if you can. We shall need every good man. But it's an awful place. So take your time and get really well. You needn't hurry. It's all quiet along the Potomac just now.'

Here the Australian joined in with his egalitarian and irreverent and extremely abashing ease. With a jovial bluntness he asked, 'But isn't it a fact, General, that we've shot our bloody bolt on the Peninsula and can do no more?'

The impudent question shivered through me. It shivered through our visitor too, I saw, but it was not embarrassment that troubled him; it was pain; pain like that which comes from a new and suspect growth within, and brings a sadness with it.

'Of course not,' I said at once to comfort him—a subaltern comforting his Commander-in-Chief.

'It is most certainly not true,' he said almost angrily. But he mastered the anger and smiled—the smile of one who did not choose to show that he'd been hurt. 'Don't you believe any such thing, but just hurry up and get well, so that you can eat your supper one day on Sari Bair. And perhaps sing your hymns sooner than you think in Saint Sophia.'

'Sing 'em exactly where, General?'

'In Saint Sophia, in Constantinople: almost the oldest church in the world. It's been sitting by the Golden Horn for centuries, waiting for us Christians to come back to it.'

'Oh, I see,' said the Australian. He quite clearly didn't, but modesty was not the chief trait of our brave and gigantic Gallipoli Australians. 'I see.'

'The legend of Saint Sophia says that, on the day Constantinople fell, the great church was crowded with people saying Mass for the deliverance of the city, and'—all those nearest us in the tent, forgetting who he was, were now gazing from their beds and listening as to some bedtime ghost story—'and that when the celebrating priest learned that the Turks had stormed into the city, he picked up the sacred elements and walked with them straight through the wall. He will return with them, they say, when the first Christian service is held there again. It's been a mosque ever since that day.' He smiled at the Australian. 'I rather want to be there and see him return through the wall.'

All that the good Australian could offer in response to this was a regretful 'Well, that'll be Okay by me, General, but I'm not sure I'm much good at singing hymns. I guess you'll have to do that part of the business for him without much help from me.' And then, not to be defeated, even by a general, he returned to his first attack, 'But everyone's saying that Sari Bair's absolutely impregnable now'.

'Nothing is impregnable.' The answer came like the snap of a rifle-bolt. Again an impatience had shown through his restraint like a chink of light when a cold draught moves a curtain. 'Words like "absolute" and "impregnable" are just slack words for avoiding new efforts and a new will. I hope you'll all come down like a hundred howitzers on any such chatter. Tell everybody that when I left England Lord Kitchener's last words to me were that once I was ashore I could burn my boats, because the Government were resolved to see this thing through.' He turned from my neighbour to me. 'After that quite incredible attack of Doughty Wylie's I signalled a message of congratulation to whoever was still alive and in command, and I got back the reply, "Thanks from all ranks. We are here to stay."'

'I know you did, sir. It was my colonel who sent it.'

'Well, his message is still our motto: alive or dead we stay. We've at least got our key into the lock of the Hellespont, and we'll turn it yet. Don't you agree?' He asked it, as if my agreement mattered.

'Abso*lutely*, sir,' I endorsed with enthusiasm—I who had left the Peninsula and doubted if I'd return to it.

'Like hell I agree, General,' said the Australian, who probably gave greater weight to his agreement than I to mine.

'Good.' He bent forward and waved away the flies that were troubling my face. 'Are these mosquito nets never coming, Major? I expcct they'll come when my eighteen-pounder H.E. does, and that'll be the year after next.' Regretting that phrase 'alive or dead', he addressed us again. 'But of course there's no question of us all dying there. Even if we had to, I imagine it would be better to die on the enemy's ground than to be butchered at the sea's edge like the Persians at Marathon.'

'Oh, yes, sir,' I said, proud that I could understand the allusion, while the Australian almost certainly couldn't.

'Yes, I think the Duke of Wellington said that. Or if he didn't, he should have done. So instead of listening to despondent talk, tell them that I know—I know from our Intelligence—that we've established an ascendancy over the Turk. We don't overtop the Narrows yet, but we overtop him. And that's the beginning of victory. Sari Bair's not a big mountain and, given enough faith, we'll move it all right.'

'Yes, sir,' I said. 'Oh, yes.'

'Tell everyone that, and just remember Doughty Wylie.

And now I must get on. We've still got your Dangerous Wards to do, I think, Major? Good-bye.' He raised a hand to the Australian. 'Good-bye.'

'Good-bye, General. Sorry I can't give you a bit of a salute. Bloody hell, I'd like to!'

'I'll salute you instead. And very rightly.' He laughed and pretended to do so. 'You're the representative here of a quite incredible crowd of heroes.' Then he touched my hand on the coverlet. 'Remember too what I said: you had a part in one of the greatest actions in all the history of war, and I envy you. I could only stand and watch with a kind of heartbreaking pride.' He gently touched the hand again. 'Well done.'

He moved from between our beds towards my neighbour on the other side, and I turned myself over to watch, for now indeed I had a hero to worship for ever.

CHAPTER THREE

My next tent in that hospital was a bell tent in the M.O.s' lines. My arm was now in good order; the wounds in my cheeks were no more than scars; but I had succumbed to some pattern of intermittent agues, and the M.O.s wanted to keep me under observation. The principal diseases in our wards were enteritis, dysentery, paratyphoid, and P.U.O.; that is to say, Pyrexia of Unknown Origin. Some of the M.O.s called it G.O.K. or God Only Knows, and I gathered that, wanting to get level with God, they were determined to know what my small fevers amounted to. But since there was no room in the wards for anyone so comparatively hale as myself, I had been put on the ration strength of the hospital's Officers' Mess and was now sharing a tent with the most junior of its doctors, an exceedingly brainy and entertaining young Jew, Lieutenant Mossy Abrams.

In this tent, overlooking the great harbour, I continued to dawdle. Soon it was a matter of weeks since I'd had any fever; seldom had I felt better after the good hospital food; but I did not draw the attention of the M.O.s to my state. I had but to recall that agony in No-Man's-Land, and my tongue stayed still. And yet I was sure now that if I wanted to I could get back to the Peninsula. But 'There's no hurry' I told myself. Everyone coming from the Peninsula reported all quiet at Suvla; all quiet at Helles. A little shelling of the trenches to show one another that one was still there; a little shrapnel in white clouds over the plateau for everyone's amusement; a few compliments from Asiatic Annie on the beaches; a little sport among the snipers on both sides—and not much else. Everyone's prospect of life on the Peninsula had increased from days to months.

So why hurry or worry? But one day in mid-October, as I

lay idly on my camp-bed gazing out at the ships in the harbour, Conscience came into the tent and touched me on the shoulder. 'Delay no more,' it said. 'You must choose now.'

My conscience entered in the disguise of Mossy Abrams, and perhaps it was appropriate that the conscience of a Protestant young man should wear that dark but handsome Hebraic countenance.

I'll say too that it was appropriate that a mild thundering should accompany its entrance. During the morning I had watched the hundreds of ships asleep on a slumbering water, but now in the heat of the afternoon a wind had come from the north-eastern hills—our old friend from Gallipoli?—and was drumming and kettle-drumming on the canvas of our tent. Sometimes it shook the canvas as a stage hand shakes the thunder sheet in a pantomime storm. The tent pole vibrated and creaked and whined. Out on the water the wind was lifting waves that dandled trawlers and tugs on their crests and insolently slapped some of the greatest battleships and liners that this planet has built.

Abrams came out of the flying dust, tossed his helmet on to his bed, shook the dust from his shirt more or less over me, and stood solemnly before my face, dressed in shirt, shorts, and a wrist-watch.

'Shimei,' he said, 'went along the hillside over against him and cursed as he went, and threw stones at him and cast dust.'

'Well, that was rather a shame of Shimei,' I said, trying to be witty like him.

'The Second Book of Samuel,' he explained.

'I don't care if it's the Second Book of the Devil.'

'I take it upon me to speak unto thee, who am but dust and ashes. We are at war with Bulgaria. And damn this wind. We declared war yesterday.'

'I saw that coming,' I bragged. 'That's why all those boys went to Salonika. They're going to stiffen up the Serbs.'

'Yes, but since you're such a master of strategy, perhaps you'll tell me what this interesting fact means to the boys on Gallipoli, who, if I'm not mistaken——'

'The old Bulgars have been flirting long enough with the Germans. It's time we—what was that you said about the boys on Gallipoli?'

'Bulgaria has an army of three hundred thousand men.'

'But they're no good, are they?'

'Those who know say that as fighters the Bulgars are worth all the other Balkans put together.'

'Well, even that doesn't total up to very much.'

'Have you a brain at all, young man? The Germans and Bulgars together can now overwhelm the Serbs from all sides, and they'll do it. The Bulgars are burning to do it. Hell take this wind!' The tent roof had struck him on the head, and he absentmindedly smoothed back his dark, almost Assyrian curls. 'The Bulgars loathe the Serbs. They think they've done 'em dirty more than once.'

'So they probably have.'

'Oh, no doubt; and now the Bulgars'—actually his word was not this, but one of a similar sound—'are really going to learn 'em how to behave.'

'Well, so far as I am concerned, they can get on with it.'

'You are very deeply concerned, my boy. So are we all.'

'How?'

'Listen. Just lie back and listen. Try to understand. The Bulgars and the Huns together will drive through Serbia to Nish. Once there, they'll have a railway line direct to Constantinople. Perfect. Our War Office has declined to send us enough shells and men, but the Germans won't be such fools. They'll send the Turk every gun, shell, and man he needs.'

'Crikey!' Slowly, like the gradual-growing darkness when a thunder-cloud comes over the sky from the north, this alarm revealed itself and overshadowed me.

'Yes, crikey it is.'

'But won't our War House'—Colonel Harby's word which I'd now adopted—'wake up at once to the danger?'

'Too late, old boy. Too late. The Germans'll be able to get munitions and men to the Peninsula in days, whereas it takes us weeks.'

'So what happens? What's the position of the lads on the Peninsula?'

'Doomed, I fear. Not a hope.' He might have been speaking, with the required professional calm, about some of his worst 'cases' in the Dangerous Wards. 'They'll last a month or two, perhaps. More than that I can't say.'

'Don't just talk like that! What do we *do*? Get them off?'

'The best people say that evacuation's not possible. Or, at any rate, not possible for half of them. Half of them would have to fight the rear-guard action, and probably die. Anything less would mean a *sauve-qui-peut*—and that's the French for a massacre.'

'Well, better, I suppose, to die on the enemy's ground'—Mossy had not heard the C.-in-C. say this, so I could offer it as my own—'than to be butchered on the sea's edge like——'

But Mossy was listening to himself rather than to me. 'And further, my son, I would invite you to take note of this wind and give a glance at the harbour outside. The boys at both Suvla and Helles will be attacked, not only by Germans and Turks and Bulgars in front, but by the seas behind. It's just about the literal truth that they're between the devil and the deep blue sea—because Germany's patently an aspect of the devil.'

Great God! Oh, but wasn't he perhaps exaggerating, as people loved to do when an alarm was abroad? Colin—the Colonel—all the Koslis—they were not really a herd of victims preserved for sacrifice? An anvil we had called the Peninsula. This man, brilliant in his way—was he suggesting that it must now become an altar?

All that evening, though I pretended to joke, and much of that night, though I pretended to sleep, I was listening to Conscience—and only listening, because I had no reply to offer. It was the small hours before I contrived to cast this bedfellow out by repeating, 'Oh, leave it, leave it, leave it. Leave it till the morning.' I repeated the words perhaps a hundred times, and then slept.

In the morning, since I as a patient had no duties to perform, I walked over the stony hills so as to get far from the sight of men and meet my unsparing mentor somewhere between the empty earth and the sky. Only in a solitude as complete as this could I bring my business to an end.

I followed a sketchy goat-track that drifted over the hills, through sun-yellowed grass, disorderly thistles and dry, broken rocks, till it brought me to a high ridge where, alone in the miles of desolation, stood a tiny square chapel of stones and mud. Before it was a trough, presumably for a donkey to find some physical comfort while its baggy-trousered master sought the higher things within.

It was open, and I went in, glad to get out of the morning heat on these barren, shadeless hills. A little room, twelve foot square, with a few tawdry icons on the walls and a woodwork screen hiding a tattered and tinselled altar. To judge from various deposits on the floor some donkeys had followed their masters in rather than stay by the trough, and some goats or long-haired sheep had also come in, hoping perhaps to find on this floor a pasture less arid than on the hills outside. The little chamber smelt of stale candle-wax, dry earth, and dung. I thought at first that since the end of my business was plain (my Baron's Court God having decided it years ago) and since this place, though small, deserted, and dirty, was a temple of sorts, I might try to gather here some strength to accept the hard decision, and to hold on to it. Small, deserted, and befouled, but not without a desire for God, how like some of us poor temples of the spirit, I thought; and especially one not too far away just now. I did not, however, remain there; I seemed to need the wide sky and the unenclosed hills, whatever their heat, for my help; so I said only a 'God give me strength' and went out again and sat on the trough.

That pain. Can you accept it again? As I asked this, the fear leapt within me like a devil in possession. It clawed at my heart.

'I don't want it again. . . .' Sweat broke from my hands and brow, and palpitations shook my heart.

Perhaps it would be a bayonet. Oh, not a bayonet, *please.*

I remembered the anguished screams of those Turks when we bayoneted them. Only a few days ago I had cut my finger deep, opening a ration tin, and instantly the sick obsessive fear had shot the sweat to my skin. Was it possible that there were others who were still unafraid of danger and pain after taking wounds that tore their nerves?

But Colin: I saw Colin in mind and longed to be with him; next second I remembered the pain and dreaded to be there. The two memories strained against each other and held me motionless.

Pends-toi, brave Crillon, nous avons combattu à Arques, et tu n'y étais pas. Famous words of Henry of Navarre which Colin had loved to expound to me. Probably he had thought of them when he told the C.-in-C. that he 'wanted to do the landing with the rest of his crowd'.

Noblesse oblige: whatever Colin's secret weaknesses and curtained sins this rule certainly dominated him. He had breathed it in the air of Castle Ivry so that now it was an attitude barely conscious. I had been taught some junior pattern of it in the Baron's Court Road, but for me it was an attitude to be acquired by deliberate practice. And now—oh yes, I wanted to do what Colin would do.

Noblesse. Honour. Only Nature's flame, perhaps, to draw redundant moths to their deaths.

Nevertheless the flame burned.

'I *must* go back, pain or no pain. Perhaps it's God's handiwork. He's saying, 'This time you've got to know what the pain is, and accept it. In that towed boat you had only fear at your side; now you will have knowledge as well. This time you will know the price. I want you to be equal to it.'

A hard master.

Noblesse. Honour. Reputation. But years would pass; twenty, forty years; and then many would know nothing of Helles, few would remember it clearly, and none would care any more about a man's absence or presence there. Evverson—if only he'd chosen to live, what would matter his shame in a forgotten gully, after forty years? So with

Lieutenant Browning. In forty years time what I did, or did not do, on Helles would be as the down on those old grey thistles yonder, long blown to nothing in the wind.

Aye, but would *I* ever forget? In forty years when I was an old man of sixty-four? On my death-bed? 'Go hang yourself, stout Crillon. We fought at Arques....'

Wearied by thought, and so a poor soil for courage, I just sat on the trough outside the chapel, gazing towards the west. This hill-top was high, and with my Zeiss field-glasses I could see in the distance, rising like a table mountain out of the Aegean, Samothrace; Thasos too; and farther to the west, a grey phantom shape on the sky, the sacred Mount Athos. Thirty monasteries on that high cone of earth. Surely it was easier to be a monk on Mount Athos than a soldier on Gallipoli?

The innocent islands seen through the haze from Lemnos or Gallipoli seemed the Islands of the Blest.

Very like life (I thought in melancholy mood) this Aegean sea; this lake of the Greeks. Nowhere on it was one without sight of mountainous islands rising blue and violet and bathed in light; but only get to one of them, and you stepped on to barren and stony soil, like this of Lemnos and our Gallipoli, with little growing there except olives, figs, and vines. Only in the brief springtime were the hills beautiful with flowers, as on that April day when we came to Gallipoli; almost at once the summer bore down and dried up everything, like middle age turning most of youth's ardent loves into dust. And still all the other islands in the distance looked like Islands of the Blest. Last in the melancholy tale, came winter, bringing torrential rains which stripped the hills of their scanty soil and carried much of it away (like an old man's memories) to sink it for ever in this encompassing sea.

Such a winter would soon be down upon Gallipoli.

And one must go back. I sought strength from thoughts of others who had gone deliberately into the risk of terrible pain. Father Finn. I saw him running from the iron shelter of the *Clyde* to join his men on the beach. Colonel Harby. He also had come running down that dreadful gangplank, his Russian boots glistening in the sun. Cass. Even poor Cassy had gone back with his box of bombs in his hands. Above all, Doughty Wylie. Had I not once, on a beach, chosen him as my exemplar? I saw him lying dead on the stones of Sedd-el-Bahr. And he, being dead, yet spoke. I saw again his sad humorous eyes: 'Come, my children.'

That gentle order of Doughty Wylie's, by mere association of sounds, carried me to another scene: Colin going down into the towed boat but turning first to me and asking, 'Coming, Gerry?' This was the most potent memory of all. Indeed it was unbeatable.

To be with Colin again—it would be wonderful. And with the men too. To go back to a welcome by them all. How strange was this desire that seized so many of us, after we'd been a few months away from the Front, whether Gallipoli or France, to get back to it, no matter how much we had hated it. A restless nostalgia for the regiment, the lads, the Line.

But not only did my love for Colin and my affection for the men help me; my vanity played a part. I had been in the Landing—'you've had a part in something you can always be proud of,' the C.-in-C. had said—I must be there at the End—whatever the End might be. I must fight at Arques.

I walked back slowly, hesitantly, and with occasional sighs, towards the camps, the ships, and the Gallipoli ferry.

It was the vain half of me that spoke when I saw Mossy Abrams standing outside our tent. 'I've made up my mind,' I said. 'I'm going back. Somehow or other I'm getting back to the Peninsula.'

'When, brave man?'

'Directly you blighters help me to. I'm perfectly fit.'

'You're not mad, by any chance? I mean, I could treat you for it. A bed in a Mental Abnormality Ward.'

'No, thank you. I'm perfectly all right. When do you think I——'

'Melancholia, perhaps? You feel unfit to live? Mudros

affects chaps like that. And all melancholiacs are predisposed to suicide. The treatment is rest and good food—quite pleasant—and unobtrusive observation. Your present idea, I take it, is to get yourself killed as quickly as possible at the hands of the Turks?'

He might be attempting humour but, as he said this, I could only see the figure of Evverson hurrying over the dark plateau towards the enemy's bullets; so I replied, unamusingly, 'No, I'm fine, thanks. *I* don't want to die.'

'I see. Then it's just plain heroism. Splendid. But something I don't aspire to. I——'

'It's not heroism or any of that nonsense,' I interrupted. 'It's just that I happen to think the C.-in-C. was right and we must get on with this business. And if I'm to do anything about it, I must get back to the Front. So now I intend to work you all like stink to get me there.'

'Helles is an awful place. Like Scott's South Pole, "My God . . . an awful place". And now it's going to be rather awfuller.'

'Can't help that. The C.-in-C.——'

'If you go back to Helles you'll be going in exactly the opposite direction to our C.-in-C.'

'What do you mean?'

'I mean,' said Mossy, with that quiet, and lack of all emphasis, which would-be clever persons affect when announcing a startling thing, 'that the C.-in-C.'s gone home.'

'Home? What for?'

'He's recalled. Which is the other word for "sacked". And if that doesn't mean the end of everything, I don't know what does.'

'The bloody, bloody shame!' I stammered. 'God damn them all——'

'A cove called Monro is coming out to take over his command.'

'Well, damn Monro.' And my indignation, my jealousy for a man's honour, my loyalty, nay, my love for a commander who'd talked to me as a friend—these flung a new substance into my resolve. It was now as hard and obstinate as any rock on this dreary isle. 'Are you sure?' I asked, seeking even now to undo such news.

'Go and look at the Orders Board.'

I hurried to this board in the Officers' Mess marquee and read a Special Order of the Day.

GENERAL HEADQUARTERS
October 17th 1915

> On handing over the command of the Mediterranean Expeditionary Force to General Sir Charles Monro, the Commander-in-Chief wishes to say a few farewell words to the Allied troops, with many of whom he has now for so long been associated. First, he would like them to know his deep sense of the honour it has been to command so fine an army in one of the most difficult campaigns which have ever been undertaken; secondly, he must express to them his admiration of the noble response which they have invariably given to the calls he has made upon them. He thanks all ranks, from generals to private soldiers, for the wonderful way they have seconded his efforts to lead them towards that decisive victory which, under their new Chief, he has the most implicit confidence they will achieve.

'I go back,' I said. My lips were tight with pity.

They will achieve. . . . But did he really believe it? Or was it words—encouraging words? I did not really believe it. And I didn't mind not believing it, for I was now just angrily, sullenly, obtusely determined, in a kind of insensate loyalty, to work my return to the enterprise which had his heart. Secretly I was proud of this loyalty.

Not at once could I work it. October was dead before a signal went across the water from No. 16 Stationary to the H.Q. ship, the *Aragon,* that Lieutenant G. Browning was certified medically fit; six more days dawdled by before my orders came to 'proceed forthwith to Cape Helles'.

CHAPTER FOUR

ON the little passenger steamer that carried me through the night to Helles I was two men: one as excited as a lover at the thought of seeing Colin again, the other carrying a heavy luggage of fear. I believed I should die; I prayed that it might be with a merciful suddenness; if not it would be that pain again. So I thought, pacing the deck of that little steamer and seeing after a time the nervous star-shells lifting up above the dark Peninsula, and the Turkish searchlights at Chanak and Kephez fingering around the entrance of their threatened Straits. But the excited man was the stronger: I was thrilled to be going back to Colin and the men, and I could still hope (since hope surges ever at twenty-four) that I should neither die nor suffer pain.

Gallipoli: there it was ahead of me in the night. The Dardanelles. Troy's edge and Agamemnon's sea. Incredible, legendary, haunted places, there in the night.

For some reason (who ever understood the reasons for the Army's delays?) we were not disembarked till it was full morning, and so I saw V Beach again, that little bay of scimitar shape, gleaming in a bright daylight, though it was now languishing, all too obviously, in the gathering dusk of the campaign. The autumn seas had begun the work which the winter rages must complete. One jetty was washed away, its bones standing like stakes in the water; a steamer lay on its side off Helles Point; flotsam littered the sands; and the whole wide embracing sea was empty, with nowhere a hint of that proud fleet which once stood here. Only the old *Majestic* remained to represent the Navy, and she lay deck downward on the sea's floor, in six fathoms of water, with a stretch of her keel showing above the surface. A lamp still burned on that whaleback keel, and the sea caressed it.

They told me ashore that the Koslis were in reserve in the Old Australian Line, between Krithia Nullah and the Gully. It was all so quiet, they said, that I could get there by walking across the open to Grey Tree Farm, where it would be wiser to drop into the communication trench which led straight to the O.A. Line.

This I did, and I was pleased to find that the air on the Peninsula, after the long quiet, and in this cool autumnal light, was almost sweet. In the first months its breath had been like that of a diseased man, so that one retched till, getting used to it, one hardly noticed it any more; now the dead were all buried, or they were white bones as cleanly dried as those on the Sicilian fields where the Sirens sang, and one could inhale the breeze on the plateau like a cool invigorating draught. When I dropped down into the trenches I found them in better condition than ever before; deep, well-drained, and served with a piped water supply. In the general quietism, devoted to passive contemplation, there had been time to dig and revet and pipe and plumb.

I found our Battalion Orderly Room in the nullah, where there sat an adjutant who knew not Gerry Browning, nor knew that such a one was returning to the battalion. To die with it. This was Captain Trevor-Brayne, and he was thirty-five at least and wore both South African war medals. As he rose (not to me but to a shelf on the wall) I saw that he was very much the regular officer, tall, supremely neat, straight as a guardsman, and with a crisp black moustache like a company of bantam bristles stiffly on parade.

I was not a little afraid of him.

'Browning? . . . Browning? . . . Browning?'

'Yes, sir,' I said. Apparently he had never heard the name.

'Browning. . . .' He let it sink in.

'Yes, sir.'

His ignorance hurt me, but he tried to be pleasant and, after thought, welcomed me with the words, 'Glad to see you.

We can do with *any* officer just now'; which didn't seem too polite.

'Straight up the Mule Trench,' he said, 'and you'll walk on to C Company H.Q.'

'And is Colin still there?' I asked, happy to show him that I was on Christian name terms with my captain.

'Oh, yes, he's there. He's one of the immortals. Do you know, that lad's never even been wounded?'

'I know, sir. And we were in the Landing together.'

'*You* were?'

'Yes, sir.' A good moment. But I rather fancied that he thought no one with a round full face like mine could have been in the Landing.

'Weren't you killed?'

'No, sir.'

'Wounded?'

'Yes, sir. Slightly.' Another satisfying moment.

'Well, don't get killed now. We're still damned short of officers. Later perhaps.'

'Yes, sir.'

'No, but I'm glad to see you back. Very glad. Unless we're much mistaken, we're going to need very soon every damned officer and man we can find—but only the Lord knows, really. The Lord and General Liman von Sanders, our most gallant and subtle foe. We'd all give something to know what that little gentleman's got in his mind—and in his pocket. Well, we shall learn soon. Good-bye—"Browning" did you say?'

I agreed it was Browning and went out with a wound unhealed.

I hurried along that Mule Trench, eager to stage a surprise appearance before Colin. 'The Moated Grange alias C Co. H.Q.' said a notice-board outside a big dug-out in the trench; and my heart greeted these words with a quick drum-tattoo. Peeping in, I saw Colin seated at a canvas table and two other officers seated on the wooden frameworks of their wire beds. And Colin was no longer the worn, emaciated lad I had left.

He had recovered flesh in the tranquil days and was once again the slight good-looking youth I had first seen on the troopship out of Devonport. A little leaner, to be sure, and browner, after eight months of a Levantine sun.

I bent my head and stepped in. 'Good morning,' I said, and, having no original wit, added, 'Captain Dester, I presume?'

'Gerry!' Colin shouted. 'Gerry, my own heart's delight!' and at these ridiculous words there was a small leap of my heart, though they were only a jest. What a balm it was, this welcome of Colin's, and of all the smiling mess orderlies, after Captain Trevor-Brayne's bewildered stare. 'Jonty! Duke! This is the one and only Gerry Browning. How often have I told you about Gerry? And he's nice and plump again. Some hearty feeding at that hospital. Gerry, have you come to call, or are you going to stay a little?'

'I've been sent to report, sir.'

'You've been sent to report, sir. Well, that's superb. Jonty, meet Gerry. Gerry and I have bin together nah for forty year, and it don't seem a day too much. He's one of our heroes. If you're shot down in the next attack, he'll get you in. He got shot to pieces trying to get poor Cassy in. The lad simply doesn't know what fear is.'

'Stuff! And what about you? I rather thought you got me in.'

'Yes, and was I terrified all the time, and thanking God you were only ten feet away? Gerry, this is our Jonty. Jonty Stuart.'

A young fourteen-stone giant, with a baby's face, puppy-cheeked, ingenuous, and shyly smiling, stood up before me as if I were a general. He had but one star on his torn and open tunic. 'How do you do, sir?' he said.

'"Sir" be damned,' I replied, feeling extraordinarily older than he. 'We're not on parade. Which is your platoon?'

'Twelve, sir—I mean, Browning.'

'"Gerry"—call him "Gerry",' cried Colin.

'Oh, I can't do that—not just yet,' smiled the gigantic boy, and I felt a liking for him; shall we say a paternal liking.

'A fine lad, isn't he, Gerry? We thought you were a big beefy boy, but our Jonty could eat you up. And that reminds me. This yonder is the Duke, our Mess President. Duke Imley. You can see why we call him the Duke.'

To be sure, I could. He was silver-haired, forty or more, slim, and with a good nose and an expression as mature and easy as Jonty's was boyish and shy. He too had but one star, and I felt ashamed to be senior to him. I found myself staring rudely at a subaltern so old. That elegant, waving, silver hair was so unlikely in a junior sub that my eyes kept returning to it.

I now felt young and callow—though not as callow as Jonty.

'Duke's a distinguished solicitor,' said Colin, 'and what he's doing here I don't know, though he'll be useful in making our wills. He's forty-five, and lied on enlisting, saying that he was thirty-nine. They looked at him and gave him a commission almost at once, feeling ashamed not to. Duke, you must fairly get the grub in now. This Mr. Browning likes his feed. He's a hearty eater. Very hearty. Besides, you've gone down a peg. Gerry's now our second-in-command.'

'Oh, but, look here,' I began, ready to offer up my seniority on the altar of such silver-haired distinction. 'What I mean . . . I . . . if you feel . . .'

'Come and sit down,' said the Duke, perceiving what I meant. 'I'm but a babe in soldiering.' He moved along the edge of his bed. 'Sit here. We've heard a lot about you. Colin's been horribly boring, sometimes, talking about you.'

Truly I think Colin was so overjoyed to see me that he couldn't stop talking now. 'You've come at the right time, Gerry. This is a health resort now. That's why Jonty's so fat. His appetite is good. Did you see our Captain Trevor-Brayne, our new Adj? He's the real Imperial model, isn't he? "And did you once see Trevor plain, and did he stop and speak to you? And did you speak to him again?" By Bob Browning, your namesake. Yes, we've made a separate peace with the Turks. The Turks don't attack any more because they've observed that if they leave it to us to do the attacking, it always ends as a victory for them; and now we've just noticed this fact too; so we sit and wait for them; *ergo*, it's peace, perfect peace for everyone. Nation does not rise against nation, nor do we learn war any more. Which suits me.'

'Then the Germans and Austrians and Bulgars haven't come yet?'

'If they have,' said Duke Imley, 'they're keeping quiet about it.'

'Oh, Brother Hun's there all right,' said Colin, 'and probably Brother Bulgar too, but the C.-in-C. professed not to mind their coming. He said it'd make no difference because there'd be no room for them to manœuvre properly on this narrow front, and I only hope the gentleman's right.'

'There'd be bags of room behind the Front for guns and planes and reinforcements,' said Imley.

The C.-in-C. I bragged at once of having had familiar talk with the great man, and I asked Colin why he'd never told me about being invited on to his staff.

'Who the hell wants to be on the staff?' was all he replied.

'Better there than here, I suspect,' said Imley.

All this time Jonty just sat without speaking, like a boy who must be seen and not heard. When he thought we'd said something funny (which was frequent, for he was a simple and happy youth, easily amused) he smiled.

Colin changed the subject. 'Gosh, isn't it hilarious to have Gerry back? Amazing how you and I last, Gerry. Most chaps lasted only a few days, but we go on for ever. I'm immortal.' I couldn't help wondering if he'd got this word from Captain Trevor-Brayne and was displaying it as his own, unaware that I'd just heard it. 'Of course in my case it's just because I'm careful to keep out of danger, but that's never applied to you. And there you stand: still on your feet. I maintain that if we've lasted so far, we'll last till the end.'

'Yes, but what's the end going to be?'

'God knows. Duke, what's the end going to be?'

'Don't ask me.'

'Jonty?'

Jonty only grinned at the humour of anyone asking *his* opinion.

'Don't imagine I've any secret information,' said Colin, 'but I surmise—I definitely surmise—that we shall soon be advertising "Positively the Last Few Weeks".'

'You mean that the whole performance'll come off,' asked Imley.

'I do, Duke. Come off with all its principal performers and go on tour.'

'Then what about us poor supers? Do we come off too, or are we scuppered?'

Colin could only shrug.

But never mind for the present this vague foreboding. For the present let me feel how fine it was to be back with the regiment and the company. I felt as if I had been long abroad on some tedious and lonesome occupation and was now returned to home and family. C Company Headquarters, wherever it might be, had become, I perceived now as never before, another home to me after that one in the Baron's Court Road, and the Company itself was another family—nor was it the less so because two of the brothers in the house were wholly new. I likened myself to a bagatelle ball which, after being displaced from its proper hole and sent wandering and cushioning and cannoning around the green parts of the table, had now slumped happily back again into its rightful home.

The next day we went up into the Line. Standing in a fire-bay, I looked through a periscope at Achi Baba. There was the old unconquered hill, a mere squatting hump with its wide shoulders stretching across the land. One could imagine eyes in the hump looking down upon our reticulation of trenches and wire like an inert but complacent spider which had all the flies it wanted in its web.

A placid, greening parapet, it spanned the narrow land, but what, and how much, was afoot behind it?

Sometimes one of our aeroplanes sailed over it to see, but we were never told what it saw.

It was not wholly true that the war had gone into a coma here. Ever and again a machine-gun raked our parapet or a bomb came over to keep us awake and assure us that the Turk was not asleep. All day the snipers pursued their sport, and if there were no caps or heads to pot at, they practised on our steel loopholes, which they knew like old friends, despite their skirts of sacking. If they could see no one at home they knocked like this on our doors and rang the bell. German Taubes flew over the hill to consider us and, looking black against the sky, might have been vultures foretasting carrion. The guns from Asia tossed their coal-boxes over, but less to offend, we thought, than to test their ranges for the Day. Overhead, though the sky was clear and blue, we saw flocks of birds flying away; and we wondered if they'd seen sinister massings behind Achi Baba and were making good their escape.

On our part, night after night, the battalions in reserve sent their wiring parties to strengthen the wire at any weak point or to build new thick screens of it. 'Thicken the wire' seemed to be the order every night.

As for me, I made a show of the old belauded fearlessness but I knew that I was having to learn courage again from the beginning. I would force myself to keep my head up as I walked the trenches before the eyes of Duke and Jonty and the men; I declined to duck it at the wasp-sizz of a bullet, though my heart dropped, my stomach sickened, and my head split for a second and healed again. I stood on the fire-step and took glances over the parapet—since death was better than loss of a fine fame. At night I went out and stood in the open, watching the work done on the wire, even when no such risk was demanded of me.

Could it be that the birds, with instincts unknown to us, had apprehended what was coming upon the Peninsula? It came before November closed.

C Company were in the trenches to receive it. The wind, blowing for a change from the sea behind us, brought up thunder-clouds and, spreading them over us, darkened the whole land. Their sudden stormburst was as loud as any bombardment. For twenty-four hours the rain sheeted down and did not stop. Such a hurricane wind and such cataracting rain seemed less a natural phenomenon than an Act of God. The water flooded the fire-bays; we stood on the fire-steps, and it reached our knees. No one minded if his head showed above the trench because the Turks opposite were climbing on to their parapets. Some were standing in the open. Since our trenches were down the slope, the flood-water from Achi Baba piled up against our parapets, broke them at last, and flooded the trenches to the brim, washing away the parados. When the torrent rushed into the trench where Duke Imley was, he leapt on to the fire-step, studied the travelling waters for a while, and then, saying, 'The roaring torrent deep is and wide. Excelsior,' toiled upward on to the parapet above. Jonty followed him, saying it was all rather fun. Soon all of us stood in No-Man's-Land together with the Turks, shivering in waterlogged overcoats, with groundsheets over our heads and hands deep in sodden pockets.

Deliberately Colin stood between his men and the Turks with a wet hand on a dripping revolver, but the Turks only grinned, waved hands in deprecation, and shouted 'War mafeesh. Germany ver' bad'. Colin, seeing their friendliness, raised a hand in acknowledgment, and thrust the revolver back in its holster; which action they approved with shouts of 'Goot. Ver' goot. German bad'.

Headquarters might have issued what orders they liked; the Government, warm in Whitehall, might be at work on its strategies; but our two front lines, from sea to sea, had made for the present their peace. In any case Headquarters on the beaches were not looking our way but at a tempestuous sea which was splintering their piers into driftwood and shouldering every vessel ashore. Even a destroyer, beaten by such a sea was cast aground. A submarine sank.

When the rain for a dozen hours had deluged down on this long ribbon of peace and sodden friends, Colin sent me and two men to the Dump in the Gully to get more groundsheets and, if possible, rum. I struggled there across the open, buffeted by wind and rain but untroubled by a single bullet and, reaching the Gully's cliff-wall, I saw the thick, deep, yellow water churning down it like a Severn bore. On its tide travelled boxes, cases, dead animals, and, yes, a drowned Turk, swinging in the torrent as he came. I watched him go sweeping and swaying by, till he was out of sight round a cape.

'We've had several of them stiffs along,' said a man by a bivouac beneath me, with wet blankets over and about him like a Bedouin's robes. 'They try to come ashore but the boys push 'em back so that they can land in someone else's parish.'

'At that rate they'll land in the sea,' said I. 'At Gully Beach.'

'I rather fancy that's the idea,' the man submitted.

My men and I were able to stagger back with some groundsheets, but no rum, because the dump-wallahs had been far too busy salving stores from the flood. Somewhere in our flooded dug-out there were bottles of whisky, and Colin rummaged in the deep water for them. He salvaged two, and he, Jonty, and I gave a sip here and there to men who were suffering the most. All were in a bad way, but I should estimate that some fifty per cent of them, though they had never heard of Sir Philip Sidney, said, 'Never mind me, sir. Give it 'im. I can stick it out.'

This deluge and hurricane were only a first chapter. The wind swung round into the north as into a cold chamber and became the coldest air I have ever lived in. It was now our old enemy the north-easter and it lanced through our clothes as with spears of ice. Instead of chastising us with rods of rain it stoned us with icy pellets of snow. Instead of water against the parapets it piled up snow, while its breath changed the water in trench or dug-out or men's clothes into ice. Soon the whole Peninsula before us was clothed in a wonderful white innocence from the crown of Achi Baba to the two embracing seas. Except where this soft white vesture was gashed by the opposing trenches or punctuated by scrub or skeleton trees, it was flawless; no shell-holes marred it nor rifle-bullets pocked it, for not a gun was firing in the silence.

Men sat on fire-steps, shoulders tight against shoulders to share their bodily warmth, but, even so, each shivered between his friends. Since officers could not well do this, they stood huddling up their shoulders and beating their arms across their breasts, cabman-wise. Colin got out of his frozen overcoat, though it was hard as wood, and stood it up stiff and erect on our broken parapet, supporting it from behind with a rifle. On the snow-white parapet it looked like a headless British soldier, and the Turks on the opposite parapet laughed and called, 'English goot. German ver' bad.'

But it was an ill time for jesting. Going along the trenches next morning, we found one sentry still standing on his fire-step but leaning forward against the trench, with one hand frozen to the butt of his rifle and the other to its muzzle. He was dead. Others of the men were frost-bitten and suffering bitterly. One was gibbering mad.

Enough. Enough to report that men to the number of fifteen hundred limped and hobbled and slid, or were carried on stretchers, ambulances, or pick-a-back, down every white gully, fissure, cleft, and trench to be got off the Peninsula—refugees staggering, stumbling, shuffling off Gallipoli. And this was only Helles. The total casualties in this battle against divine artillery were ten thousand, with three hundred drowned.

And then a Monday morning, November 29th of blessed memory to us all, broke upon a white world, sunny and warm. Under the sun the fields of snow lay in patches of bleached gold and pale blue-greys. The sun brightened; the shadows on the snow turned into dove-blues and mauves; the first drainings of the thaw came down the slopes in strings of sparkling water more brilliant than diamond-cut glass. But if there seemed a new mischief in the sun's eye, and a laughter in the sparkling snow, well, this cynical amusement was nothing unacceptable to us, for, we soon perceived that, even as the Great Fire of London smoked out the Great Plague, so its opposite, the Great White Blizzard on Gallipoli had destroyed the last of our manifold plagues. No more flies, no more dust, no more dysentery; only fine weather and warm. And if we had suffered ten thousand casualties, the Turks, less well clothed, less accustomed to cold, had suffered more. The blizzard had frozen the hearts out of them. Thus December came and stood upon the Peninsula with a benign smile, distributing sunlight and stillness and a clean healing air.

CHAPTER FIVE

LIKE the battle for Sari Bair this battle with the elements was decisive. On the Peninsula and in the islands we knew nothing, but far away in a London street, somewhere between Westminster and Charing Cross, the decision was made. The orders came thence that plans were to be prepared for an attempt to get the armies off the Peninsula. To get some hundred thousand men and several hundred guns down to harbourless beaches, with an unbeaten enemy behind and a moody sea in front—it looked to be as dread an operation as the first invasion of those beaches from the edges of the sea and beneath the eyes of an army entrenched.

That it was to be attempted we couldn't believe, though rumour came running into every dug-out with talk of hospital ships lying empty, and the greatest Cunarders and White Star liners waiting at anchor, and an assembling everywhere of small boats that were to snatch from the beaches as many as possible of the living and the wounded, leaving the dead where they lay.

Of casualties we had none till Sunday, December 19th, when our line at Helles launched a violent attack once again. Our Koslis were not in that attack; we stood behind it, amazed and guessing. Our guess was that we, once again, were containing the Turks at Helles while something happened at Suvla, and how right our guess was the next day showed.

It was a bright clean morning, cold beneath a December sun, but pleasant. I was standing with Colin in a support trench outside a dressing-station, talking to the M.O. A battalion runner came down the trench slope and, with an abbreviated salute and the words, 'C.O. sent me round with this, sir,' handed Colin a pink telegraph form.

Colin took it, read it, and exclaimed, 'Christ!' And then 'Oh *no*!'

I had been looking at the message over his shoulder, and I too said, 'Oh *no*!' in protest against incredible news. I turned to see what the M.O. thought, but he had gone back into his dressing-station, not imagining that an order to a combatant officer had any interest for him.

The telegram stated that the whole army at Suvla and Anzac had been evacuated without casualties.

'Oh *God*!' I lamented, not thinking of our danger on Helles, but of something less personal. I was thinking: My country shamed. That great world champion felled. Knocked out. I was feeling an uprush of love for my country in this bitter shaming, as for a sick mother. For a moment, a brief moment, I felt eager, angrily eager, to fight for her anew . . . die for her if that would win her fame again. I thought of the C.-in-C. and his statement that an evacuation was 'unthinkable'; and, jealous for him, angry for him, I was ready to fight furiously on Helles, offering myself, if necessary, as an oblation on that poor broken altar, in honour of his abandoned cause.

Whether Colin was thinking bitterly or sadly, I don't know. Still holding that loaded telegram, he was saying, 'How the hell . . . It's never been heard of. How can they have brought off eighty or ninety thousand men without a single casualty? People don't do such things.'

I turned my eyes in the direction of Achi Baba. 'Not twice,' I said.

He too looked in that direction. Down in this deep trench we could not see that long-shouldered hump, but it was there, Still there. A defensive rampart for many months, but what now? A sally-port for thousands of men?

'O.K., Harry,' he said to the runner, returning the telegram. 'Very interesting.'

The runner went, and Colin stayed silent. I suspected from this silence that he, like me, was feeling the sudden loneliness. Some eighty thousand of our friends had gone. We were alone on Helles.

Still looking towards Achi Baba, he said, 'This'll double their army there. At this very moment all their hordes from Suvla are probably marching south to deal with us. Bringing their guns behind them.'

'How many are they, d'you suppose?'

'Only about a hundred and twenty thousand.'

'No! Nothing like as many as that?'

He shrugged as one who knew no certain truth but could deal in probable estimates. 'They had twenty divisions at Suvla.'

Twenty divisions. Seeking comfort, I asked, 'Isn't there anything in what the C.-in-C. said about there being no room to deploy them properly on this narrow strip of land?'

'More in what the old Duke said about there being heaps of room for immediate reinforcements in all the nice unspoiled vales and gardens behind Achi Baba. Heaps of room for guns. German guns. With German shells in 'em that really go where they're supposed to go, and go off properly when they get there.'

'Oh, well . . .' I said, since there was nothing else to say.

That was December 20th. Not a doubt in the next days that the Turk's C.-in-C. had marched his Suvla armies south. From hump and shoulders of Achi Baba the new guns spoke with quick little serpent-tongues of flame. They searched our front line from flank to flank and our retreat lines from trenches to beaches. It was a spendthrift, gay disbursal from a wealth of shells. Those licks of flame, paled by the satirical winter sunlight but sharply bright under the night sky, seemed like signals telling the doom of Helles. The might, inexhaustible, of the Central Empires, was there in front of us; the sea, untrustworthy and deep, behind. Our friends were gone, and their guns gone with them. We felt like a lost people on a Limbo.

Limbo, Colin said, was the right word, because Limbo was an abode on the borders of Hell, designed for those to whom, though the fault was not theirs, the benefits of redemption could not apply. And beneath December's pale moonshine our headland, cooped in the arms of the sea, looked like a place for ghosts. Well it might: it was already a graveyard and a charnel area for men's bones. You came upon them, sooner or later, wherever you walked. White, disconnected, lonely bones.

A Special Order of the Day told us that we were to 'Have the honour of holding Helles for the Empire'.

So? But—how far was this a lie to deceive the Turks? Why this slow thinning of our units? Why did those who left the Peninsula for one reason or another never return? Why this nonsense of boats full of men leaving the beaches but, should an enemy plane appear overhead, instantly turning round and coming back towards them? Why came the order that no tents or huts were to be taken down, even though empty? Why were the Indians told to drive their mule gharries up and down all day, making as much noise and raising as much dust as possible beneath the spying planes? Great the skill with which these smiling muleteers converted the resentments of their touchy beasts into clouds of dust and many excellent bangs. Why this lighting of fires at the usual meal-times in places where no one was now cooking? Why this movement of guns from here to there, to fire and come back again and fire again from somewhere else?

The more our companions left without returning, the lonelier we felt; but not unhappy; laughing, rather, in a kind of dull fatalism. Suspense was no longer any part of our daily thoughts: we seemed to dwell like good friends together in some place on the other side of Suspense. Soon we heard that all the French had gone; and we were but four British divisions facing Achi Baba; four lost tribes. Colin would look at our narrow bridge-like headland and quote, 'Life is a bridge; pass over it, but build no house there.' I, wandering along the nullahs or over the plateau and thinking apathetically that I might soon be dead, would see in imagination a goatherd many years hence leading his goats through the scrub, or perhaps a peasant driving his ox-drawn plough through the grey unfriendly soil, and neither of them knowing or caring that I had once been here.

. . . . .

'All officers to C.O. at once.' On the second day of January (or was it New Year's Day? It is all so far away now that I cannot feel sure) the runner gave Colin this message.

'Right-ho, Dicky,' he said, and to us standing by: 'Now we shall know something.'

Battalion Headquarters, in the Eastern Mule Trench, was a fine and roomy dug-out because it had once been a Brigade Headquarters. It had a roof of corrugated iron covered with sandbags and, positively, a front wall of mortared stones. Ducking under the entrance, we went down several stone steps to its floor.

The Colonel sat sideways at a long table awaiting us with his legs crossed. He was in his working dress: the high grey sweater and high Russian boots; but the sweater was now rotted in places and the boots mapped with scratches and gougings from the wire. Nevertheless his batman had done all things possible with them, even, it was said, giving them a touch or two of urine along with the polish, and they shone.

The Adjutant, Captain Trevor-Brayne, sat on his left, and he too shone—from everywhere, from badges of rank, tunic buttons, and Sam Browne belt. Whether his batman applied the same anointing to his belt and boots we didn't know.

'Well, gentlemen. . . .' The Colonel glanced round at us. 'Are we all here? Sit down. There are some cigarettes there.'

Colin sat on the Colonel's right, I beside Colin, and Jonty and the Duke on the opposite side of the table, with officers of other companies.

The Colonel, since this in its way was a parade, now put his legs beneath the table. He drew a paper towards him from before the Adjutant. He lit one of his tiny cheroots, studied the paper again, and, raising his eyes from it, said, 'Gentlemen, we are going.'

What else could there be but silence?

Duke Imley, one of the most junior officers present, was yet the oldest. Almost a contemporary of the Colonel's, he had ease in his presence. Unlike the rest of us. Thinking it wise to break the silence, he asked, 'You mean, from the Peninsula?' He even, on opening the discussion, forgot the 'sir'.

The Colonel looked at him. Colonel Harby didn't wear glasses, but the angle of his head and eyes now was exactly that of a man looking over his spectacles. It was not an angry look; I felt that he was considering the Duke's silver hair and wondering about these New Armies which flung up junior subalterns of forty-five, and others like Cass who withdrew too soon, and fellahs like Dester who sat in their trenches reading Greek.

'Yes, Imley. Of course. From the Peninsula. And in a few days' time. In what order we shall go I have not yet heard.'

Silence from us all. Now that the order to go was given us I do not know if we were glad or sad, or both at the same time. To leave this curst but familiar land—it was like the moment when a man, who has dreamed of leaving his wife, must take the final step and realizes that if it's hard to live with the woman it'll be hard also to live without her. We had some sort of love for the old ill-tempered place—once (before our marriage to it) the most wonderful place on earth.

'We may not be the last to go,' pursued the Colonel. 'There are some forty thousand men to be got away and over a hundred guns.' With a small lift of his head he announced, as if it were simply an item *de fide* of his creed, 'We never abandon guns.'

'When do you *think* we shall go, sir?' asked the Duke, and I was astonished at his irreverence.

Once Evverson's irreverence had worried me, but the Duke's was different. It was not as a junior subaltern that he talked with Colonel Harby, but as a social equal. Indeed, with his greater height, his fine nose and silver hair, he might have been the social superior of our little colonel. I began to feel that the Colonel might at any moment be asking him for his advice. Which would surely be uncomfortable for us all. I fancied that Captain Trevor-Brayne, the Adjutant, and a regular of regulars, was as surprised as I at Imley's ease, and as dubious about it.

'When?' The Colonel lifted helpless shoulders and displayed an empty palm. 'I haven't the faintest idea, Imley, except that it'll be soon. Naturally I've asked that we may be among the last, as I know you would all have wished me to do. But there's a lot of competition for this place.'

I glanced at the officers along the table and wondered how many would really have wished him to do this; how many were relieved that there was some competition. I don't think he had misinterpreted the wishes of some of us, because, whatever fears and doubts might now be seated in my heart, the hope leapt up that we might be among the winners of this competition.

'Dammit, we were among the first ashore,' said the Colonel, 'and I take it that if there's to be a last stand, we have a strong claim to share in it. I think so, don't you?'

'Yes, sir,' said Colin, the senior company commander; others murmured their 'Yes, sir'.

'Now as to the methods,' he said, taking the cheroot from his lips (it had gone out) and looking down at the paper. 'There are to be silent periods in the trenches—absolutely silent—every night. For about two hours at first but increasing steadily. This is to train the Turks for the silence there'll be after we've all gone down to the beaches. Dammit, we shouldn't like his rest to be disturbed by doubts and suspicions just then, ha, ha. Ha, ha, ha.'

We laughed too—most of us in duty, but Jonty loudly. He had the same simple humour as the Colonel. The Colonel looked towards him, and was pleased.

'These silent periods will be spaced about between dark and dawn until the night before the end, when there'll be one from eight o'clock till three. There's to be no nonsense about this. Not a sound, *if* you please. The men's boots are to be wrapped in sacking or rags, and where the trench floor is hard, either soften it up with your picks or—if it's rock or planking—lay down blankets. No talking whatever among the men, and you, please, will speak only in whispers. No smoking or light of any kind. And for God's sake tell the men not to rattle the bolts of their rifles.'

The Duke spoke again. 'Are the men to know what it's all about, sir?'

'Yes. Yes, you can tell 'em now.' He relit the cheroot.

'But, sir, if the Turks get suspicious about the silence and come over to see what we——'

'Then you'll give them all you've got straight in their faces. That'll "learn" 'em not to come over when we're not there, ha, ha. Ha, ha, ha.'

The Colonel looked towards Jonty, where a laughing response seemed most likely. This time, however, Jonty only smiled most amiably.

The Duke waited for the Colonel's eyes to come back to him; then submitted, 'But, excuse me, sir, our line on the map is about four miles from W Beach——'

'We go from V Beach,' said the Colonel, a correction which didn't answer this objection at all, since the beaches were side by side.

'Yes, sir; four miles, and if the men are in full equipment——'

'—and carrying ammunition boxes,' added the Colonel, as if to make it worse. 'All the ammo is to be brought down.'

'Precisely, sir, and it'll take two hours at least to get to the beach; three if it's raining and the trenches are gluey.'

'Four,' Colin improved.

The Duke nodded agreement. 'Quite. So what, sir, if it's pouring with rain, and there's a heavy sea?'

'I don't know,' said the Colonel. 'The Padre's praying for fine weather.'

'May he keep at it,' Colin whispered, and someone else muttered, 'I'm joining in with him.'

'But, sir,' persisted the Duke, and I gasped at his impudence. The man was cross-examining the Colonel as if he were the defendant in a court of law. All the officers were watching and listening, and one part of me, even if worried, felt proud of Imley, our solicitor. C Company *should* take the lead like this. I think Colin was proud of him too. 'If the Turks guess and come over in strength, aren't we certain to be overwhelmed? The rear parties, at any rate?'

'The sappers will pull barricades of wire into the trenches behind us.'

'But there's the open,' submitted this socially-gifted and fearless man.

'The sappers are mining the whole width of the Peninsula, and as we go down, they'll join up the trip-wires behind us.'

'Glad o' that,' murmured a voice, and another whispered, 'God bless 'em.'

'Yes,' said the Colonel, who'd heard. 'That should make the Turk think.'

'But the rear-guard, sir?' continued the Duke. 'What about the rear-guard?'

'You said someone would be overwhelmed,' the Colonel reminded him, as if this were the price they'd agreed upon together. He had probably forgotten the Duke's junior rank and was enjoying this discussion with an intelligent man. 'To be frank with you all, it may be that we shall have to turn round and fight; if so I take it that we shall—well, fight, and, as they say, sell our lives dearly.' Not wishing this to dishearten anyone, he added, 'But we hope it won't come to that. They got 'em all away at Suvla—how the hell, no one knows. Still, they did it.'

The Duke nodded. He allowed that his colonel was right! But in this same moment he seemed to awake to the fact that this was not a clubroom argument between elegant silver hair and sparse grey hair, but a subaltern disputing the odds with his commander. And probably conduct prejudicial to good order and discipline. So he said no more, but all of us *felt* his unspoken comment, 'The Turks are warned now, sir.'

'All that Imley says is right,' said the Colonel (and I was proud again), 'and it gives point to the only thing I can say.' He raised a serious finger to say it. 'Repair the wire. Repair it just as fast as they break it down, and each time, if possible, leave it even better than it was before—for God's sake. Any further questions?'

'No, sir. No, sir.' The murmur went round.

'Very good, gentlemen. One other thing only: try to tell

the men that we haven't altogether failed. Tell those who were in the Landing that they took part in one of the greatest battles of the world that'll live in memory for all time. Tell the others that all our reports show that our long fight here had utterly exhausted the old Turk. It's drawn all his men here—half a million of 'em—so that his fields are untilled and his industry and trade in ruins. We've broken his arm here—before we go. Tell 'em that. They're good fellahs and should know it. And tell 'em that we've defended Egypt and the Suez Canal and the Persian Gulf and the Russian front *here*, on his own ground——'

'At the price of two hundred thousand men,' I heard Colin whisper.

'As the C.-in-C. put it, and the fellah was'—he coughed and corrected himself—'the C.-in-C. was a bit of a poet, you know; and he put it'—the Colonel halted as if he, a soldier, was not quite happy about speaking poetical stuff to his troops—'he said, 'We've kept a dagger over the Turk's heart—only a little way in, but we've bled him to death there.' Quite a good way of putting it, really,' he apologized. Surprising that poetical stuff should express things as well as that! 'It'll be months before the old Turk can stage any sort of fight again. But he's a great fighter at his best, as we've all had reason to know, and it may be we shall meet him again at Suez or on the Tigris or somewhere. If so, I have no doubt that we shall be pleased to resume the battle. I think that is all, gentlemen.'

CHAPTER SIX

SINCE I was now allowed, indeed ordered, to tell the men, I went to this task with all the enthusiasm of a young man in possession of notable news. Some received the news with unashamed delight; most met it with shrugs and silence. In those silences I guessed there was some dismay mingled with their wonder how the thing could be done and their nervousness lest they should be among those who, all too often, got killed in the last hours before a war ended. Though none of them ever spoke their patriotism aloud, preferring the sound of sedition, it was clear to me that they did not bear easily the thought that their country had taken the count and must go beaten from the ring.

None of us had much interest in the world beyond our slim headland: our horizon was the sea. Death might be close to us, but I dare say that most, like me, shielded themselves from its neighbourhood and its breath by the facile thought, 'Not me. I shall be all right. Not me.' When reason dismissed this comfort, I felt only a strange tranquillity in the knowledge that my time *might* be short, and that I might never see the Baron's Court Road and my mother again. It merely seemed strange, even interesting, that my life might be finished already, with all its sins and doubts and pains.

The next few days taught us some of the tricks that had achieved the bloodless evacuation of Suvla. Along the front line rifles were fixed on brackets with two tins or buckets attached to them. The upper tin had a hole in its bottom and, when the hour came, it would be filled with sand or water that would drip into the lower one. The lower one, when heavy enough, would fall, pulling a string attached to the trigger and so firing the rifle though no one was near it. Or candles were used to keep rifles and Very pistols firing long after the trenches were empty. String with a weight at one end and the trigger at the other was tied round the candle, so that when the flame burned down to the string, the weight would drop and rifle or pistol fire. My men spent absorbed, even delighted, hours making these amusing appliances. One of the craftiest was a string of cartridge clips attached to a candle, with a small night-watchman's brazier at a little distance away. On the flame's burning of the string the cartridge clips would shoot down a groove into the fire and all their cartridges go off like jumping crackers on Guy Fawkes night. They would not injure any Turks, but they would maintain the music of a machine-gun while its usual soloist was marching down to a beach.

The enemy's planes were numerous now, and up and watching us keenly; we were ordered to fire at, but not hit, them, so that they might see boats loaded with men coming towards the beaches. Every man was to fire, and fire rapidly, so as to give the impression of large numbers ashore, and of machine-guns firing where no machine-guns were. I enjoyed much sport firing at speed all round these visitors. So did my men. The Indians, on word of them, rushed to their gharries and with grins drove them inwards, before unloading beneath these enemy eyes all manner of empty boxes and tins.

We kept the trenches noisy in the normal periods, to emphasize the silence of the silent ones. I shall never forget these silences during our last days. I would walk along my sector, my boots thickly wrapped in sacking. The sentries in each bay, and the men sitting on its fire-step, were motionless, soundless ghosts. If one made a creak, I did not say 'Hush!' but lifted a warning finger after a frightened frown, for my heart had jumped. Ghostly steps approaching from behind a traverse set the heart palpitating again. 'Turks?' But probably it was only Colin and the S.M. drifting around, or a pale-faced messenger, but whoever it was, they passed, grey phantoms, speechless and soundless. A silence so total was a host for breeding these quick, unjustified fears. At these whispers of footfalls beyond a traverse I was a small boy again in that far-off Baron's

Court house lifting an ear above my bedclothes to make sure it wasn't 'robbers' creeping along the passage to my door.

Because of our silence every sound in No-Man's-Land was sharply audible: ration tins shaking on the wire; a breeze playing a tune along its strands; a small animal scurrying from crater to shell-hole. And not in No-Man's-Land only: sometimes we heard the night sounds in the Turkish trenches: their footsteps; their rifle-bolts; some of them singing—perhaps a chant to Allah but more likely a bawdy rhyme. And behind the Turkish trenches—listen! Sinister sounds that might mean anything. Bullock wagons crunching and camel teams padding. Bringing what? Gun limbers drawing what new guns? Orders spoken. To what end?

There was never such a time for deep meditation. Walking along the silent trenches during my turn of duty with no one to stay the plunge of my thought, I would tell myself, 'Think sensibly. Death within the next hundred hours is rather more likely than not, so am I glad that I came back? Yes. Yes, I am glad. I am still afraid of pain, horribly afraid, but I'm glad I did what seemed unselfish even though I was helped to do it by vanity and by my longing to be with Colin again.' The silence had hours to run, and I walked on, head bent, whenever possible, to think. 'This is another period for self-dedication if only I can bring it off. I'll try to bring it off as I did in the boat; I *will* bring it off'; whereupon I felt a secret deep happiness below my fear. Perhaps I would look over the parados at the ravaged plateau behind us, with its few tormented trees yet standing and its white hospital tents on the distant hills above the beaches and I would think of it as the garden provided from on High for my self-abandonment. Surely it could be counted good to die in a moment when one was shriven by self-offering and worthy of the Presence. To be assumed into that Presence (if such there were) before one could backslide again. 'Just remember Doughty Wylie,' the C.-in-C. had said. 'It must be quite good to die when you're standing on the summit of yourself.' Oh God, if Thou wilt, help me to get a little nearer to the summit. . . .

These were one young man's thoughts in those famous silences. I wondered if Colin's were similar but knew he would never speak of them. On the fifth day of January we learned that our Koslis would leave on Saturday the 8th, the last day, but would not be the last of all; nor would any of us be part of the rear-guard of honour. This rear-guard was to be sixty men from each of the four divisions left on the Peninsula; two hundred and forty men, and the volunteers for these places had been numbered in thousands. So there must have been others with thoughts like mine in the silences, and I mused how in all men, even the coarsest, a frustrated saint lies sleeping. No doubt some of them were relieved as well as disappointed that they were not among the chosen. I think I was, though ashamed to be. For Colin and I had offered; and the Duke too, and Jonty with his biggest grin. 'It'd be fun,' Jonty had said, though his voice tripped once, hinting at an unstable heart.

In the evening of that day Colin did say to me all that he could bring himself to say. I had felt for some time in our company dug-out that he wanted to speak to me alone; and now he watched the Duke and Jonty go out to their men—he waited till they were far up the trench—and then spoke.

'Well . . . next Saturday night it is . . . if we live to see it. The old Turk'll attack before then for a certainty. Between you and me we're down to twenty thousand men and a few worn-out guns, while he's got about a hundred thousand chaps and heaps of new artillery. He'd be a pretty poor ass if he didn't come. It's the only gentlemanly thing to do.'

Ever a speaker of pleasant wishes rather than hard sense, I rejoined: 'But they say the old Blizzard froze all the heart out of him.'

'That was weeks ago, Gerry. He has crowds of new men now. I say he'll come at any moment. If not tomorrow or Friday, then on Saturday just before we go—which would be the worst time of all. Yes, quite likely it'll be Saturday. Johnny was always a sportsman, and he knows we like a game on a Saturday.'

'On their home ground,' I said, pleased to fill out the metaphor.

'Why, sure. We're certainly the visiting team. Yes, it could well be that they'll kick off on Saturday, just when we've got everything else to do.'

'And if they do——'

'If they do, it'll be a coarse business.'

'I suppose it will.'

'Bound to be. Look, Gerry, if by any chance I'm *for* it, and you get away, I'd like you, when you get home, to look up Olwen and give her my love. Make it easy for her. I'd like you to tell her that I tried to do my best. She knows all about you from my letters and always says you sound nice. Actually she says "sweet", which is pretty silly, you must admit. But she'll make a devil of a fuss of you. Olwen's that kind of girl. And perhaps you'd say something of the same sort to the old man too—my father, I mean. It's the sort of thing the old boy'd like to hear. He'd give you a tremendous welcome at Ivry.'

All these words had flung me into a slough of sadness. I had to struggle out of the slough by saying, though I knew the wish was father to the comfortable assertion, 'It's odds on that nothing's going to happen to you, or to any of us.'

'My God, the odds are the other way round. I should say it's a thousand to one that we shan't all get off—if any of us do.' Then, since a commander must not create despondency, he quickly changed key. 'But it may be all right. You never know. And Gerry, if by any chance I should be the lucky one, I'll do the same for you and your people.' He said it easily, as was only right, but I could see that, with all his real affection, he would not suffer as much for me as I for him.

'Thanks,' I said.

'Not at all,' he laughed, and tore a sheet from his field message book which lay on the table. 'What the hell's your address?' He poised a pencil over the sheet.

'Oh? My address?' I saw his Castle Ivry and felt ashamed of a little grey house in Baron's Court Road. Quickly I cast this shameful feeling away and answered, '59 Baron's Court Road. Do you know Baron's Court?'

'Afraid I don't. Sounds respectable.'

'Well, do you know Earl's Court?'

'Indeed I do. Spent many a wild night there.'

'Baron's Court is two stations further on, and as its name suggests, it's two grades lower down.'

'I'll find it, old boy. Don't worry.'

'Thanks,' I said again, with a laugh, though my heart for a moment fell as deep as I could wish, because he had said the words so easily. I said no more but remembered some lines he had once spoken, laughingly, about his love for Olwen, 'His folly has not fellow Beneath the blue of day That gives to man or woman His heart and soul away.'

Then it was January 6th and in some sixty hour's time, in the darkness of Saturday the 8th, we would be creeping down the Krithia Road towards Sedd-el-Bahr and V Beach (the Turk permitting). With luck we should be taken off V Beach that night. With more luck the last men, rear-guard and all, would come on to the sea in the small hours of Sunday the 9th, and Gallipoli would be history.

The Krithia Road was no more than a cart track running between the ever-uncaptured village of Krithia and the little ruined town of Sedd-el-Bahr above V Beach. For most of its way it was called the Krithia Road, but a mile or so from Sedd-el-Bahr it became the Sedd-el-Bahr Road. Whether our swaddled boots would ever disturb the dust of the Sedd-el-Bahr Road we took leave to doubt.

Colin spoke not another word to me or to anyone about his anxieties, but it was plain that with every hour his suspense increased. He could not but be anxious, like all of us, about himself, but in the main it was his responsibility for his men that was lying heavy on his thought. As a young show-jumper on a fine-mettled horse longs to do a 'clear round', as an artist strives for a composition without blemish, so Colin was living with the fixed hope of getting all his company off without loss.

He was for ever getting on to the fire-step and looking at the wire.

That evening the Turks, seeming apprehensive too, loosed a bombardment on our front that might mean anything. When it ceased and nothing followed but the silent dark, Colin leapt on to the fire-step again. He jumped down from it, two feet together like a schoolboy, and brusquely ordered me to find fatigue parties 'for a whole night's work on the wire'. During the night I noticed that he hardly slept at all. He tossed, and more than once rose from his chicken-wire bed to go and look at the working parties and across at the Turks.

January 7th came up out of Asia and hung bright over Gallipoli. It was known as 'Y Day' because tomorrow, the 8th, was 'Z Day' and closed the alphabet of Gallipoli.

'One day more,' said Colin, looking up at the friendly sky as we walked to a fire-trench. 'Is the weather really going to play fair? There's a wee bit of wind,' he said, grimacing at me. 'On the whole I'm glad we can't see the sea from here.' Then he gazed through a periscope at the Turks' black sandbags wandering west and east under the softly wintered sunlight and across the melancholy dust. 'Surely,' he said, 'they'll come today.'

But all the morning they remained quiescent, and we were able to make preparations for our departure in the dark tomorrow.

At midday the thing happened. The Turks opened a bombardment heavier than any we'd known. They had the guns now. All afternoon it went on, and our Line stood alert from Fusilier Bluff on the Aegean to the brinks of Kereves Dere on the Dardanelles. Fingers at triggers, it waited for the guns to stop and the enemy to come. The old Eski Line behind us was manned lest they went over us and through. These were hours as anxious as when we lay under the sandbank eight months before. We hardly believed we could hold them, for we had now only about fourteen thousand rifles available, and they—what? Probably a hundred thousand. Surely they would come, wave after wave.

'We've *got* to hold 'em,' said Colin to the men in every bay. 'Fight as you've never fought before, boys. Remember it's a fight for the chance to go home. We've just *got* to hold Johnny this time, blast his soul.' He walked up and down our sector throughout the bombardment, with his revolver holster open, his fingers feeling the pistol butt, and his teeth set. Often he peeped to learn the state of the wire and bit his lip to see it being battered down.

I think it was about three-thirty when the bombardment stopped and the Turkish bayonets sprang above their parapets, a long irregular uprush of silvery shining blades. Behind them came the Turks bellowing 'Allah! Allah!' They had a hundred yards to cross and Colin leapt on to a parados where most of his men could see him and shouted, 'Rapidest fire ever. If ever you've learned rapid fire, show 'em what you can do. Give it 'em all.'

I yelled, 'Come down, Colin! Come down! Get down!' but, this being a bayonet, not a bullet, attack, he stayed there for several seconds, shouting, 'Give 'em all you've got. Faster. Faster. If you love your Mums and want to see 'em again, fire, fire.' Then came down with a brief grin.

Did they respond? I have never seen such a fire from machine-gun and rifle. It swept that hundred yards like a storm-driven hail. I heard one of the men say, 'There's no one like our Collie,' but the real storm behind the hail was their passionate need to guard tomorrow. All that Colin had done was to cheer and encourage the storm. To our joy and excitement some naval guns from the Aegean sent over a grand contribution. Monitors, we imagined. But the Navy was there, as it had been at the beginning, and as it had striven to be all through. The same yesterday, today, and for ever.

'Keep it up! Keep it up!' yelled Colin, running along the trench. 'More. More.'

Astounding: the Turks wavered. Their officers, before being shot, were trying to urge them on with threats and blows, but the men hesitated and, halting, were shot down too. 'Keep it up! Keep it up!' The more they fell, the more their mates flung themselves on their faces, sick of the war, and were shot—riddled—where they lay. 'Keep it up! Keep it up! Full speed ahead.' Colin was on the top of high spirits. 'Fire, fire. Think of your Mums and fire. Fire, fire. Kill 'em. There's nothing else for it, poor devils. Go on. That's the game. Who's for 'ome? Who's for home and beauty, boys? Good old Sussex. Sussex by the sea. Remember the Downs and the Weald? What's wrong with seeing them again?'

The attack melted away before our eyes. So it did before our whole line that day. Every other sector, it seemed, had fought with the same desperation to guard their hopes of tomorrow. Such Turks as survived scuttled back like hares to their holes. We stood waiting for a second wave but it never came. The Turkish Line went silent. Dusk advanced over that long stretch of martyred soil between our wire and theirs, gradually veiling from our eyes those Turkish corpses that lay like boulders on the dust everywhere.

Before the evening was much older the Colonel came to congratulate us and told us that the British casualties along our whole width of front were no more than about fifty killed and a hundred wounded.

'Our only casualty is the wire,' Colin told him, 'and luckily that can be healed at once. As soon as it's dark, sir, we'll do some good surgical work on it and make it a better man than it was before. Man enough for anything.'

'That's right,' he said. 'Can't be too careful, but I've never been so optimistic, Dester. After that costly fiasco I think they'll wait before they come again. They must think that we're very much stronger than we are. And if they wait only thirty hours they'll wait too long. Well done, all of you. I'll just go along the trenches and say a well-done to all the men. Grand fellahs, you know; they really are. *What* a show they put up! Should think you're proud of 'em.'

'They want to live for tomorrow, sir,' said Colin.

And the evening and the morning were the last day but one.

CHAPTER SEVEN

My three hours of duty were finished, Jonty Stuart had relieved me in the trenches, and I could rest till stand-to at dawn. I came into the dug-out and saw Colin lying on his bed in breeches, cardigan, and unlaced boots. His tunic and revolver were on a box beside him. I hoped he was sleeping at last. He had been out with the wiring parties for much of the night, and they had now returned without loss, the Turk seeming subdued after his treatment in the day gone by.

But though I tiptoed in, he opened his eyes. 'One more night, Gerry,' he said, as I too removed coat and revolver. 'This time tomorrow we should have shoved off from the shore.'

'It's already tomorrow.'

'So it is. What's the time now?'

'Nearly three o'clock.'

'That all? Still, it's Saturday now. *Der Tag*, as Brother Hun says. Though I shall be quite sorry to leave the old place. I felt sad walking along the trenches with the S.M. They're beautiful trenches now, and it seems such a pity to leave them.'

'I am reconciled to it.'

'Wonder who'll be rooting about in this dug-out tomorrow. Some smelly old Turk. He'll be sitting on this bed. I hope we did that wire all right.'

'Of course you did.'

'Well . . . good night, Gerry.' Did I imagine it or did he say it more affectionately than usual because this was our last night in a place where we'd been so long together?

On my bed I shut my eyes and waited for sleep, but thoughts and doubts kept harrying it from me. It may have been an hour later when I heard Colin moving about and opened my eyes. He had put on his tunic and was leaving it loosely open while he slung the lanyard of his revolver round his neck.

'What the hell . . .' I began, blinking at his candle-light.

'Go to sleep. I'm going out to look at that wire again. There's one part I'm far from happy about.'

'There's nothing to worry about. It's——'

'If it's not too good . . . well, it's a quiet night, and we can start doctoring it.'

'Oh, give it a rest.'

'That won't do, sonny. It may be touch-and-go tomorrow night, and I intend that for my boys, at any rate, it shall be "go". I don't know what the other companies are doing, but I propose to get my company off intact. Let that be perfectly clear to you and to Brother Turk and to everyone else.'

'The wire's all right.'

'Maybe, but I have another idea too—a rather bright one. I'm not bright really or I should have thought of it before.'

'What is it?'

'I'll tell you when I come back. May be nothing in it. Now go to sleep like a good boy, and have a nice time.'

I could see that he was overburdened with apprehension on such a night as this; and, judging from myself, I suspected that it was an apprehension both selfless and less than selfless. He was eager to get his men safely away both for their own sakes and for the sake of earning praise. But, draping all the anxiety in merriment, he said only 'Sleep on, my boy. We shall be busy tomorrow. Tomorrow is our wedding-day And we will then repair Unto the Bell at Edmonton . . .' and after giving me a careless wave, blew out the candle's guttering relic and went out into the darkness.

I tried again to sleep; I dozed . . . and woke with a fearful start as a hand touched me. A voice was speaking, 'Can you come, sir?'

It was the S.M. 'Mr. Imley sent me to fetch you, sir.'

'Who?'

'Mr. Imley.'

'Why?'

'The Captain hasn't come back.'

I could hardly breathe my '*What!*' for fear of his answers.

'He went out to look at the wire——'

'I know——'

'—and Corporal Haynes says they saw him leave it to look at some of the dead. He went on looking at them, and we can't see him anywhere now, sir.'

My heart was empty of all but a deathly alarm as I leapt from bed. 'Been any firing?'

'Only once, sir.'

I slung my revolver and suffered as I remembered Colin doing this an hour or so ago. I walked out, the S.M. following me along the communication trench. Sure that I was walking towards what must be a death of the heart, I felt as a man must who is walking to his execution. I looked up at the stars in a sloe-blue sky as if they were something that had little interest for me any more. Never a more perfect Gallipoli sky, but what was it to me? Nothing. Nothing but a sickness on the edge of death.

In a fire-trench I found both Duke Imley and Jonty. In the diluted darkness I could see that Imley's face looked grey and strained. Jonty's round face showed no more the boyish smile, but only a boy's frightened stare. 'Thought you'd better come, Gerry,' said the Duke. 'If anything's happened to Colin, you're next in command.'

'What *could* have happened to him?' I asked angrily.

'He said he'd be back in a few minutes, but he's been gone nearly two hours. He said he was going to look at the uniforms of the dead Turks so as to learn exactly what regiments were opposite us. He seemed satisfied with the wire and walked on looking at the Turks.'

'He's probably still doing it.'

'None of us can see him anywhere.'

'It's dark. . . .'

'Not as dark as it might be. Besides, Gerry, they sent up a

star-shell about an hour ago, one of the brightest ever, and there was a burst of machine-gun fire. As if they'd seen something.'

'Oh . . . God . . . Christ. . . .'

'He may be all right, Gerry.'

'I'm going out to look.'

Fear or no fear—and I had a great fear of that machine-gun—I knew I must go out and look for him. He was Colin; and not only that: had he not once come out to get *me* in? In this moment of my life I knew, for a while, that all the weight of fear in the world did not equal love. Not that my imperfect love cast out fear, but that it carried it along with it, like a burden in a traveller's hand. I clambered over the parapet and through the wire, thinking defiantly, angrily, 'That machine-gun may tear me up, but what's my love worth if I won't take an agony for it and even die for it?'

I was now in No-Man's-Land, the place of my dread. The S.M.'s voice followed me: 'Be careful, sir'; and Imley's: 'The night's too bright for this sort of game. . . .' Someone else said gruffly, 'E's mad.' I paid no heed to them, but went on. In this wide No-Man's-Land the bodies appeared to be lying left and right, and everywhere—as far as my eyes in this darkness could distinguish them from a scrub. If Colin was one, how could I hope to find him among a hundred? Still, I wandered on, from each to each. Ten, twenty, thirty I visited. All were Turks, and little use could their uniforms have been to Colin. They were nearly all in parts of *our* uniforms, salvaged, no doubt, from the burning Suvla stores: Australian tunics, British tunics, Indian drill tunics; all with badges removed but buttons in place. Some bodies had our puttees swathed round their boots or round their plump bellies like cummerbunds. Familiar British Army boots; and each of these limp or stiffened wearers had been alive in the morning, lacing his boots.

Useless. Useless to attempt this task alone. And morning was coming nearer. I went back to organize a search party.

Imley looked dubious: he had not been Colin's friend so long as I. I asked for volunteers and there were many, for the boys had loved their captain. Jonty was importunate to be one, but

I said No, just myself and six men. 'Better send for the C.O.,' I said to Imley, and led them out. Spread in extended order we crept among the bodies, searching. But did the Turks hear our feet? Or was the day brightening? Did I once speak too loud? A Very light shot up in a high parabola, green in the deep grey night, and the machine-gun sought us in its glow. Four of my six men fell. Two, Jim Haley, a boy of splendid spirit, and Wal Trenter, a lively and loyal 'old sweat', were dead. 'Get back,' I said. 'Get back.' Despairingly I ordered them back. 'Get back.' But only for a little while, I thought, only for a little, as we dragged one of our wounded in, the other being able to walk.

In the trench was the Colonel. 'No more,' he said, as if displeased. 'Unless you've any others wounded.'

'No, sir. We're all in except Haley and Trenter. They're . . . killed.'

'Well, no more, Browning. You must leave him.'

'Leave Dester, sir? But we don't know that he's dead. He may be lying wounded.'

'Hardly likely. The Sergeant-Major says no one could have lived through that machine-gun burst.'

'Three of us lived just now, sir, without a touch.'

'Don't argue with me, Browning. That was but a small burst. The other was terrible, the Sergeant-Major says, and while it lasted, No-Man's-Land was as bright as day.'

'But . . . he must be still lying out there——'

'Browning, that'll——'

'There have been no Turkish patrols. No one's moved in No-Man's-Land. He must be lying out there.'

'No doubt he is. And dead. That'll do, Browning. It'll be light soon, and I'm not having any more of my men killed and wounded—tonight of all nights.'

'He may be alive, sir.'

'If he's alive, and it's almost as certain as dammit that he isn't, he'll be taken prisoner by the Turks. And the Turks are gentlemen.' Probably as much to comfort himself as me in a harsh but necessary decision, he averred in his romantic way,

'The Turks are the most gentlemanly enemy I've fought in *my* lifetime. We must gamble on that. You've done all you can. You've done your best.'

'I cannot leave him there, sir.'

The Colonel blanched. Never before had I seen such a white anger on his face. 'You can do anything I order you to, and nothing else.'

'He may be only wounded.' I didn't even add the 'sir'.

'Browning!'

'I'll not leave——'

The unfinished sentence was my mutiny. For some seconds the Colonel stared at me. Then he said, 'Browning, I didn't hear those words, and you can thank your stars I didn't. Do you want to be sent down under close arrest? Now kindly do exactly what you're told. In this battalion my orders are obeyed.' Gazing into my face which probably showed some childish angry tears, he softened. 'For Christ's sake, boy, don't spoil your fine record. And just at the end too. On the last day of all. It's ridiculous. We've had one dreadful disgrace in this battalion. Don't give me another, I beg you. . . . I beg you. . . . No one else, officers or men—nobody at all is to venture out of this trench.' Abruptly he turned and went; in mercy, I know, that he might not hear more suicidal words from a sufferer.

He was gone, and I paced the trench, hands gripped behind my back, and telling myself, 'I will *not* leave him. I will not. He came out and got me in. "Jonty, this is our Gerry. He's one of our heroes. If you're shot down, he'll get you in." "Coming, Gerry?"' No, my God, I wouldn't leave him there! Unvisited. Not till I knew he was dead and beyond my help.

In this moment, as I halted and stood still with this vow, the old Peninsula, that spiritual counsellor of mine, gave me another of its revelations. I saw vividly that my daily desire to be an attractive personality, offending no one, pleasing all, must, if for ever yielded to, end in my becoming no personality at all but a fluid sham. And since in this moment I knew that I could never live with the knowledge that I had not gone out to Colin, it seemed plain to me, inevitable, unarguable that tonight for once in a way I must be myself and disobey the Colonel and take whatever came to me: court martial . . . cashiering . . . imprisonment. To hell with what happens to me. The love which I had no difficulty in feeling and the selflessness which I found so difficult to sustain seemed to meet and blend and bless my mutiny.

'It'll be light soon. I must go quickly.' Once again I clambered over that parapet and went on into No-Man's-Land, ready, in my grief, anger, and deliberate self-abandonment, for death (though hoping it would come without pain). I heard Imley's voice behind me: 'It's madness . . . but for the Lord's sake pass it down that Mr. Browning's out there.' The word went along the trench: 'Pass it down. Mr. Browning's out there . . . pass it down. . . . Mr. Browning . . . What? . . . Pass it on. He's out there. . . . Christ! . . .'

I could feel the eyes of the men watching me in silence, and I'll not say that in the heart of all my grief and anger there wasn't a pleasure in the thought that they were seeing me and probably repeating the sweet reputation, 'He doesn't know what fear is.'

All very quiet. It was getting near dawn, an hour when guns and rifles slept. In a great fear, I crept on among the bodies, crouching more for a fool's comfort than in hope of safety thereby. And then my fear lessened as—oh, the true comfort of it—as an early morning mist came travelling over me from the north-east. When I had last looked up at the sky the stars had seemed like glow-worm lamps hanging in a topless blue hollow; now those that could still be seen were like tiny moons, each in a nimbus of gold.

Walking upright now, I went from one quiet enemy to the next, an instinct telling me that Colin would have gone towards the left, for it was there that the Turks' attack had started and most had been slain. Probably he had gone on and on with a boyish conceit, unwilling to be beaten by the dark and determined to find something helpful which he could tell to the Colonel proudly.

I too went on and on—on and on—ever disappointed but not

to be beaten. Time mounted into hours, or so it seemed, and I began to feel, along with a mad anger against fate, a desperate fear lest my protector, the night, should get ready to abandon me, having no longer permission to stay. But at last—over there—pale whipcord breeches on a prostrate form. They were not unlike those I had last seen on Colin's bed. Oh, could that be—I ran there—and yes: Colin. Colin lying prone but with his grey-white face resting sideways on the earth. Shot through throat and body. His blood spread beneath him. It stained the earth at his side. I guessed a bullet through an artery—and he had bled to death.

'Colin . . . Colin . . .' I besought, but of course the figure did not answer.

Colin lying with the Turks whom, only a few hours before, he'd urged his men to kill and kill.

Oh, it would happen cruelly like this. Twenty hours, and he'd likely enough have been safe on the sea. But . . . killed at the end. And not even in a battle, but in an excess of anxiety and duty; in an over-ensuring of his men's safety and his own; in an over-eagerness for praise.

Damn Heaven. Damn fate. Damn God—but there's no God.

Side by side, in the troopship steaming through the Mediterranean sun, he and I had attended the lecture on First Aid and been taught how to determine if life was extinct, but I had not thought then, in that gilded ship's-saloon—I would not have dared to think with Colin whispering jests at my side—that one day I should apply this knowledge to him in an empty darkness, far ahead of our Line.

Kneeling, I got my hand on to his breast, still warm: but no beat in his heart; no beat at all. I held his wrist: no pulsing there. I looked into his eyes: no recognition of me; only death's dull ignorance. Lustreless but glazed, and finding some light from the sky, they stared into mine, unseeing, uninterested, uninformed with anyone's life, anonymous, just as Evverson's had done, and no more brightly than his.

Passionately I flung myself forward and, being alone in the

night, with no one to see or hear, let the sobs tear through me and sound however they cared to, in the dark.

When I felt better for this I looked again at that body by my side. I had known nothing of Colin's secret life but I was sure that, with a mind of his quality, he must have counted the likely cost of his every bold action and secretly made ready to offer it. 'Nothing,' I thought, 'is ever quite perfect in this world—not even at moments on Gallipoli—and there may have been traces of vanity in this last act of Colin's—who am I to know?—but in the main, I'm sure, oh yes, sure for always, that it was a sense of duty, and a love of his men, that sent him forth tonight.' Yes, the pieties of such as he were secret, but their works were public. Here at my side was Colin's public behaviour. Good then, perhaps, to die so near the summit.

My diminishing sobs swept up into mind a distant memory: myself reading of Achilles above Morto Bay and how he cast himself down on hearing of Patroclus' death and, flinging dust upon his head, and drenching the ground with tears, vowed to die with him. I had imagined myself putting on a fine Achillean act should Colin ever be killed. And here he was beside me in the darkness. And all I should do would be to get up and walk away. And a few hours later walk right off the Peninsula, leaving him to be swallowed into its soil, in some shared grave with his enemies.

'Colin . . . I will get you back if I can.'

Let me try to get a bearing so that, if possible, I could find him again. I stood up and thought I could descry, away there in the south-west, the torn or decapitated trees of Twelve Tree Copse. I got them in line with a lift of the Turkish parapets, and that was the best I could do; but it was good to do something.

No reason to kneel again. I stood there, looking down upon him and in my heart believing, though I had spoken of coming back, that this was the last I should see of Colin. It was difficult to turn away. I don't know when I would have turned away if I hadn't suspected a thinning of the mist. Then I said almost aloud, 'I must go, Colin,' but this seemed such a poor good-bye that I decided I must do something to make a better one—something that would defeat this sense of impotence and failure; and since no one could see me, and no one would ever know, I knelt and put a kiss on his temple before coming at last away.

In the trench; the darkness lifting; the mist shredding slowly aside. I could leave him where he lay or I could ask the Colonel if I might take out a party to bring him in. But I had disobeyed the Colonel's order, an offence which might mean my arrest and disgrace. Just so: and almost for this reason, since it would prove that my love for Colin was more than my love for myself and, moreover, since I was feeling sullen with the Colonel for having spoken to me sharply and forbidden me to do what I wanted to do, I resolved to go to him, tell him how I had found Colin, and ask his permission to bring his body in for burial. I wanted, by some such desperate action, to save, to keep, to complete and crown (I hardly know the exact word) a love which death had sought to snuff out for me; and I heard myself mumbling such fate-defying words as 'I'm not going to be beaten by death. . . . *I* don't mind *what* happens to me. If I didn't have to suffer for it in No-Man's-Land—*all right!* I'll cheerfully give up career and reputation for it now, and even go to prison for it. Yes, and in spite of all that Evverson once said about the horror of being bricked up in a prison—like hell I will. Oh, *yes*. *Yes*.'

But it was not yet day, and neither my love—for all my love of it—nor my huffiness—for all its festering possession of me—was of the kind that could wake a colonel out of his sleep. I delayed till morning; and even till the Colonel should have breakfasted. Then I walked—rather slowly—towards Battalion Headquarters. Though obstinately determined to go there, I was not less afraid than when I approached the beach on that April day, or when I led my men out of all shelter in the fight for Sari Bair. I came upon the Colonel in the Headquarters Mess, where he was seated with the Adjutant.

'Sir . . . ?'

My heart pounded in protest within me, but my will, unsparing, insisted, 'Go on. Remember Colin.'

'Yes, Browning?' He spoke gently, not, I think, because he had forgotten my insubordinate manner of last night, but because he was remembering it.

I could not at once speak. Two regular officers: the Colonel, for me the summit of command; the Adjutant, with a crisp black moustache and dress of military correctness; regulars of regulars both; and I was afraid of what must come from them.

'Yes, Browning?'

'I have found Dester's body, sir.'

'You have *found* it?

'Yes, sir.'

'How? How, pray?'

My voice trembled. 'I went out to look for it, sir.'

It was the announcement of mutiny.

'You——'

'I knew Dester so well, sir, that I felt sure which way he would go.' My limbs might be trembling before these two, but it was with a trace of schoolboyish pride that I reported, 'I walked straight towards him, sir.'

The Colonel's eyes fixed on me, above lips which anger had locked. He did not speak. The Adjutant who had been looking down on his papers suddenly looked up at him because of the silence. He continued to look at him, as the toe of the Colonel's Russian boot tapped impatiently.

The Colonel said, 'Leave us, Trevor.'

Surprised, but too good a soldier to show his surprise for more than a second, the Adjutant said, 'Yes, sir,' and rose. As he went out I felt exactly as I had felt ten years before when my headmaster shut his room door on my caning, which must be private.

The Colonel for some time left me standing there with my apprehension. His mouth worked, as if he were clamping his teeth together. I fidgeted and he spoke.

'Did I not tell you, Browning—my God, did I not tell you that nobody, officer or man, was to leave that trench?'

'Yes, sir.'

'And you deliberately disobeyed my order?'

Shifting my eyes away, I said, 'I could not leave him there if he was only wounded.'

'God and to hell, man! *I'm* in command of this battalion and decide these matters! I decided to risk no more lives. He was dead, of course?'

'Yes, sir.' And as I thought of him still lying there, defiance helped me to say, 'I came to ask if I might take a party out and bring him in.'

'You can certainly do nothing of the sort. *Will* you be quiet! God——' I saw in his eyes what seemed the fury of a small bull suddenly teased beyond bearing. 'It is now daylight and you'd all go to certain death. God damn it, Browning, what has happened to you? Have you gone mad? You coolly disobey my orders and then come and tell me you've done so and ask permission to be even more idiotically disobedient. By all that's holy, you stage your disobedience the very moment you get command of a company. You could be shot on the field for it; and ought to be. I simply don't understand you New Army officers. You seem to imagine you can think twice whether you obey an order or not. To a regular officer there's no crime more shocking than to disobey a superior officer in the presence of the enemy. God alive, man, here you are, on your own testimony, guilty of wilful disobedience to a lawful command! Do you know that for this a General Court Martial could give you a sentence up to penal servitude for life?'

I bent my head.

'It's time some of you realized this. I'm in two minds whether to put you under instant arrest. I ought to. It's my duty to.'

'I am sorry, sir.'

'If I do, it's a court martial and a cashiering for certain.'

'Yes, sir.'

'And, upon my soul, you deserve it.' He got up, walked some paces forth and back, and sat again. 'But I cannot bring myself to do it, Browning. No, no, not after all your fine service with the battalion. . . . No.'

A pause. Not for the criminal in the dock to speak.

'I suppose that was why I sent Trevor-Brayne away. If anyone knew that you had deliberately disobeyed my orders I should have no course but to put you under arrest. But I cannot . . . I cannot bring myself to do it.'

If I had felt like a boy about to be caned, I now felt like a boy in disgrace who, because he is spoken to with kindness, is ready to cry. My throat filled; my mouth shook.

He just mused in his chair; he picked up a pencil and doodled on a sheet of paper, saying at last, 'No,' and shaking his head. 'Damned if I'll court-martial anyone who was on V Beach with me.'

His booted foot kicked the Adjutant's chair another inch from the table. 'Sit down.' He ordered this angrily as if the sounds of anger would harden lenience.

I sat down clumsily, eyes still cast down.

'And you were wounded,' he said gruffly, 'when Colonel Doughty Wylie led us in that assault from the beach, weren't you?'

'Only slightly, sir,' I said, with drooped head.

'Still . . . still . . .' he mused, in softer voice. 'Yes. . . . Poor Doughty Wylie. . . . What a job he did that morning. . . . Makes one proud. . . .'

He said no more, and I sat wondering that V Beach which Colin and I had shared together, should be saving me now, and that Doughty Wylie, long dead, should be acting for me as Prisoner's Friend.

There was a silence, only a minute long, but to me it seemed as if it would never stop.

'No . . .' he began, but went silent again, and rose and walked about, before returning to his chair. 'No. Nor can I—don't think I'm pleased with you; I'm angry; very angry indeed—but I cannot bring myself to punish any young man brutally because he loved his brother officer. You were fond of young Dester, weren't you?'

'Well, yes, sir.'

'*Very* fond of him, I think?'

'Well . . . yes . . . I suppose so.'

'Yes. I know. I understand. You were with him from the beginning. And once he got you in, didn't he, when you were wounded? Yes, I can understand how you feel about him lying out there.'

He thinks he understands, but he doesn't, I thought. Not quite. How can he? Who would?

'I feel the same myself, Browning. But look: let us forget for a minute that I'm your commanding officer. I'm old enough to be your father, and I'd rather speak to you like that—if I may. May I?'

I bent my head again, not lifting it quickly; and he continued, 'You won't mind? Good. Thank you. I don't want you to be too unhappy about Dester. He was one of the best young company commanders I've ever known in thirty years of soldiering—a splendid young fellah—splendid—and would he have wished any of his men to be killed, getting him in? Weren't you nearly killed once, trying to get Cass in?'

'I was wounded, sir.'

'Terribly wounded. Would Dester have wanted you to go through that again or be killed?'

'But when it is dark, sir?' I ventured. 'Tonight.'

'When it is dark tonight we shall be occupied with the living. I'm sure he would have wished us to save all the men we could, even if it meant leaving him there. There's another point. The Turks have asked for a five-hour truce to bury their dead, and the C.-in-C. has refused it.'

I felt a shock of disappointment. I wanted to think that we were not less chivalrous than the Turks who had such a reputation as generous enemies.

'It can't be helped; we can't grant it,' said the Colonel, seeing the shock in my eyes. 'For two reasons. One is that it's a toss-up whether we can get away tonight without disaster, and we can't risk having the Turks near our trenches, seeing what's going on. They may be magnanimous fellahs, but there's a suspicion that during the armistice in August Mustapha Kemal, one of their generals, who's a very sly fox, took the opportunity, while officially supervising the recovery of the dead, to see all that he could of our trenches, ha, ha, ha. The other's a subtler reason. It seems that the Turks have a superstitious hatred of advancing over the bodies of their dead, and that means that all those lying out there—including young Dester, come to that—are helping to guard us from attack in the gravest hour of all. I don't believe young Dester would have minded doing that. Do you?'

'No, sir. Not if Colin—not if Dester knew about that, sir. No.' There could be something in what he was saying, I told myself: Colin lying out there, along with Brother Turk, as he used to call him, and both of them doing a little to cover our escape.

'Try to think of him doing that. The Turks will bury him after we've gone. Now give me your promise that you'll attempt no more private mutinies. I shall want all your loyal service tonight. Do you promise?'

'Of course, sir.'

'Good. And remember: only you and I know what has passed between us. Like you I have, I suppose, disobeyed the orders of my superiors. I ought to have handed you over to judgment and damned well you deserved it.' He smiled. 'So you will kindly mention this talk to no one for the next forty years, by which time I shall long have been comfortably dead and forgotten. I have no desire to be cashiered in my old age, ha, ha'—but this was not one of his heartier laughs; it was weary. 'And now I think you must have much to do today before you bring your company off tonight. Bring them off safely, all of them if you can. That was what young Dester wanted to do, eh? They've been good lads and they deserve it.'

'Yes, sir.' I rose. 'Thank you, sir. Thank you for everything.'

He just shook his head. I saluted, about-turned with a particularly smart movement since such was the very seal and signal of a devoted military obedience, and went back to my company. And as I went, some of the love which Colin was no longer there to receive, took a direction towards the Colonel and filled the well of my affection for him to overflowing.

CHAPTER EIGHT

THERE was little we could do in these our last twelve hours on Gallipoli. Those in the fire-trenches watched our front uneasily, sometimes walking from loophole to loophole and firing from each, to give the impression that our bays were largely manned. Behind us the men packed kit-bags, valises, ammunition, and stores for the journey through the dark. This was the uneasiest day of all that we had known on this stretch of wasted headland between the seas. How slowly the hours marched by, while the thought beat in all of us: 'Since the order is to get off, the sooner we go, the better. I don't want to be killed in these last few hours.'

But no fire from the Turkish Line, no aeroplanes rising above it, suggested that any suspicions were active there or any abnormal hostility preparing. Their whole line, undulating along with its brown and black sandbags beneath the slopes of Achi Baba, seemed comatose or only sporadically awake. Good; but why did the sun stand still like this? We were not Joshua, wanting the sun to stand still over Gibeon while we avenged ourselves on our enemies. All we wanted was for it to quicken its dilatory pace and get from Gibeon before our enemies avenged themselves on us.

All of us felt easier when we found things for our hands to do, though there was a certain sadness, as well as the excitement of unbelief, about doing some of them for the last time. One thing we all found a merry business. This was to write farewell messages to Johnny Turk and pin them up in our dug-outs. Jonty particularly enjoyed this, so much so that he could not stop composing them, nor did he worry if their humour was of an elementary order. 'Good-bye, John,' he wrote. 'Sorry we can't stay. Thanks for the entertainment.' And, 'Saïda, Abdul. Love to Mrs. Abdul and the kids.' He signed them 'Jonty Stuart'. One he even headed 'To Johnny Turk from Jonty Stuart'. I played my part in the game, though thinking all the time how Colin, out there, would have enjoyed it. My own inscription on our walls was, 'Good-bye, Johnny. A lovely summer. Enjoyed every minute of it.' Imley, a scholar and showing it off a little, wanted to put '*Plaudite, amici, finita est commedia*', which he assured me were the last words of Beethoven.

In the afternoon I decided to go to the little wired cemetery in the Gully where Bay, Cass, and Evverson lay with some of our men. All these were but names to the Duke and Jonty, so I left them in charge of the Company and with my batman and the S.M., who said he'd like to come too, made my way to the great ravine. Our company sergeant-major was a youthful, pleasant, and understanding person for such a rank, and not at all like the robust and raucous figure of the home-made cartoons in our little army paper *The Peninsula Press* (in the men's terms, 'The Gallipoli Liar'). The sight of the little cemetery touched us all with sadness, and we went into it as silently as into a church. We set the graves in order, straightening the case-wood crosses, rearranging the borders of upturned cigarette tins or white Gully stones, and replacing the sodden pith helmets (where such had been laid on a grave's breast) putting stones on their rims to hold them down.

'A mutt's game, sir,' said the S.M. 'The old Turk'll take them for souvenirs. You can bet your life he will.'

'Maybe not,' I said. 'John's a gentleman.'

'Well then, the wind'll have 'em,' said the Sergeant-Major.

On some of the graves there had been sprigs of Gallipoli's flowering heaths, either erect in empty shell-cases or lying like lovers' sprays above dead breasts: these the wind had already sent far adrift. We put them back in their places, though the Sergeant-Major shrugged at the futility of this reinstatement.

Other men from other units were engaged in the same last piety towards their friends, and it was to be noticed that my batman and the S.M. gave as much care to Evverson's grave as to anyone else's in that small wired compound.

'Well, that's that, sir,' said the Sergent-Major when we had done; and we stood for a last look at the graves and came away.

As I walked back I perceived with pleasure that the sun was going down.

At last. The night had long been dark—oh, why had we not moved; why this delay, this delay? For long the wind had been rising, bringing new fears with it—why no orders, no orders? —but now the moment was here. 'Right,' I said, standing at the mouth of the communication trench. 'Lead on, C Company. Silence. Absolute silence.'

Imley leading them, my company filed past me with hardly a sound. Their boots, wrapped in stockinet, sacking, or rags, made no noise loud enough to compete with the low moaning wind. A tired and tatterdemalion army they looked, with their uniforms torn and stained and their pounds of equipment dragging down their shoulders or bowing their backs. To Jonty, waiting as the junior sub to follow behind the Company, I said, 'Very much an after-the-battle crowd.'

'Still . . .' he objected, not wanting his romantic soul to be hurt, 'they've done a job.'

'Oh, quite,' I assented. 'A job of sorts. Now follow on, Jont. I'll follow you.'

I let him go several yards before I followed him. Then I came out of the Line, the sole survivor of our bright cheering April company. Bill Drewer, Bay, Evverson, Cass, Colin—I alone came away in the company of strangers like Jonty and the Duke. Outside the chapel at Mudros I had been so sure that I should die but instead, here I was, the only one still alive, though not certain yet that I would get safely on to the sea. Surely the wind was rising?

In the communication trench I brushed past them all and took the lead with Duke Imley and the S.M. The S.M. was looking at the cross-cuts and mule saps as we passed them.

'A fine trench system we made at last, sir,' he whispered. 'Sad to leave it. Sad to leave it.'

I remembered Colin saying something like this, and I gave the same reply. 'I am reconciled to it.'

'The Turk'll never keep 'em nice,' he deplored. 'He'll muck 'em all up.'

Strictly he should not have spoken at all, but I was not strong enough to rebuke a sergeant-major, even so slight and amiable a one as ours.

'He'll grow something good here one day, I should think,' Imley suggested. 'We've dug his land deep enough for him.'

'Quiet, Imley,' I ordered.

'I don't think anything'll ever grow where the Scotties have been,' murmured the S.M., and I conceive he meant something rude.

This time I managed to say, 'Silence, everybody,' but I addressed it to everybody; not to the Sergeant-Major.

Here and there a shell-burst had broken the trench wall, and I could see out into the open. Out there it was a wide grey night again, as it had been twenty hours ago; the shadowy clumps of brushwood, the low heather bushes, and the few, shell-thrown trees reminded me of the many dark bodies which I had approached last night. All those indeterminate shadows out there, sometimes becoming clearer in the falling glow of a star-shell, seemed like a visible kindred of the shadowy but audible shufflings of our feet. The illuminating light might have come from a Turkish trench or, on its own, from our uninhabited Line. Once, in such a light I saw a lonely wooden cross canting aside before the north-east wind and so pointing towards the beaches.

The Sergeant-Major had seen it too and asked, 'How many chaps d'you suppose we shall leave here, sir, dotted about all over the place?'

'Forty thousand,' I conjectured. 'Fifty, perhaps. Of ours. And about fourteen thousand Frenchies, I believe.'

'Pity to leave 'em,' he said, just as he had said about the trench system; and together we walked on through the night.

Ancient night was down upon the Peninsula, I thought, as it was when Xerxes crossed it with his defeated army two thousand three hundred years before, marching them to the Hellespont, to get them home by boats. As it would be tomorrow night and for thousands of years to come.

For a time none of the men behind me even whispered. Then a muted voice said, 'Steal away, steal away to Jesus.'

'Stop that talking!' hissed the S.M.

A spent bullet struck one of the men on his cheek, drawing a loud note from him, as when a bell is struck.

'Shut up!' said the S.M. unsympathetically. 'And keep closed up, all. Don't straggle. Pass the word to close up.'

'How one can do anything else but straggle with the kitchen curtains round one's boots,' murmured the first voice, 'buggered if I know.'

'Stop talking, I said! Didn't yer *hear*? And, anyhow, mind your language.'

Silence again, but later a man stumbled over a blanket spread on the trench floor; he nearly pitched on to his nose; and the ammunition box he was helping to carry fell to the planks with a clatter to wake (so we declared) the whole Turkish Army.

'Christ!' exclaimed someone. 'That's torn it. That's the end.'

'Hell and be damned to you!' cried a voice, almost loud enough to complete the resurrection of the Turks. 'Stop that tittering!'

'The Colonel!' whispered that first erring and unteachable voice.

The Colonel had come from in front to join us. By rights he should be in front of A Company, but I think he came and walked near me because of our quarrel in the morning and my grief for a friend abandoned behind us. His Russian boots were swathed like all of ours, and their thick bandaging caused him to walk as if on low gentle springs. Inside his tunic was his famous grey jersey leaving the Peninsula for good work somewhere else; and though it was winter now his civilian topee was in the best place for its porterage tonight—on his head.

'All rather sad, Browning, isn't it, what?' he said.

'Yes, sir,' I answered, pleased to be liked again, and needing it tonight.

'Still, as I told the men, we broke their arm. Yes, I shall always think that. Given the men, we could have gone through. Gone through, and, in my humble opinion, ended the damned war. Not but what the old Turk did his stuff damned well. We must allow that. All things considered, I say he deserved to win, what?'

'Yes, sir.'

A great silence among the men, now that the Colonel was walking with them—even though he himself was saying a bushel. But we were getting far from the enemy and when the Turk started to fire back at our empty but active Line, a voice commented 'Silly ass', and the Colonel did not interfere. Indeed, after meditating on this comment he accorded it his usual delayed 'ha, ha, ha'. Hearing this appreciation from such a high quarter, another man announced to the night, 'First time I've worn my stockings outside my boots. I don't know what Mother'd say'; and again the Colonel digested this and duly laughed. 'Outside his boots, ha, ha, ha. . . . What his mother'd say. . . . But they're good fellahs, Browning.' Moved to humour himself, he said to the Duke, 'No one so good as the British at evacuating, Imley. It's the one thing we do really well, ha, ha, ha. Corunna . . . Mons . . . Suvla . . . and now this. It's terrific. I had plenty to criticize in the Staff's management of the Landing, which, in my humble opinion, left much to be desired, but this is wonderful.'

'In fact,' suggested Imley, ever unafraid of colonels, 'nothing in our battles becomes us like our leaving of them.'

'Eh, what?' begged the Colonel, for the allusion was beyond him. 'Damn this wind. Yes we know how to retreat. We've had so much practice at it. And why? Because we invariably send far too few fellahs far too late and then have to dig 'em out.'

'That's about it, sir,' said Imley cheerfully.

We passed the rear-guard of honour, manning, I think, the old Eski Line. They lifted their hands to us as we went by, but said no word.

The Colonel raised his hand to his topee and kept it there

till he was out of their view, then explaining to me, 'Fine fellahs, Browning. Bloody fine fellahs.'

'We'll get them away, sir,' Imley promised, comforting his superior. 'Everything's going fine.' Such easy, almost flippant, words to address to a colonel.

But the Colonel seemed unperturbed by, and even to expect, this easy familiarity in his one silver-haired subaltern. 'Mebbe, mebbe, Imley, but what's this wind doing to the sea? We've fifteen thousand fellahs to get off.'

'We'll do it, sir,' Imley assured him, as a parent might soothe a worrying child, or a hospital orderly a patient. 'I'm sure the old Turk's still in the dark.'

'Yes, hark at him firing away at our Line. Wasting some of his best ammo.'

We passed the check point, where officers counted us as if we were schoolchildren passing the ticket collectors on our way to a treat by the sea.

We had come out of the Mule Trench now and were on the Krithia Road, giving farewell glances at old familiar landmarks: Clapham Junction, Roman's Well, Pink Farm in the distance with its solitary tree, and the relics of a Royal Naval Division Dump, known as 'The Army and Navy Stores.'

'Sad to see the last of 'em,' said the Colonel.

Now, in the open, we could see other files of columns of men draining down towards the sea along Road No. 2 and Road No. 3, which was 'Princes Street'. I turned to look back towards the Line and remembered a favourite quotation of Colin's, 'Men who march away 'Ere the barn-cocks say, Night is growing grey,' but he had spoken it of men who marched *towards* the battle, 'pressing to the field ungrieving'; not of those who marched softly from it. 'Leaving all that here can win us; What of the faith and fire within us Men who march away?' The words beat along with our feet. 'Faith and fire within us. . . .'

He lay there, left behind. Not far from me on my left now was Morto Bay above which I had sat imagining the fine scene wherein I, like Achilles, vowed to avenge my friend. Instead I was stealing away through the night. Steal away to Jesus. Only this: I had struggled with the Colonel for Colin's body as Achilles for Patroclus's. And lost.

'If anything happens to me, Gerry, and you get away, you must look up Olwen and make it easy for her. . . .'

('Damn this wind,' muttered the Colonel again, looking up at the sky, where clouds were forming.)

Gallipoli's north-east wind, unfaltering from the first, and now contemptuously blowing an army away.

Like that dust in the summer we drift out to sea.

'Tell her I tried to do my best. . . . And tell the old man too.' A duty that had got to be discharged now, but an unhappy, an uncomfortable one, surely. How little at ease I should be with the old lord, her father, and how shy with Olwen herself, perhaps, in her lordly home. How would she take my story, that I had left him lying there? 'Make it easy.' Would it not be better to lie and say he was 'missing, believed killed'? But this might keep a hopeless hope alive. No, better the truth. . . .

('Getting near now, Imley. This is the Sedd-el-Bahr Road. All depends now on what the sea's doing.')

Better the truth, and I could tell her that I too in this matter had tried to do my best. But were women ever reasonable about those they loved? Could they accept and understand and forgive?

('The Sedd-el-Bahr Road.' The word travelled down the column behind me. 'The Sedd-el-Bahr Road. Gor-blimey!')

Ahead of us the light reflected from the sea. That means the beaches. Yes, we're passing the Torres Lines. Soon now. If we do get off, I shall be free from the need to be selfless and dedicated. Free from the strain of it. I can leave it here with the destroyed ammunition. Free from that hourly threat of agony—oh, how wonderful! Maybe I shall have done with it for ever, because we're going to Egypt, everyone says, and it'll be months before the Turk can attack us there, with his broken arm.

And so on towards V Beach in silence. A silence like that with which we came towards it from the sea. Would the silence burst, as then, into a hail-storm of death? Was the Turk waiting his moment, as then? We went down a slope towards the beach, no more knowing what would happen there than when we came up to it out of the sea.

Our dead Line behind us still fired occasionally or shot up a Very light. A monitor or a destroyer—or both—or many—fired over our heads. One was almost certainly a monitor, for its heavy shells had an avalanche roar. The Navy still watching; still our father and our mother.

V Beach once again, and for the last time: the shattered fortress of Sedd-el-Bahr, a ghostly ruin in the dark; the low sandbank; the scimitar curve of the sea. And far out at sea the green lights of our hospital ships, waiting; the only lights on the water. But the sea was wind-driven and high: were we only just in time? So it looked, but they halted us under the lee of the fort, and we sat down on the slope of Hill 141. Sat and waited... and waited... watching the hurricane lanterns move on beach and jetties. The Duke and Jonty sat—or reclined—by me and I told them the story of Doughty Wylie, how he led an exhausted company from that sandbank there, including Colin and me, up this very incline to capture beach and hill.

Doughty Wylie, as I talked, was lying somewhere behind us in a grave in Sedd-el-Bahr.

And I was looking down that slope while Colin remained where he was—but no: only his body was there; he had evacuated the old Peninsula a day ahead of me.

Ever and again a single bugle-note from the fort told us that the watcher there had seen a gun-flash in Asia and we had thirty seconds to take shelter while the dilatory shell came loitering over the Straits. But there was no shelter: all we could do was to put our heads towards the ground. Fortunately the gun was overshooting and the shell either burst in the sea, sending up a waterspout, or plunged into the sand, forcing up a gusher of flame and stones.

'Which gun is it?' asked Jonty of me, the expert.

'Asiatic Annie,' I said, pleased to be an authority. 'Or Helen of Troy.'

'It's Creeping Caroline, I think, sir,' said the S.M.

'It's Bloody Mary,' amended a voice behind.

All this time men were pouring down on to the *Clyde* causeway or the jetties and being taken away in trawlers, tugs, and 'beetles', which were new motor landing-craft capable of holding five hundred men. As the men went off in their hundreds, I looked inland and thought of all those populous boroughs in ravine and nullah and along the Gully walls, or in the earth itself, which were now empty. Thinking this, I saw against the night sky the humped sarcastic rampart of Achi Baba.

The wind rose, the surf dashed, the lighters rocked. Would they ever get us off? Would they get us off at all? Would the orders to embark be countermanded till the sea fell? Might we yet have to turn and fight?

It was now past midnight, and Sunday.

But here was the Colonel, coming up the slope. Coming, we supposed, from the Military Transport Officer on the *River Clyde*.

'Come, men,' he said, and turned to lead us down.

They were the words he had used when he led us charging up this slope behind Doughty Wylie.

'Come, boys,' I said, pleased, as a commander of sorts, to echo him, and half-remembering that these had been Colin's words when *he* came charging up the slope with me. How almost perfect, I thought, the contrast between this January Sunday and that April Sunday. Then we came up from the sea in a spring dawn; now the sea takes us back in a winter midnight. Then a thunder of guns; now a shuffling silence. Then our thousands slain, and the sand filtering blood, and the sea laced with it and flushing red; now we get away with no blood on the shore except that of our poor toiling mules who have come through the scrub to their sacrifice.

I led my men down to the beach, in Doughty Wylie's steps, but the opposite way.

Thanks from all ranks to C.-in-C. We are here to stay.

On the *Clyde* causeway, under the high prow of that faithful old hulk, which we must leave here to rust with its memories, the men piled into a beetle behind those of a sister battalion. A few of our C and D Companies could not be embarked and we had to wait for a trawler which was fussing around the bay, picking up remnants from the jetties. The beetle chunked out on to the heaving sea, and the scrubby little trawler came rocking alongside.

'Any more for the *Skylark*?' said its skipper, stepping ashore. 'If so, come quickly. My old tub's getting the wind up, and so'm I. Come along, brother; put a jerk into it. The sooner I can get away, the better I'm pleased. I'm a nervous type. Wasn't built for this sort of thing. Lor' love you, I bin nearly hit twice already by that bloody Annie.' It was my friend from the North Sea fishing beds who, when taking me off before, had said his name was, not Nelson, but MacHasty. 'Jump to it, lads. Come along, all.' As then, he laid a grimed hand on many a soldier's back, waving them in with a captain's welcome and offering instructions and encouragement. His peaked cap was still on the back of his head, as if he'd had no time to move it during this busy campaign. 'No waiting, please. First class forrard, gentlemen; second class aft, and dump your baggage down till we find you your state-rooms. If you want anything just ring for your steward. Ladies downstairs. Lead on now——'

'Ta,' said a man in gratitude for the physical help of that hand.

'You're welcome. I apologize for the dark, but we ain't allowed any lights; not for tonight, anyhow. Got a bad knee, brother? Mine's a hip. Rheumatics. But mustn't grumble. Watch your step, all. We lose a lot of customers just here. Hurry up. Thank you. . . . Now sailing. No one in the dining-saloon or the dance hall, please. This way, sir——' This to a most palpable, officer in silvery middle-age, Duke Imley, with a parental hand on his back. 'Pass right down to the end of the car, sir, and God be with you. Hold tight and have your fare ready. Off in a few minutes, gentlemen, and thank God for that. Seen you before, have I, guv'nor? Well, hope it's the last time, eh? I expect you feel the same about me. But don't mind my patter, sir. All visitors ashore, please, when the bugle goes.'

As usual, I was alarmed that he should shout flippant orders in the presence of our colonel, but the Colonel only turned abruptly, looked at him, and seemed to realize that he was one of those odd phenomena which the New Navy, like the New Army, tossed up in these most irregular days.

Colonel Harby waited on the causeway till the very last of his men had embarked. His romantic soldierly mind, I knew, would insist that he himself must be the last off the bridge, the last to seek his safety on the sea. Satisfied that all, without question, were safely aboard, he turned towards the Peninsula and saluted, keeping his hand at his pith helmet and his heels together for several seconds. Whether he was saluting the dead left behind, or the Peninsula itself as an honourable foe, I never dared to ask. Perhaps, being our Colonel Harby, he held it his duty, on leaving the field, to salute the victor.

This courtesy completed, he stepped briskly among us, and I shivered to see the skipper rest that hand on his back, as on any private soldier's, welcoming him in. For a moment I feared the grizzled old hearty might accompany the hand with some such words as 'Come along, Dad' but he had tinges of respect in him and allowed the hand to say all.

The trawler pushed off from the jetty and puffed and fussed past the *Clyde*, while its captain chanted rather lugubriously and abstractedly, 'Eternity, Eternity, Where will you spend Eternity?' and so sang us away to sea. Looking back at the Peninsula, I could just discern, like spectral things, the square white tents of No. 17 Stationary still standing on and around Hill 138, because we had struck no standing tents if they were under the eyes of the Turk; we had left them for him to visit in the morning and find empty. Our trawler nosed its way towards an old Folkestone cross-channel steamer, waiting for more passengers in the darkness out at sea. As it went rocking towards her, I could only keep my eyes on those diminishing beaches and think of a towed boat going the other way with so many of my friends in the breathless April dawn.

My wife and I stood upon that beach with the young grinning Turk beside us. The three Turkish women were still sitting on the low sandbank, sitting (as Brother James would have said) 'the quiet waters by'. They watched us silently, inquisitively. Well, nothing to do now, I supposed, but get into our queer Turkish craft and come away—as those summer visitors of forty years ago had come away. But never in my life have I less wanted to leave a place and take what must certainly be my last sight of it. I waited yet another few minutes, I sighed, and then said, 'Well, that's that. Come, Olwen dear, we must be going.

'I suppose so,' she said, but not moving; gazing at the empty green slope and the crown of what was once Hill 141.

'I've been wondering,' I said, 'whether Colin would know me if he was an old man too and came down that slope. I think not. He would pass me by like a stranger.'

'Me too, perhaps.'

'No. I'm sure he'd look twice at you, and pause, and look again.'

'And why not at you, Gerry?'

'Because he must have known your face so much better than mine, having a slightly greater interest in it. Besides, a man's youth dies so much faster than a woman's.'

'What nonsense! The very opposite is true, my pet.'

'Not at all. There's still a girl in your face, but whatever youth was once in mine has been dead these many years, and, come to that, will all too soon be dust. Let us go. Come along, all, as the trawler's skipper said. Could it be that he's still alive, an old gentleman of ninety and more? No, Captain MacHasty, of the lively prattle, has long since gone, I think, to his last jetty. Come, dear; it's all over. This was but a visit to his youth solemnly undertaken by the remains of Gerry Browning.'

With my wife in a pensive mood and following me slowly, I limped back to the boat, which tossed gently by the spit of rocks and against the remains of what could only be the old *Clyde* causeway. We got in and the boy at engine and tiller turned its bow towards that current which, in Othello's melancholy line, 'keeps due on to the Propontic and the

Hellespont'—oh, but not so fast, boy; let me look back once again at the slow-paced waves that idle up towards the sand-bank. Never again will such flotsam lie on that beach as once I saw; never perhaps in history again will such a retreat be achieved as those waters knew, for we got every man away, rear-guard and all, without a single death. Not, though, without great loss of stores, ammunition, and animals—those beasts of burden who lay destroyed on their lines or by the sea's brink to which they'd come doing their last service for their masters.

But the boat curved away; it curved over the very sea-bed where the *River Clyde* once rested, hard aground; and as we turned into the channel between Sedd-el-Bahr and the Plains of Troy, the quiet uplands of the Peninsula came into full view. I gazed through the limpid Aegean air at that silent headland where I had known a love that dared not speak its name, but whose elegiac memory was now sweet and pleasant in the heart; and where, for once or twice at any rate, I had conquered most of my selfishness and known, amid every weariness and terror, the happiness of the dedicated. I don't think I have ever recovered that self-offering, because life has been too kind to me; but I have known all along that it was the truth.

It left its legacy with me.

So quiet now, that long narrow land. And yet once upon a time there had been mounted there a drama of violence, horror and, to myriads, death. Now—a silence of scrub and sand and pines. Only the earth and its scars remained, and some French and British dust. As our bows cut all too fast towards their home at Çanakkale, I remembered the chorus of Argive Elders in the *Agamemnon*, which Colin, with his usual joyous relish, had once recited to me, proud that the verse translation was his own. 'So fair in form they lie In graves by Troy's wall; Their foe's calm earth has shrouded all.'

38 L
105